THE PICCOLO FESTIVAL MURDERS

By M.W. Burdette

© 2017 M.W. Burdette

All rights reserved.
Printed in the United States of America.

ISBN-10: 1544667353
ISBN-13: 978-1544667355

Original Publication Date: March 23, 2017

This is a work of fiction. Names, characters, businesses, places, events and incidents are either the products of the author's imagination or used in a fictitious manner. Any resemblance to actual persons, living or dead, or actual events is purely coincidental.

For Martha

CONTENTS

INTRODUCTION

Prologue

PART I: THE BODY IN THE THEATRE
1. The Beautiful City of Charleston
2. Mysteries of the Battery
3. The Gaillard Center
4. Mayor Anderson's Office
5. Negotiations
6. Leadership
7. The Coroner
8. The Team
9. The Investigation
10. The Morgue
11. Slightly North of Broad
12. Comparison of Notes

PART II: MOTIVATION FOR MURDER
13. And Then There Were Three
14. Potential Suspects
15. Lawrence Baker
16. The Student List
17. Blood's Lessons
18. Jacuzzi Consultations
19. Out on the Town
20. The Mayor
21. The College of Charleston
22. Full Speed Ahead
23. Suspects
24. A Veiled Threat

PART III: IT ALWAYS ENDS IN THE MORGUE
25. An AWOL Rookie
26. The Real Suspect

27. Finding Juliet
28. Interrogation
29. Deal Making
30. Polygraph and Hypnotism
31. Terror at the Hospital

Prologue

Margaret Adams Watson, Maggie to her friends, was the chief murder investigator for the small city of Rowlette, Illinois, located about fifty miles southwest of the megacity of Chicago. Many of the residents of Rowlette worked in Chicago and commuted to and from there every day. Maggie had no desire to live in a large city, and in fact had grown up in Rowlette before going off to Loyola University, where she received her bachelor's degree in Criminology. She and an old friend from college had solved the mysterious murders that centered on the local cathedral, and she believed she deserved a rest from last year's craziness.

Her right hand man in those investigations and old friend from Loyola was Jonathan Pembroke. After a somewhat rocky start to their renewed relationship after college, they became inseparable. Jonathan was a very successful real estate investor and attorney, and his wealth afforded him the opportunity to remain in Rowlette and become one of the strongest allies that Maggie had in the Rowlette Police Department. He had virtually saved Maggie's life at the end of the cathedral murder investigation, and he shared the belief that they both deserved some downtime away from the local townspeople.

It had been a rather frustrating and tiring fall and winter for Lieutenant Maggie Watson, the Chief Homicide Detective for the City of Rowlette, Illinois. The crimes at St. Aquinas Cathedral had taken a toll on her and the entire police department. She needed a vacation: Memorial Day 1996 approached, and she decided to get out of the state and cleanse her mind and soul of the carnage of last fall's drama. The scenes from St. Aquinas Cathedral would play in her head for years to come, but that didn't mean she couldn't introduce new positive images to help blot out the bizarre behavior of an insane stalker who had almost killed her. And after all, she had a new friend to enjoy the slow times with these days.

So here she was, packing for a short vacation trip to Charleston, South Carolina, one of the oldest cities in the United States. She had made arrangements with a teenager she knew to care for Molly, her beloved West Highland Terrier. Nothing was too good for Molly. Other than her beau Jonathan Pembroke, Molly was her best friend in the world. Always happy to see her, Molly never failed to smother Maggie with kisses every day when she returned home from work at the precinct. Boldly—for her—Maggie had invited Jonathan to make the trip with her to Charleston. Why would anyone go to a romantic city for a getaway without all the amenities that you needed to make it a perfect weekend? At least that was her logic. Jonathan, of course, agreed to accompany her to Charleston. Airplane tickets were made, reservations at the oldest historic hotel in the city were confirmed, and they were now just minutes from landing at Charleston International Airport in North Charleston.

This would prove to be a historic trip for both Maggie and Jonathan—more so than either of them had expected when they left O'Hare International Airport.

BOOK I: THE BODY IN THE THEATRE

Chapter 1

The Beautiful City of Charleston

What most people know about South Carolina's history is that it was one of the original thirteen colonies of the United States. After being made a crown colony in 1719, it split off from North Carolina in 1729. After the invention of the cotton gin, the state gained prominence and financial wealth by successfully developing plantations that were cultivated and harvested principally by slave labor. This economic history put South Carolina on a direct path to the historic first shots of the Civil War fired on Fort Sumter in April of 1861. Although an immediate victory for the South at the time, the attack and subsequent four years of the Civil War brought devastating effects upon Charleston and the State of South Carolina. Charleston went from being the 22nd largest city in the country in 1860 to a city in one of the poorest states in the Union for the next century. The white ruling class who had dominated life in Charleston and other successful cities in South Carolina before the war was decimated by the effects of the Carpetbaggers and the Reconstruction, which was anything but reconstruction.

Jim Crow laws, the Civil Rights Act of 1965, and violence between racially active white and black citizens raged in South Carolina. Somehow, Charleston and its focus on historical correctness in architecture, literature, and the arts became a phoenix for the state. With the Battery area in full renovation by the 1970s, Charleston became once again a jewel in the crown for South Carolina. Many of the historic homes and houses of worship in the downtown Charleston area that had survived the war were restored to their pre-Civil War elegance. This reconstruction reinvigorated Charleston was the city that Maggie Watson and Jonathan Pembroke flew into, with summer well underway.

* * *

"I think that the temperature has to be hovering around 100 degrees," Jonathan complained as he secured their luggage from a porter at the airport baggage claim.

"Oh, what a baby!" Maggie chided him, while giving him one of her sexy smiles. "You are from New York, where it gets 100 degrees every summer. What's so different about the weather here?"

"First of all, the humidity in New York is not 100% to go along with the high temperatures. And second, we have about six weeks of warm to hot temperatures, and then the weather becomes more manageable. From what I understand about Charleston, the average temperature here year 'round is in the mid to high sixties. The average low is 38 to 45 degrees, and that is only in January and February. Geez, I think my shirt is already soaked with sweat. Do you like sweaty lovers, Maggie?"

"Right now, I like air-conditioned cars, hotels, bars, restaurants and anywhere that I can breathe! You are right about one thing, Jonathan. It is sticky here. I guess the locals get used to it, but it does limit one's wardrobe. Maybe I should break out my hot pants and halter tops!"

"I think I have a better solution. We can check into the Gaslight Inn on Meeting Street and stay inside, where it is cool, making love all weekend. There's an option I would be up for," he said with a wicked smile.

"Jonathan, one thing I have learned about you these past few months is that you are always up for it. And you know the IT that I am referring to!" She leaned over and gave him a peck on the cheek.

Their rental car was idling and cool when they reached the auto rental facility. The fact that the car was thirty degrees cooler than the outside air and the humidity nonexistent earned the car rental attendant an extra ten dollar tip. They piled their luggage into the mid-sized sedan and headed south on I-26 toward downtown historic Charleston.

"You know, since neither of us has ever been to this city, this could be an adventure for us both," Maggie said boldly. "We can find the haunted houses, walk in the steps of some of the signers of the Declaration of Independence, and take a dinner cruise past Ft. Sumter, where the Civil War began. How does that sound to you?"

"It sounds fine, but I wouldn't mind ordering dinner in the room, wine and cocktails on the patio, and several hours of exploring what's under the covers of a four-poster bed. That sounds even more exciting to me."

"Jonathan, we can fool around under the covers anytime and anywhere. We are in one of the most romantic cities in the world, at least in the United States, with over three hundred years of history and intrigue. Don't you want to make a few memories of our own to take back to Rowlette when the winters are approaching ten degrees below zero and the snow is two feet deep? Don't be a spoiled-sport! Tell you what I'll do. I'll plan the events, and you can pay for them!" she said with a big laugh. She was so much fun when he could pry her away from her official duties.

"Here it is," she said, looking at the picture of the hotel on the flyer and the pink stucco, three story hotel on her right.

The Gaslight Inn was somewhat unique in Charleston in that there was a Jacuzzi was in the courtyard where everyone checking in and out of their rooms, or even those going out to dinner or a festival activity, could observe patrons in the hot, bubbly water. It kept those who had thoughts of romantic but risqué behavior in check, as well as prevented the hotel from having to install individual Jacuzzis in the quaint and historic rooms. The really convenient thing about it being in the courtyard was that if the hotel employed a stringed instrument or other classical combo playing in the common outside areas, that music could be enjoyed from the bubbly experience.

"Welcome to the Gaslight Inn on Meeting Street! We are about to have an adventure of a lifetime!" Truer words were never spoken.

Chapter 2

Mysteries of the Battery

"Let's walk down to the Battery, Jonathan. I understand from the brochures in the hotel room that this is where the Confederate Army fired the first shots that started the Civil War. Supposedly, there are still cannon placements mounted exactly where they were when it all began in 1861."

"And this is important, how?" Jonathan picked at her.

Maggie gave him one of those "Don't push your luck" looks. He immediately got the message—"Whatever you want to do is just fine with this New Yorker!"

They walked down Meeting Street past the Circular Church that was founded in 1681 when Charleston was still "Charles Towne." The church had the oldest burial grounds in the city. Captured in 1780 by the British, members of the church were illegally exiled to St. Augustine, a Spanish settlement, and then the historic building was used as a British hospital until left as a shell of its former self. The third structure on this site, built in a circular design in 1804, burned in 1861, in a fire unrelated to battles of the Civil War. It was rebuilt and completed in 1892 using bricks from the original structure. Three hundred and twenty-five years of history in a city of many historical places, Circular Church was well placed in Historic Charleston in the middle of the hustle and bustle of Meeting Street.

As they approached the unique facility, they could hear the beautiful sounds of an a cappella choir performing classical Christian music. The sounds ringing in the old building tempted them to investigate the choir's performance. According to the banner that was hanging on the ornamental iron fence surrounding the unusually designed building, the founder and director of the choir was Dr. William Barker, a self-made man who had built his organization from nothing but blood, sweat, and tears. Although tempted to squeeze into the venue to hear this nationally known chorus, their desire to have a glass of wine motivated them to pass on by the church.

"Maggie, watch your step," Jonathan warned her, almost too late. She just narrowly missed stepping in horse manure from the passing horse-carrying cart for tourists. "You really have to be on your toes, literally, in this town if you are going to negotiate these streets and remain unsoiled," he laughed as he guided her around another pile of manure. Many of the streets of the old historic city were still paved with the rocks that had been off-loaded from the early merchant ships, which had used them for ballast purposes, before filling up their cargo hold with rice and cotton for their return to Europe. This particular street had rocks that were huge and did not fit well together, making the path somewhat treacherous.

"Rumor has it, Maggie, that when they have to make repairs on these ancient streets, they number the rocks and return them to their original placement."

Maggie gazed at him with admiration at his extensive knowledge of every place they visited. He obviously had done his homework on the history of Charleston. "Why on Earth would they do something like that?"

Jonathan laughed and said, "I know what you're doing, and it won't work! I have done my homework on Historic Charleston, and you're going to have to listen to every word of it as we move our way through the city."

"So you're going to keep me safe and clean while we are visiting here?" she asked him with a smile.

"Well, someone has to do it," he said as he placed his arm around her waist. "I guess I am qualified to be a protector of the innocent, helpless traveler."

"And you really think that I am innocent and helpless?"

"Not on your life," he laughed and kissed her tenderly on top of her head. "However, I will protect you if you will let me," and this time there was a sincere look on his face. Maggie squeezed his hand a little and continued to walk toward the little park at the Battery.

"From what I have gathered in my limited research about this city, this Battery Park has some mystery associated with it that is worthy of mention," she said.

"Really?"

"It appears that a pirate and his entire crew were hanged here in the 1700s as a punishment and an example to those who might have similar ambitions to rob from the rich and keep the bounty for themselves," she said. "It has also been documented by spiritualists that the souls of those hapless sailors walk the Battery after midnight wailing and moaning."

"Spiritualists, huh? I guess that's about as authoritative as we can expect from such a suspicious lot."

"Don't make fun, Jonathan. Don't you believe in the spirit world at all?"

"Ask me that question after we have been here for more than just a few hours."

"Have you ever seen the play *Porgy and Bess*?"

"Can't say that I have, but then we don't get those types of plays in New York very often, unless you want to go down to the theatrical district and rub elbows with all the artsy people."

"Actually, Jonathan, *Porgy and Bess* was first performed in Boston in 1935, and then in New York City shortly thereafter. Although written about events in Charleston, the racial tensions in the 1940s through the 1960s prevented it from being performed here until 1970. And you're in luck, because I have secured us two tickets this evening for the musical. In fact, it starts in about thirty minutes, so we can go to the play and then enjoy dinner at one of Charleston's fabulous restaurants afterward."

"I'm in. Then can we go explore what's under the covers of our four-poster bed"

"Don't you ever think of things other than sex?"

"Actually, no."

"I give up. Let's walk off some of that energy that you seem to have in abundance while we are waiting for the play to start at the Gaillard Center, a small playhouse on Calhoun Street, a few blocks east of Meeting Street. While we wait for the curtain to rise, we can walk up to Liberty Square, which appears to be a park on the edge of the bay."

"OK. By the way, what's all this advertisement about the Piccolo/Spoleto Festival?"

Maggie looked a little sheepishly at Jonathan, and it was now obvious why she had wanted to come this weekend. He had picked up on it immediately. As he had told her in the past on several occasions, she should never play poker. Now she would have to come clean about why she wanted to come to Charleston for Memorial Day Weekend.

"OK, Maggie, spill it!" he said and looked at her knowing that she couldn't keep a secret any better than he could. "You knew about this festival before we ever left Rowlette, didn't you? Forget answering that question, because the answer is written all over your face. I am assuming you have us booked for plays, musical group performances, and fancy dinners. Tell me I'm wrong," he said, staring at her.

"Nope, I can't lie to you. You may not get much rest on this trip, but most of our activities won't be in the bed at the hotel. Sorry," she said, without any pity in her voice. "You need to be educated culturally, Jonathan, and Charleston is just the place." She leaned over and kissed him.

"Are you sure you want to see this play?" he asked her with the hope that she would say no. He was out of luck, because she didn't come over a thousand miles to just play house in the hotel room. He resigned himself to the fact that he would be enjoying spending most of the time with his favorite girl, outside, not inside.

"OK, let's hurry back to the Gaillard Center. The play starts in ten minutes, and I don't want to be late." She began pulling him down East Bay Street.

"OK, OK," he said and picked up the pace to match her steps.

They arrived at the theatre at 2:50 PM, just before the curtain was scheduled to rise at 3:00 PM. As they approached, a crowd of several hundred people had gathered around the ticket booth. What made it all surreal to them was that the crowd was absolutely silent, just staring at something on the ground in the entrance area of the playhouse. With Jonathan well over six feet tall, and Maggie almost five-feet-ten, they could both see a body lying on the terrazzo floor. With no police or rescue people there, and the accident or murder scene being trampled on by curious bystanders, Maggie went into detective mode, pushed to the front of the crowd, and began to isolate the fallen soul at her feet.

Chapter 3

The Gaillard Center

The Gaillard Center was somewhat of an anomaly for Charleston. Built in 1968, and designed as a modern performance hall, the "modern" Gaillard, with glass, steel, terrazzo and concrete, was not what one would expect after seeing The Dock Street Theatre and other historical sites in the old city area. However, Gaillard was where the local symphony performed, as well as where many off-Broadway plays and musicals appeared in the "Low Country," the area around Charleston that sat below the Fall Line. Areas to the north of Charleston, such as Aiken and Chesterfield Counties, were referred to as "Up Country." The distinct differences in these areas of South Carolina reflected more than just geological differences in the terrain—they represented dramatic cultural differences as well. For starters, cuisine was totally different in Columbia and Greenville than in the swampy, mosquitos-laden areas around the rice and cotton farms near Charleston.

When Maggie and Jonathan observed the crowd in front of the Gaillard, it took a minute for the scene to register in their minds, and then Maggie jumped into action.

"People, please step back from this immediate area. Jonathan," she called to him, "please help me with crowd control."

He immediately took his position by her side and kept the crowd back from the body. It was a daunting task, because there were people inside the theatre trying to leave, as well as people still trying to get into the building.

"Has anyone called the authorities?" she asked as she looked around for someone with authority at the Gaillard. Everyone seemed stunned to see a body lying in front of the theatre, and no one answered her. Unexpected deaths just didn't happen in the historic area of Charleston. Two older ladies in white dresses with nametags, "Piccolo Festival Volunteers," were both as pale as their dresses. Maggie opened her cellphone and dialed 911. The operator came on the line. "What is your emergency?"

"My name is Lieutenant Maggie Watson from Rowlette, Illinois, and I am visiting in your city. There has been some type of accident or incident at the Gaillard Theatre. We need some emergency equipment or a BUS here immediately. There is at least one person down on the concrete floor, but we haven't been inside the building to see if there are other casualties."

"Please hold the line," she said and was gone for at least two or three minutes. When she came back on the line, she asked, "Can you stay at the site and help secure the scene until the police and ambulance get there?"

"Absolutely, not a problem," Maggie said. "My associate and I will try to keep the scene from being trampled as best we can, but we need some police tape and some officers to help us seal off the area in case this is a homicide."

"OK, Lieutenant Watson. Our officers will be there shortly."

Maggie and Jonathan managed to move the crowd back about fifteen feet from the body. Maggie asked Jonathan if he could control the crowd while she checked out the inside of the theatre.

"Sure, Maggie. I've got this. As soon as the authorities get here, I will come inside and join you."

Maggie had not brought her Glock with her, so she decided she would be more cautious than usual as she checked out the interior of the Gaillard.

"Is there anyone here?" She began to pan the small theatre with her small flashlight that she never traveled without. There was movement to the right of her, and before she could identify who or what that movement was, she was struck on the head with some instrument. She only got a glimpse of her attacker before she fell to the floor and passed out.

As Maggie began to come to, she heard Jonathan calling to her from the entrance of the theatre. "Are you all right?" His voice was the only sound in the building. He didn't have the benefit of a flashlight, so he went down to the front of the stage and groped for a light switch or another way to illuminate the hall.

He found a battery of breakers, threw one into the active position, and the footlights on the stage illuminated the entire space. He saw a shadowy figure slinking out the rear exit of the theatre into the alley that ran behind the Gaillard. He spotted Maggie lying in the center aisle. He picked up his cell phone and called 911 again.

"Send an ambulance immediately—officer down, officer down!" he yelled into the phone.

He rushed to her side and felt for a pulse. It was strong and steady. He grew concerned about a possible concussion. The paramedics and the local police arrived at the Gaillard within seconds of each other. He told the uniformed policeman what they had observed, and he watched while they began to put yellow crime scene tape around the building entrance.

Since Maggie was his first concern, Jonathan rode with her to the University of South Carolina Hospital, located on Ashley Street near the harbor. The paramedics took her into the emergency room, and he shared Maggie's personal information with the admissions clerk and admitting nurse. He sat in the waiting room and watched the hands of the clock move very slowly as it clicked off the seconds and minutes while he waited to see her. He had to wait over an hour to hear anything about her condition.

"You may see your friend now," the attendant told him, and he escorted Jonathan to the ward where Maggie had been admitted for observation for the evening. "Don't stay too long, because the doctor says she needs her rest," he said with a parting word of caution.

Jonathan slowly pushed open the door to a room that had two beds separated by a curtain hooked to a track on the ceiling. No one was in the other bed, so he felt as though he could talk to her without reservations.

"What happened?" she asked with a dazed look in her eyes.

"You don't remember?"

"I remember going into the theatre with my flashlight, looking for clues. I saw something or someone out of the corner of my eye just before he clobbered me. Then I remember waking up here a few minutes ago. How badly am I hurt?"

"You have some lacerations where you fell against the seats in the theatre, and you have a nasty bump on your head. Other than that, you appear to be fine."

"Do I have a concussion?" she queried.

"Not that the doctors can see from the X-rays, but they want you to take it easy and stay in the hospital overnight for observation. I think it's a good idea," he said as he brushed the long strands of hair away from her face.

"Not going to happen," she said in her typical stubborn voice when she had already decided what course of action that she wanted to take with a problem. "I've got to get back to the Gaillard to make sure these locals don't destroy any evidence that we may need to track down this maniac."

"And you think it is a good idea for you to be investigating a murder so soon after a head trauma? This is not your city, nor your case. Let it be, and let's go back to the Gaslight Inn and rest until you have your strength back."

"Look, Jonathan, whoever attacked me made this personal for me. Unless the local authorities prevent me from helping them solve this crime, I am going to do my best to help in any way possible to find and prosecute my attacker. By the way, what happened to the person on the street in front of the theatre?"

"Pronounced dead on the scene by the local coroner. It appears from what I have overheard with their preliminary investigation, the murdered victim was a local actor who had reported to the theatre for rehearsal just before the doors opened to the public. When the first patrons began arriving to take their seats for the show, this guy wandered out of the hall into the entrance and collapsed. By the time anyone got to him to check out his vital signs, he was not breathing and had a big knot on the back of his head, much like yours. It appears that he did not fare as well as you, since the coroner pronounced him dead at the scene at 3:14 PM, about twenty minutes or so after we arrived at the theater."

Maggie began getting up from the bed so she could find her clothes to get dressed to return to the Gaillard. Jonathan just looked at her with a mixture of disbelief and admiration. This woman was as determined as any person that he had known. She was going back to the theatre if it killed her!

"Since you are determined to go back to the Gaillard to follow up, I am going with you. We will probably need to make a courtesy call on the mayor's office or the chief of police to ensure they have given us their blessing to remain in the city after this incident."

"That's fine with me. I always try to follow protocol."

Jonathan just rolled his eyes, surprised as ever by Maggie's courage and strength.

Chapter 4

Mayor Anderson's Office

"Mayor, the off-duty police Lieutenant from Illinois who found the body of the actor is here in the outer office to see you. Shall I send her and her associate in to see you?" the receptionist asked Leon Anderson, the long-time mayor of Charleston.

Anderson had been elected to the office of mayor almost thirty years ago. He was a local son, having graduated from the College of Charleston in 1964. He then graduated from the University of South Carolina Law School in Columbia, a two-hour drive up I-26. Leon remembered well the drive to Columbia from Charleston, because when he was traveling to and from Columbia and Charleston, he had to use a two-lane state highway, and the trip could take upwards to three hours in bad weather or on holidays. If anyone appreciated progress in Charleston, it was Mayor Anderson.

The mayor's office was located on the second floor of an historic building at the Four Corners of Law, at the intersection of Broad Street and Market Street. Each of these buildings represented a different level of government—the Charleston County Courthouse, state law; the U.S. Post Office, federal law; St. Michael's Episcopal Church, God's law; and the Charleston City Hall, municipal law. This was just one of the many oddities of Charleston, a city with over three hundred years of colorful history.

Leon, a likeable gentleman, was originally elected to the mayor's office after a racial scandal had rocked this historic city in the late 1960s. The scandal involved a prominent African-American pastor who had had an affair with a Caucasian woman, a newspaper columnist with the *Charleston Beacon*, the major local newspaper. She was not from the Charleston area originally, which was a strike against her for Charlestonians, and the infidelity made her seem more like a pariah than she would have been otherwise. Besides the sensitivity of interracial relationships in the South at that time, there was a secret child between them. To further create instability to the situation, both the pastor and the columnist were married. A very prominent civil rights leader made a trip to Charleston to help calm the anxiety, and Mayor Anderson became the negotiator between the races on that fateful day. It took a special touch with the locals and their institutions to be elected mayor of "The Holy City" and to be reelected for so many years. Anderson fully appreciated what Edward Gilbreth, a columnist in a major local Charleston publication in the 1800s once stated, *"Any city that is full of sacred cows, worshipped by its inhabitants and envied by the rest of the world, would inevitably become known as the 'Holy City.'"* Anderson appreciated Charleston's "sacred cows" fully!

The racial stress in Charleston was fateful for Anderson, because it propelled him into prominence in both the black and white communities surrounding it. Mayor Anderson was so popular that no one attempted to run against him when the election rolled around every four years. Since there were no term limits to the mayor's term of service, he just kept coming to work trying to represent his city for all those years. There were typical problems with theft, larceny, and other crimes in and around Charleston, but very few murders occurred in this historic place. The downtown area of Charleston from Calhoun Street to the Battery was considered off-limits for local troublemakers because of its commercial value to the city. As improbable as it would appear to a statistician, downtown Historic Charleston was a non-combat, off-limits zone for local criminals. It was just understood by everyone living there.

Although Anderson was short of stature, five-feet-six inches or so in height, he made up for it in his bigger-than-life personality. His distinguished gray hair and seersucker suit created the perfect picture of a Southern gentleman for Maggie and Jonathan as they were ushered into his office.

"First of all, I want to thank you myself and on behalf of the entire City of Charleston for coming to our aid yesterday at the Gaillard Theatre. It was an unfortunate situation, which I am glad to say is under control at this time. I do hope you weren't injured too badly," he said in a smooth, but heavily accented Southern drawl.

"Oh, I'm fine," Maggie responded. "Just a bump on the head—nothing serious, I'm glad to report. Can you tell me what leads you have on the attacker and possible murderer?"

The mayor squirmed a little in his overstuffed leather chair and replied, "Well, we are looking into the details of the incident, but at this time we really don't have any leads to follow. We don't know that this was a murder because the actor could have fallen and hit his head before staggering out into the open area of the theatre. I have turned everything over to our Police Chief, Major Gerald Pinckney. I'm sure he will handle things tactfully and in good time," the mayor finished his thought and stood to indicate that this pleasant conversation was coming to an abrupt end.

"Before we go, Mayor, I wanted to ask a favor of you. Jonathan and I have planned a two-week vacation here in Charleston, and we have pre-paid our lodging at the Gaslight Inn on Meeting Street for that period of time, and I would like to consult with Major Pinckney about the progress of the investigation while we are here. I am assuming, since I was a victim in this ordeal, that you would have no objections to my talking with him unofficially."

"Well, I don't see how it can hurt, Lieutenant Watson. There is one thing I want you to keep in mind, though. The Piccolo/Spoleto Festival is an annual celebration that has been taking place in Charleston for the past twenty years, and it has a major economic impact upon our businesses and residents, with visitors and their revenue coming from around the world for two weeks every year. Although it is unfortunate that the young man died at the Gaillard Theatre, we will probably not get into a full-fledged investigation until the festival concludes later next week. I'm sure you see my dilemma here," he said with a concerned look.

"I understand the sensitivity that the economic impact of this murder could have on your city, but if you wait ten days to two weeks to begin your investigation in earnest, many clues about the murder may have vanished by then," she said critically.

"Why don't you speak to Major Pinckney about your concerns, and then we will go from there? Now, I really must get back on schedule. I have meetings all day with organizers of the festival that I must keep. Mrs. Warrenton will show you out," and almost magically, Nancy Warrenton appeared at the door to escort them out of Anderson's office.

As they were walking back up the street toward the Gaslight Inn, Maggie looked at Jonathan and asked, "Am I the only one who felt like we were politely told to get lost and forget that all of this happened?"

"No, you're not. However, we don't have any jurisdiction here, and if the mayor wants us to keep our fingers out of the pie, I guess we will have to do so."

"The hell you say," she said emphatically. "You're not the one who was attacked by the murderer and who had to make an unplanned visit to the hospital for X-rays! Let's see how willing they are to consider a lawsuit by a tourist during their precious Piccolo/Spoleto Festival!"

"Maggie, are you sure you want to go down that road? Once you throw the gauntlet down in that manner, you really can't reverse your course of action very gracefully. And from what I have noticed about every local Charlestonian, gracefulness is a quality that they all aspire to here in Charleston.

"In answer to your question, you're damn right I plan to go down that path. They have no idea what they are dealing with in regards to the murder of the actor, and also I have a right and a duty to help find whoever knocked me out so rudely!"

"Do you think you should call Captain Culpepper and let him know about the sensitive nature of the events down here before you get knee-deep in the affairs of such a sensitive situation?"

Captain Josiah Culpepper was Maggie's boss and the top cop in the Rowlette Police Department back in Illinois. He was a no-nonsense sort of guy, and he didn't like his officers to make waves that upset his calm working relationship with the mayor of Rowlette, Elijah Ridgeway. She was not officially representing the City of Rowlette while she and Jonathan were on vacation in Charleston, but she was a high profile person who seemed to attract attention no matter where she was and what she did.

"Look, Jonathan, we are simply tourists on holiday, just like everyone else here in Charleston this week. The fact that I have been involved in a crime that no one seems to want to acknowledge should not impact my relationship with my boss back home. Am I right?" And she looked to him for some indication of approval.

"Maggie, you should never go into politics. The first thing you have to learn is that you are always being observed, and the smallest slip that you make can, and often will, come back to bite you in the ass!" he said rather dramatically.

"I never claimed to be a politician! I want no part of politics in my job or anywhere else, but I have to say that 'right is right' and 'wrong is wrong', and that's all there is to it."

"Maggie, Maggie, Maggie," he sighed. "Whatever you decide to do about this situation is OK by me. I have your back, and I always will have your back, but this episode could get really messy if you're not careful."

"So, I'll be careful!"

"Right," he said softly. "Like a bull in a china store!" And he couldn't help but smile at this beautiful, determined woman that he was falling head-over-heels in love with.

"Let's go see Major Pinckney and talk some sense into him. Why does that name sound familiar to me?"

"Other than his great-great-great grandfather being a signer of the original U.S. Constitution?" he said and smiled at her sweetly.

"Oh yeah, I knew I had heard that name before. I will act impressed with his family history if you think that will put me in his favor," she said and gave Jonathan a devilish grin.

"You are too much, Maggie Watson. Just much too much!" he said and kissed her gently on top of her head. She was a handful for sure, but she was his handful at the present time, and he was going to enjoy it as long as it lasted.

Chapter 5

Negotiations

"We are here to see Major Pinckney," Maggie informed the desk sergeant, Abigail Lawton, at the Charleston Police Department front office. "We just visited with the mayor, and he suggested that we stop by and visit with your chief," she concluded, twisting Mayor Anderson's direction.

"I will see if he is available to visit with you. And what did you say your name was?" "Just tell him that Lieutenant Maggie Watson from Rowlette, Illinois, would like to see him about the murder at the Gaillard Center yesterday."

Abigail raised her eyebrows. "Give me a minute to see if he is tied up in a meeting, and I'll be right back," she said and disappeared into the back offices.

Jonathan looked skeptically at Maggie, hoping that this situation was not going to turn into a controversial visit. He knew that although Maggie had good intentions, the visit could go badly. Pinckney would have to believe that she had some legitimate right to see that something was being done to find the person who had injured her. The door to the lobby opened, and a large, well-built man in a very ornate uniform entered the room. He was over six feet tall, muscular, but not overly so, with tanned skin and a full head of red hair. His uniform had clusters of stars on his shirt collar, his jacket fit him perfectly, and he sported a highly starched white shirt under the decorative jacket.

"Good morning, Lieutenant Watson." He extended his hand in a gesture of friendship to her and Jonathan. "What can I do for you today?" he asked and motioned them to a grouping of chairs in the lobby, where he indicated they might sit and talk.

"Good morning, Chief Pinckney," she responded in kind to him. "I was thinking we might want to discuss this situation in a more private setting," Maggie suggested to him.

"Well, Lieutenant Watson, there really isn't anything to discuss at this time," he said rather matter-of-factly. "We are analyzing the situation that took place yesterday, and we will move forward when we have more information. That's about all I can share with you about the events at the Gaillard Center yesterday. And by the way, your Chief Culpepper has asked me to have you call him at your earliest convenience."

"So, let me see if I understand you, Major Pinckney. You want me to forget that I was attacked and put into the hospital by someone who murdered someone in your city? And you think that putting pressure on me from my boss in Illinois will get you off the hook? What have I mistaken about your comments so far?" she asked with color rising in her cheeks.

"Lieutenant Watson, you have no legal authority here in Charleston, that is unless I grant that to you, and at this time I don't see the need for such an action. I suggest that you file a complaint against the unknown perpetrator and leave the crime fighting in Charleston to us," he said more emphatically than before.

"I guess I am supposed to turn a blind eye to the fact that you and the mayor are ignoring the fact that a murder was committed in Charleston yesterday, and by the very person who attacked me? Is that what you call 'crime fighting?'" she exploded with as much anger as she thought she could get away with under the circumstances.

"As the mayor may have shared with you, we haven't decided that the young actor was murdered. It could have been a coincidence that you were attacked shortly after the young actor died. The coroner will determine those facts, and we will move forward once we have the probable cause of death. However, that is no concern of yours," and he stood to dismiss her.

It appeared to Maggie that the mayor and Major Pinckney were conspiring to get her off this case and out of town. She wasn't buying into their scenario, and she was a little concerned about speaking to her boss back in Rowlette.

"I'll tell you what I am going to do, Major Pinckney. I have prepaid for two-week's lodging at the Gaslight Inn on Meeting Street, so I will continue to visit in Charleston until that time expires. If at any time during my stay I feel like I have any leads on whoever hit me on the head, I will make sure you are made aware of those facts." and Maggie stood up to leave.

"About that lodging at the Gaslight Inn, they have graciously returned the full amount of your charge to your credit card, because it appears the hotel is overbooked, and your room is no longer available for you at that hotel. The manager wanted me to tell you that they are very sorry for the inconvenience, but your bags and personal effects are now waiting at the concierge's desk."

"Do you actually think that running me out of town is a charming thing to do for a city with the reputation that Charleston has, Major Pinckney?" she asked with an unbelievable look on her face. "Unbelievable!" she said in a volume much louder than was normally heard in this charming city.

Just as she and Jonathan were getting up to leave, the booking officer asked Major Pinckney if he could speak with her briefly. She also asked Maggie and Jonathan to stay until she had finished her conversation with the chief. She handed the telephone to Major Pinckney, and he listened to the conversation on the other end of the line without comment. He finally said, "OK, Mayor," and hung up the phone.

"Could you please come into my office?" Pinckney asked them and held the door for them, directing them down the hall to his personal space. Maggie could only look at Jonathan with wonder and disbelief, all the while hoping that she and Jonathan would not be incarcerated for some unknown reason. She wouldn't put it past Pinckney to do anything unlawful at this juncture.

"I just heard from Mayor Anderson. It appears that another actor has been murdered at the Strand Theatre on Church Street. We have agreed to let you help us investigate these unfortunate situations, with a few caveats, that is, if you are still willing to get involved in our local affairs," and Major Pinckney's attitude was totally different from what it had been just a few minutes ago.

Maggie looked at Jonathan, and they both nodded in the affirmative. They were almost mute, they were so shocked.

"Mayor Anderson has spoken to your Chief Culpepper, and he has arranged to loan your services to us for an indefinite period of time, assuming you are willing to help us. He said that your vacation is rescinded, and you are officially on duty. We, of course, will see that all of your expenses are borne by the City of Charleston."

"So what about our reservations at the Gaslight Inn?"

"I'm sure under these circumstances your room can be secured again, what with this being an emergency and all."

"Sure, we will be happy to help fellow officers of the law," Maggie said with commitment. "What caveats do we need to comply with to be willing to join your team?" she asked suspiciously.

"Lieutenant Watson, Charleston is not a rough and tumble city like most major cities in the USA. Things are not done the same way here as they are in New York City, or even in your small town of Rowlette, Illinois, for that matter. We have old traditions that we need to try and uphold as we are investigating this unusual crime spree. I understand that some things will have to be done that might be considered less than discreet during this investigation, but please keep in mind that many of our patrons are visiting our city from various other cities in the country, and from foreign countries as well. We want them to feel safe, and we don't want them to think that they are in danger walking the streets of Charleston. Just keep that in mind, and we will get along fine," he concluded.

"We will do what we can to downplay the investigation, Major Pinckney, but the hard, cold facts are that your residents and visitors are not safe walking the streets of Charleston as long as this person or these people are killing people with no regard for decorum," she added with a small smile.

Major Pinckney nodded his head in acceptance of the unspoken truce between them. Now they both needed to coordinate their efforts to stop this danger to everyone in Charleston. Maggie and Jonathan headed up the street to dress for an investigation, and Jonathan thought he might jump in the Jacuzzi for a few minutes while Maggie was getting ready to go back out. She was pretty efficient at getting ready, but he probably had time for a Jacuzzi nonetheless.

Chapter 6

Leadership

"Captain Culpepper," Maggie spoke to her police commander from the Gaslight Inn in Charleston for the first time since she and Jonathan had arrived in this beautiful historic city. "Do you want to give me instructions about this assignment, or would you like for me to ask questions?" She wanted to find out how he had come to know about the situation.

"Well, when Major Pinckney called me the first time about your potential to meddle in their affairs, he was curious about how aggressive an officer you were." Maggie made no reply.

"And how did the conversation move from that point to the request for me to be temporarily loaned to the City of Charleston as a murder investigator?" she asked with real interest. "They were getting ready to run me out of town on a rail!"

"Funny you should ask, because within an hour of my original conversation with their Mayor Anderson, I received another call from his office. That second time, butter wouldn't melt in his mouth, especially when he found out about the cathedral murders that you and your task force had just solved. Let Pinckney tell you, but I think he wants you to be a special independent investigator for them. I can spare you as long as you're needed because of the fine job you did bringing Jo-Ellen along as a junior investigator. She can't replace you, but she is as sharp as a tack!"

Jo-Ellen Broussard was a recent graduate of the Police Academy in Rowlette, and even though she had gotten off to a rocky start with Maggie at the beginning of the cathedral murders investigation, she had matured into a fine investigator over the past few months. She was one of two young investigators on the St. Aquinas Cathedral case, and she was head-and-shoulders above her associate Leroy Cannon, who had graduated in her class at the academy. He would probably never make lieutenant, but Jo-Ellen was well on her way to bigger and better positions, having already earned the rank of sergeant for her excellent work on the St. Aquinas Cathedral murder cases.

"It's good to know something positive came out of those murders. That seems like a century ago."

"Keep your nose clean down there, Maggie. Is Jonathan OK with an extended stay in Charleston as well?"

"Oh, I think he can get accustomed to multiple five-star restaurants on every street, along with a Jacuzzi in the courtyard of our hotel available to him most of the day and night. He's really roughing it, if you know what I mean." She laughed and looked out the window at Jonathan sitting in the Jacuzzi with the jets bubbling water everywhere. When she hung up, she was ready to get started with the investigation.

"What do you want to do first, Maggie?" Jonathan asked when he came in from the Jacuzzi. "Should we check in with Major Pinckney at headquarters before we proceed with any investigations?"

"Yes, even though Captain Culpepper has said they want me to head up this investigation, I haven't heard it officially from anyone who has authority here."

"OK, let's check in with Major Pinckney and see where things stand."

As they were walking to the police station, Jonathan just chuckled a little. "I think I could get accustomed to this city if I were I enticed to move here for some reason."

"What brought that up?"

"I just feel comfortable and relaxed in Charleston. I could see us buying one of these historic houses, sitting on the piazza sipping sherry, and watching the kids play in the backyard."

"I'd love to see a New Yorker like you trying to adjust to the pace of a Southern city like Charleston. You would be meeting yourself going and coming. They don't get in a hurry around here for much of any reason. Also, you would be bored to tears! And who said anything about kids? We haven't even talked about marriage!"

"Surely you've thought about it, Maggie. I might just surprise you and become super domesticated!" He kissed her full on the mouth.

"We don't have time for that right now, but bring the subject up to me again in the Jacuzzi after the day's work is over."

"Promises, promises."

* * *

They walked into the police station, and this time Abigail Lawton called for Major Pinckney before they could announce themselves.

"He will be with you shortly. He is expecting you."

Pinckney came through the door with his hand outstretched to both of them. His attitude had completely changed from a few hours earlier.

"Come on back to my office," he said warmly. "Can we get you anything to drink?"

"No, we are just fine," Maggie told him. "I wanted to make sure we were on the same page on how you want me to help your investigation."

"I think the mayor wants to speak to you about that as well, so can you two walk across the street and meet with us together?"

"Sure," she said.

They got up to leave his office, and Pinckney said, "Please accept my apology for our earlier meeting. I was simply following my orders from the mayor. Everyone here is very sensitive about crime and how it may affect our festivals and tourist trade."

"Think nothing of it," she said. "If I had been in your position, I might have reacted the same way. We just want to help you get the perpetrator off the street so your citizens and visitors alike will feel safe again."

They walked across the street, and the mayor's administrative assistant, Nancy Warrenton, rose, immediately went into Anderson's office, and brought him quickly back into the lobby to greet them.

"Come inside, come inside," the mayor repeated and ushered them into his office. He motioned them to sit on the leather loveseat that was directly opposite his desk. Chief Pinckney took a wing chair off to the side of the mayor's desk to complete the circle. "I appreciate your agreeing to stay on for a while here in Charleston to help us solve these two murders. I am afraid we have never had to deal with anything quite like this since I was elected some thirty years ago. Lieutenant Watson, I would also appreciate your taking the lead on the investigation, if you are comfortable with that task. I understand from your Chief that you and your friend here recently solved a very difficult murder case in Rowlette," and he motioned to Jonathan to make sure Jonathan knew that he was considered part of Maggie's team.

"Well, I have to admit, Mayor Anderson, I could not have succeeded without Jonathan. He is a great sounding board for my ideas, as well as a pretty decent investigator on his own."

"Oh, are you a licensed investigator as well, Jonathan?"

Jonathan laughed. "No, but I studied criminology at Loyola University, which is where I met Maggie," he said and grinned at her.

"He's neglecting to tell you that he also graduated from Harvard Law School and that he completed post-graduate studies in psychology. As I said, he is extremely helpful when it comes to second-guessing a crime scene."

Unlike a tactful Southerner, Mayor Anderson asked, "And are you two engaged?" He was venturing into a more personal area than either Jonathan or Maggie felt comfortable discussing. Hell, they hadn't even discussed that subject formally without joking between themselves at this point in their rekindled friendship, so how could they civilly answer the mayor's question?

Jonathan got them off the hook by simply saying, "Maggie and I have a very special relationship. Let's leave it there for the time being," and he indicated in his tone that any more questions about their personal situation were off-limits, even to the mayor.

"Maggie, I want to ask a special favor of you. We don't get murders around the Historic Charleston District very often. As I may have mentioned to you earlier in the day, I can't remember a murder during one of our annual festivals, much less two murders. We don't have the expertise to go about the research and investigative techniques that are probably very common to you in Rowlette. So, I have asked your captain if you might serve us as a special investigator until we have solved these Piccolo Festival murders. As much as I want to dismiss this as a freak accident or some other anomaly, it is pretty obvious that this is something much more. Culpepper told me that the decision to stay and/or serve as a special detective for us is your decision to make. He will support your decision, and we will pick up your expenses, but the final decision is yours and yours alone."

"Well, not quite," she said, and she turned to Jonathan for his input. "You will be as involved as I am if I take this assignment. Are you up for it, or did you really just want to come to Charleston to rest?"

"I'm game," he said. "But the mayor and chief will have to understand that I will need to be deputized to be able to help defend you, if the situation arises where that is required. We will need some supplies that we did not bring with us, but I'm sure they can be procured from the police department property room if the chief is amenable to our requests," and Jonathan paused for everyone to get on the same page.

"Do you know how to use a sidearm or a Glock, Jonathan?"

Jonathan produced his concealed carry permit for them to inspect, and Maggie chimed in quickly, "He can put a three-inch pattern of rounds in a target from twenty yards away, unless he is using a sniper rifle."

"And are you also qualified with a sniper rifle, Jonathan?" Anderson asked.

"Qualified or not," Maggie jumped into the conversation to answer for Jonathan, "he can hit a bull's-eye target from sixty yards with a scope. I know because he saved my life a few weeks back doing just that!" and she beamed at him.

"I have no problem deputizing you, Johnathan," the Chief said. "Let's go back by my office, make you eligible to carry a weapon for the City of Charleston, and get both of you dressed out with the proper gear to help us find the lunatic wrecking our beloved city," Pinckney said somberly.

"That works for us," Maggie said, and they shook the mayor's hand as they exited his office. Once outside, Maggie turned to Jonathan, "What a difference a few hours can make when you possess what someone really wants!"

Chapter 7

The Coroner

"Major Pinckney, do you have a roster of your people available so I can review their personnel files? I want to choose my own team of investigators to help me solve these crimes, but rather than having you tell me who is available, I would like to choose two of your people and see if they can be made available to me for this investigation," Maggie said, showing her leadership abilities to take charge of the situation.

Maggie had been instructed by the mayor that she could have anyone she wanted on her team of investigators, but having no prior knowledge of anyone on the police roster, she knew she would have to depend on Major Pinckney to help her determine the best two officers to join her team. She had parameters that had worked for her in the past, and she thought that sticking to that protocol would probably give her the best chance of solving these murders. After all, murder was murder, whether it was in Illinois or South Carolina.

"I will get Abigail to generate that list for you now, so you can have it in the next couple of hours. Do you know who or what type of members you want?"

"Not really at this time, but when I see their personnel jackets, I will know who I want. It's just sort an innate thing that I do when I am selecting out a team to help me."

"There is no one in the department that you cannot have, especially if choosing the correct people will help us solve these crimes quickly."

"I can't promise you if or when we will be able to solve these two murders, but I can tell you that we will leave no stone unturned until we have exhausted every effort to determine the suspects. That I can promise you," she said and looked him in the eyes in such a way that he had no doubts. He knew Lieutenant Maggie Watson was someone special as an investigator in his city.

"First, what has been done to preserve the crime scenes from the two incidents today?"

"We have placed crime tape and barricades at both theatres, and we have moved the events for the next few days away from the affected venues. Other than that, we really didn't know how to preserve the crime scene," he admitted.

"OK, we need to get a couple of your best street patrol officers on the scenes and have them stay there until the coroner and I can make sure that all the potential evidence is retrieved, analyzed, and cataloged. That needs to be done immediately, because people may have already have contaminated the crime scenes with foot traffic, in and around those theatres."

"We'll get that done now," he said and had Abigail get on the police band radio and move a couple of officers into place at the affected venues. "What else do we need to do now to help you?"

"Jonathan and I will both need a Glock, ammunition clips, a Kevlar vest suitable to our body sizes, and a battery of bright, portable lights delivered to each scene, one at a time. By the way, can you get the coroner on the phone for me and give me an introduction? I work very closely with the coroner when I am analyzing the statistical probability of why something happens or doesn't happen."

"Sure. Why don't we walk over to the University of South Carolina Hospital on Ashley Street so you can meet her? Her lab is in the basement, and she is there most of the time. I will call ahead and make sure she is available before we go. It's about a fifteen-minute walk, unless you prefer to drive over."

"Walking is fine. I need to walk off some of the calories from this Low Country Cooking that I have been consuming since I got to town."

The chief picked up the telephone and called a number that had been programed into his desk set. "Louise, are you busy right now? Good, I want to bring someone by to meet you. I will have a Lieutenant Maggie Watson and her associate Jonathan Pembroke with me. We will walk over, so it will be about fifteen or twenty minutes before we get there. Will that work with your schedule?" He listened again and said, "OK," and hung up the receiver.

"Are we ready to go?" Maggie asked him.

"Yes, I thought we would introduce you to Dr. Louise Henshaw, and then I will come back and get your weapons and Kevlar vests. With this maniac running around killing folks for the pleasure of it, you both need to be armed."

"I agree," Jonathan chimed into the conversation. He had not interrupted Maggie or Gerald Pinckney as they were talking strategy, but he just wanted to make sure everyone knew that he was for getting armed and protected before they launched their own investigation.

"Abigail, please make sure you have those personnel files on the desk in the conference room so Maggie can go over them when we return from the coroner's office."

"Yes, sir," she said compliantly. Abigail rarely spoke in Maggie and Jonathan's presence, but when she did say something, it was usually a necessary and important bit of information. "Shall I set them up in the office that Joe Waller used before he retired last fall?"

"Absolutely, and make sure that they have adequate chairs and other items necessary in case they want to use that office for interrogation purposes." They exited the police station and headed west down Broad Street and took a right turn on Ashley toward the hospital and the morgue.

* * *

Major Pinckney inserted a special key into the control panel of the elevator to activate the basement button. Maggie and Jonathan thought that it was a bit unusual that the elevator had to have a special key to access the basement. This was a new security procedure, Major Pinckney explained, that was enacted after some relatively innocent interruptions into the morgue a few months ago. They exited the elevator and were met by an attractive young physician in her white lab jacket with Dr. Henshaw stenciled on the pocket.

"Dr. Henshaw, this is Lieutenant Maggie Watson and her associate, Jonathan Pembroke. They will be working with us on the recent murders of the actors in the Piccolo/Spoleto venues. Maggie is a successful investigator from Rowlette, Illinois, and

Jonathan is a freelance inspector in his own right," Gerald Pinckney made the introductions when they had arrived at the coroner's lab.

Louise Henshaw held up her gloved hands, indicating that shaking hands would not be appropriate, as she had excused herself from the autopsy room to meet with them. She gave an appraising glance at Maggie, but she stared intensely at Jonathan's face, as though she had met him before.

"It's nice to meet you both," she said politely. "I'm sorry I can't sit and talk with you at length right now, but I have two bodies in the cooler that need to be autopsied as soon as possible. They are the two unfortunate actors who were killed at the Galliard Theatre and the Strand," she said.

"We understand, Dr. Henshaw, and that's one reason we are here. In Rowlette, I have been able to sit in on the autopsies of recently murdered victims while the procedure was being performed. It gives quite a different perspective to the crime when the actual body of the victim is being diagnosed for cause of death. If you don't mind, and if your policy is not such that I cannot attend your autopsies, I would request that both my associate and I be able to be present when you perform the procedure on the two actors."

"Well, what I have found over the years is that well-intentioned detectives often find themselves throwing up in my preparation sink once I have begun my surgical procedure. Do you think either of you would have that reaction? If so, I'd just as soon not have you in my operating room until I have completed the procedure."

"I can guarantee you, Dr. Henshaw, that neither Jonathan nor I am the least bit squeamish when it comes to dead bodies or their dissection. We both studied criminology in college and attended many autopsies during the course of our final year of studies. We both witnessed autopsies recently after a crime wave in Rowlette. The reason I am making this request is that your expertise in explaining why the color of the tissue—the coagulation of blood and bruising of the body occur—can help us find who committed the crime."

"Under those circumstances, I am more than willing to have you present in my autopsy room. Also, please feel free to ask any questions that might arise while we are performing the operations. I will have an assistant coroner helping me with the dissections, and I will be dictating my results into an automated voice recorder. That recorder is the official record of the autopsy, and a script is generated from the recording. Don't worry about stopping me to ask questions, as they will be edited out of the final report. Any questions?"

"When do you plan to perform the first of the two autopsies?" Maggie asked.

"I'm finishing up on a couple of cases today, so I had planned to get to the first death, the one in the Galliard Theatre, tomorrow morning around 9:00 AM. You're welcome to attend. Just come to the elevator and ask the guard in the lobby to grant you access to the basement. He will have to use his passkey."

"So, is this floor secured from the remaining part of the building and the hospital on a routine basis?" Jonathan asked.

Dr. Henshaw grinned a little and said, "Well, we had to restrict access to this floor when innocent bystanders would inadvertently come to the autopsy room by mistake and pass out or throw up. It became a logistical problem, so I asked for the keyed access button on the elevator. We are the only operational office on this level of the hospital. Everything else is mechanical, storage, or otherwise non-patient related."

"We will be here no later than 9:00 AM tomorrow morning, Doctor. Thank you very much for accommodating us," Maggie said to her before they parted.

"By the way, Jonathan, are you related to the Pembroke Real Estate Company in New York City?" Louise asked.

Jonathan looked at her in disbelief but answered courteously, "Yes, in fact, the founder and recently retired owner is my father. Why do you ask?"

"It's a long story, and I will be happy explain at another time," and she turned to go back into the autopsy room. Jonathan had an uneasy feeling about her question, and he pondered why she might be knowledgeable about his family's past.

* * *

Louise Henshaw was an attractive lady, approximately the same age as both Jonathan and Maggie. She lived alone and was consumed in her work. The only living being that she ever had time for was her St. Bernard dog, named Lucky, who was lucky that his owner could afford to feed him eight to ten cups of dog food a day. She walked him around the streets of Charleston, and she felt very safe when Lucky was leading her down the historic streets. A two hundred pound dog certainly kept strangers away. Louise often thought about him during the day and looked forward to their walks for relaxation from her job.

Louise's mind moved from her thoughts of Lucky, as she looked at Jonathan leaving her morgue, wondering if her thoughts of his family name were accurate. She would cross that bridge later, if forced to do so.

In the meantime, Maggie, Jonathan, and Major Pinckney reentered the elevator, arrived at the main level, and walked back to the police department building. Once there, Maggie was pleased to find that Abigail had the police officer personnel folders displayed on the conference room table, all alphabetized and in neat stacks.

Chapter 8

The Team

Putting a discovery team together in one's own city and police department had been a job in itself, but doing it a thousand miles away in an unfamiliar city made the task even harder. Maggie had no concerns that the mayor's office and the police department were now completely behind her efforts to solve these two murders quickly and efficiently. Her greatest barrier at this point was determining the best people to include on her immediate team of investigators—people she could totally trust to do their jobs without direct supervision. She hoped Major Pinckney would be of assistance helping her construct her team.

Abigail's stacks of personnel folders, six or seven high on the conference room table, held probably fifty or more files. She calculated that she and Jonathan could do their first sorting of potential team members in about an hour.

"Major Pinckney, thank you for the introduction to the coroner, and for your help in getting these files to us for our consideration. If you could give Jonathan and me a little time to look over these briefly, we will select four or five files for final consideration. Once we have narrowed down the two officers that we think will be most suitable for our team, we will ask that you have them meet us here at the station so we can interview them. Is that suitable to you?"

"How many officers do you think you will need for your task force, Maggie?"

"We normally work with a very limited number of officers for a couple of reasons. First, the fewer people involved in this type of investigation, the fewer unauthorized leaks make it to the news outlets. I'm sure you will agree that keeping this investigation out of the public eye for the time being is critical."

"Absolutely, we want it no other way."

"Second, by keeping the team small, everyone can be brought up to speed on what the other team members are doing very quickly. What we have discovered in the past is that time is generally not on our side with cases like this. Anything to minimize the loss of time in the investigation puts the odds in our favor that we will succeed in finding the perpetrator."

"That sounds reasonable to me, but what can I do personally to help? This is my city, and the safety of the public and my citizens is my ultimate responsibility. I want to help, but I don't want to impede your progress in any way with bureaucratic bullshit," he said and smiled knowingly at them.

Maggie had been in the same position in the past in Rowlette, so she knew exactly how to answer his question. She wouldn't lay it on too thick, because Gerald Pinckney was no backroads country lawman, and he would see through false praise. However, a genuine compliment always made the sledding easier.

"Actually, Major Pinckney, we really do need your help with this investigation. We need you or one of your lead officers to coordinate officers at the sites of the crimes, to control foot traffic in the areas of the affected theatres, and to be ready with SWAT teams or other special services that we may need once we corner whoever is causing all of this grief for the City of Charleston. Is that something you would feel comfortable doing, or would you want to delegate that chore to someone else in your command?"

"I will be happy to handle the coordination of support for your team. This is important to me, the mayor, and the very livelihood of our city going forward. As you have probably noticed, this is a town driven by tourism. 'As tourism goes, so goes Charleston,' we say. Many years ago, the city fathers directed the city's services to accommodate the travelers and tourists who visit us each year. In the 1970s, when Gian Carlo Menotti, an Italian-American composer and Pulitzer Prize winner, proposed that the Spoleto Festival U.S.A. be in Charleston as a compliment to the Spoleto, Italy, Festival, it really put us on the map. Now, every year about a half a million tourists come to our city to celebrate the arts during the festival. The city sponsors and runs the Piccolo portion of the festival, and those concerts and arts displays are more local or regional in nature. However, everything is coordinated between the two festival boards, that is, the Spoleto Board of Trustees and the Piccolo Arts Committee of Charleston.

So you see, we want this crime wave over as soon as possible. It is imperative to the economic health of our area. We will give you 100% support in your efforts to find and prosecute these criminals. All you have to do is ask!"

"Thank you, Major Pinckney. We will look over these personnel jackets and get back to you soon," and she proffered her hand for him to shake, unofficially dismissing him from his own conference room. He got the picture and left them alone with the files.

"So, just what are you looking for in a couple of investigative officers, Maggie? I am assuming the length of service, merit accommodations, and history like that are not as important as other things. Am I correct?" Jonathan asked.

"Precisely. What we need are enthusiastic, energetic and hungry officers who want to make their mark in this department. That doesn't mean that we cull everyone over the age of thirty years of age, but history tells us that recent academy graduates, those with the best aptitude and attitude, are our best choice for assignments like this. And they are pretty good at taking orders and carrying out directions without having to have every detail explained to them. In other words, they don't know enough to be a pain in the ass!" She laughed at her own statement.

'So, I guess we get started by culling everyone over thirty!"

* * *

"How many of the officers have you set aside for review, Jonathan?" Maggie asked as she closed the last personnel file remaining in her stack.

"We both had twenty-five folders, and I have three that I think are worthy of consideration. How many do you have?"

"I have three as well, so we will need to do a little more trimming to get down to just two people. Why don't you take my three, and I will take yours? We can use a new set of eyes on each file, and if we still have more than two at the end of that procedure, we can discuss them."

"Excellent idea, Lieutenant Watson," he said with a sly grin. "You should be in charge of this investigation—oh, wait, you are in charge of the investigation. How quickly one can forget!" he chuckled.

"Well, aren't you in a good humor today?" she said and gave him a seductive look. "If you keep complimenting me, you might get lucky tonight!"

Jonathan just smiled his goofy, lustful smile that made her feel sexy.

They both poured over the remaining six personnel jackets, eliminating one from each stack in just a few minutes. They had difficulty narrowing the field further without some discussion.

"Give me the number one officer of the two that you are considering, and I will do the same for you," she said. They exchanged files, looked at each other's choice and both nodded in the affirmative. "Here's what we are going to do, Jonathan. These two officers are going to be members of the task force, and the other two will be reserve members, in case something happens to keep the first two from serving until the crimes are solved. What do you think?"

"Excellent choice. Unless we need to reconsider one or both of the reserve members, there is no reason to spend a lot of time considering who will be next. Unless Major Pinckney has a problem with either of these officers, I think we have found the best team members for our appointed task," she said.

"OK, let me see if he is in his office and can come in here to confirm our choices for helpers," Jonathan said, and he was out the door and down the hall before Maggie could respond one way or the other.

Major Pinckney picked up the two folders for the officers that they had chosen. "I congratulate you on two excellent officer choices. Both Juliet Robinson and Joey Lancaster are somewhat new and inexperienced, but both of them finished in the top tier of their class at the academy, and they both have excellent instincts. Juliet Robinson scored one hundred percent on her firearms qualification. She could actually become a sniper, if we were a large enough department to specialize in those kinds of skills."

"Thank you for your confidence in our choices. Can I assume you would have no objection to both of them serving on our task force?" Jonathan asked.

"No problem, but let me ask you about these other two folders that you have kept back with the two you intend to use. What's the story about them? Have you changed your mind about how many officers you'll need for your task force?"

"No, not at all. However, over the years we have learned to have some reserve players in line, just in case someone gets sick, has an emergency in the family, or some other unknown reason keeps the original people from carrying out their original duties," Maggie responded.

"I don't have any problem with the two officers that you selected, but can I ask why you chose inexperienced officers over experienced ones, with all the other factors being similar?" "Don't take this wrong, sir, but with new officers, you don't have to un-train them before you train them to do what you want them to do. The other two officers would have been our first choice had these recent graduates not been available. We understand that we lose something with inexperienced eyes over officers that have seen similar situations in the past. However, newer officers have fewer preconceived ideas about what results they should be getting during an investigation, whereas sometimes more experienced officers are looking for a certain result and might overlook other evidence if their mental picture of the desired result is already set in their minds. That is no reflection on your department or your training techniques, but in the ten years or so that I have been doing these types of investigations, newer eyes generally give us a more honest, clearer opinion of the data that we gather during the operation. For example, we just wrapped up a very complicated murder scheme in Rowlette a few weeks ago, and of all of the people on the task force, the rookie cops were most effective. One of them was effective enough to earn a promotion to sergeant once the operation was over. The other new officer was effective, but pretty run-of-the-mill when it came to creativity and innovation. They both benefited from the experience, and I now have two more experienced officers, where only a few months ago they were still rookies, stumbling and bumbling around my crime scenes. I took a chance with these two rookies, and we got the job done in record time. If I had to make the choice again, I wouldn't do anything differently."

"Pardon me for being too inquisitive, Maggie, but will you share with me your age and time in law enforcement?"

"Not a problem, sir. I turned thirty-two years old this year, and I have been in the criminal investigations division for eight years. When I first graduated from Loyola University with a B.S. in Criminology, I figured I could use a little more training before I jumped into the fire, so I attended the police academy, focusing on criminology and forensic investigations. The additional training was very valuable, and it has helped me in my career path. Why do you ask?"

"As you two can probably figure from my gray hair and middle-aged paunch, I have been at this a little longer than you, eaten a few too many donuts, and lost a few too many foot races with some perps. And in all of those years, I have never met anyone your age with so focused an approach to crime solving as you. It's enough to make me want to try and recruit you to join us permanently here in Charleston."

"I appreciate the compliment, Major, but I'm too much of a Midwesterner to ever fit into this conservative and relaxed city. I do like a challenge, and it looks as if this is definitely going to be a real challenge for us all. Jonathan will tell you, I get bored pretty quickly if there is no real serious crime to solve. From what I have gathered from the Mayor's comments, and yours as well, this situation is unusual for Charleston. Living close to Chicago keeps us on our toes in Rowlette. We are only fifty or so miles southwest of one of the largest and violent cities in the country, if not the world. As much as I could get used to these fabulous restaurants in Charleston, I would probably get bored with the peaceful setting that you have here most days of the year. Also, I would have to purchase a new wardrobe every year eating in these great restaurants!"

Major Pinckney just looked at her and nodded. However, he thought she would make one hell-of-an inspector for the Low Country. He was jolted back into the present when Maggie asked, "Do you think that you can have the two officers report to the station tomorrow morning around 8:00 AM?"

"They will be there, ready to follow your lead, Lieutenant. See you then," and he stood and wished them a pleasant evening.

* * *

As Jonathan and Maggie walked back toward the Gaslight Inn, Maggie said, "Let's get some of that famous Low Country cuisine. I've heard that the 82 Queen Restaurant is one of the best in Charleston for She-crab soup and shrimp and grits."

"That sounds good to me. I understand that more wine is consumed in the Historic District than water, tea, and coffee combined!"

"Where did you get that statistic?"

"Why, from the Internet. Where else? By the way, I predict that this Internet thing will catch on, and we will no longer need phone books, address books, or newspapers in the distant future."

"Pretty bold prediction, Jonathan. What makes you think people will put their trust in something that they see on a computer screen over something in print? It would be a revolution."

"Just a hunch, I guess."

Seated at 82 Queen, they were able to sit in the garden area surrounded by small ornamental trees, sparkling white miniature lights, with plants and flowers all around. Their particular table had a white ceiling gently circulating air over them. They didn't know how long this place had been in business, but everything around them looked like antiques.

"What will you have?" the server asked.

"What do you recommend to visitors from Illinois?"

"Is this your first time in the city?"

"Actually, it is. We may be in town for an extended stay, so we want to get the best of the cuisine offered while we are here."

"Our specialties are She-crab soup and shrimp and grits, but everything on the menu is delicious. Would you like a few minutes to decide? How about some wine while you ponder your choices?"

"Excellent idea. What would you recommend?"

"If you are thinking of seafood or fowl, I recommend the 1976 Pouilly Fuisse. However, if you are contemplating pasta or beef, I suggest a nice Bordeaux from the old country."

They ordered the Bordeaux, had a fabulous pasta and shrimp dish, and were too full to order dessert. They walked two blocks north on Meeting Street to their hotel, let themselves into their room, and collapsed on the four-poster bed with hand-carved bedposts and a lace canopy. They dozed off to sleep and woke a few hours later, still in their clothes from work.

"I think we need to get up, get a little more work done, and then hit the Jacuzzi out in the courtyard," Jonathan said.

"Do I have to?" she moaned and rolled over in the queen-sized bed.

"Yes," he said and snatched the cover from her. "If you stay in bed now, you will be awake at 2:00 AM, and that just won't do, so get moving!" he joked, pulling her out of the comfy bed.

"You are so mean to me," she said, joking back. "I guess you're right—we have a lot to do before we meet our team members in the morning."

They gathered their materials, went to a lovely, glass-topped ornamental iron table in the courtyard and began their background research on the two officers who would be joining them the next morning. The courtyard at the Gaslight Inn was typical for a historic Charleston hotel—bubbling fountains, ornamental iron everywhere, live plants in urns adorning the space in the piazza area, and a single cello player lost in his playing of Bach. The culture in this city was so much richer than that of Rowlette, Illinois, that they discussed Charleston as a desirable place to retire when that time presented itself.

"Let's put this information on paper, so we can refer to it tomorrow when we have our first meeting with the two newly added officers in our task force," Maggie said to Jonathan.

"Our first special officer is Juliet Robinson. She is a first-year officer who graduated from the College of Charleston with a B.A. in History, and she entered the police academy immediately following her graduation. She has been assigned to patrol duty for the past three months in the North Charleston area—not a particularly good area to be walking solo, according to the crime statistics for the past few years. She worked in plain clothes as she walked her beat—not sporting a uniform of any kind, much less that of a police officer." He handed the dossier to Maggie, and she read the dossier.

"It looks like Robinson has been on the force for six months and has had twelve collars in that time period. She also finished near the top of her class, and she qualified as an expert with her service pistol," Jonathan read out her personal information from the dossier.

"Any family to speak of?" Maggie asked.

"It appears that she has a brother who is also in law enforcement, but no one else in the family has any history of law enforcement or military service. It would probably be good to find out just why she joined the police department. Sometimes there is a motivating factor that can either help or hurt an officer's advancement, and we don't need complications on this team."

"Good point. Do you see anything else that you find helpful or questionable in her past that we should consider?"

"She appears to be an excellent athlete. She ran track competitively in both high school and college, and she played intramural basketball while at college. As we both noticed initially, she finished with superior marks at the police academy. It appears that she was the top rookie in her class at the rifle range. The only thing that concerns me is that she is very young and very inexperienced."

"That can work for us, as well as against us. It's like having clay and deciding how to mold it. If we are lucky, she will turn out more like Jo-Ellen Broussard, and less like Leroy Cannon. We just won't know how she will react until she comes under fire in the field."

Jo-Ellen Broussard and Leroy Cannon were the two rookie cops whom Maggie and Jonathan had employed as part of their task force back in Rowlette, Illinois, when they were trying to solve the St. Aquinas Cathedral murders. Although they were both recent graduates from the police academy, Jo-Ellen had taken charge and was very instrumental in helping Maggie and Jonathan solve the complicated crimes perpetuated upon the people of

Rowlette. Leroy, although a good officer and dependable, showed no leadership characteristics throughout the investigative process.

"Well, unless she says something in the interview that is over-the-top, she will do just fine," Maggie said. "Now, let's look at officer number two."

Jonathan pulled out the personnel jacket for Jerome Lancaster. He was also a rather new officer, just a year out of the academy, and nothing much special denoting his service so far with the Charleston Police Department. He had good marks at the academy, but he didn't finish at or near the top of his class. He was from the Charleston area, and his family dated back several generations in this area. He had attended the College of Charleston, just off Ashley Street in the Historic District, but he had not finished his degree. They might want to challenge him on why he had started a program but did not finish, although Maggie truly believed that some people were just not meant for college studies. He was a perfect marksman, scoring no less than 100% efficiency at the range. He also had letters of recommendation in his file that indicated that he was a very personable young man. He might be the "buffer" for Maggie and Jonathan when it came to smoothing over miscues during the investigation to come. These Charlestonians seemed susceptible to possibly judging people more harshly if they weren't approached with that Southern charm that people from Illinois just didn't understand fully.

"OK, give me positives and negatives on our Officer Jerome Lancaster," she said, with pen in hand.

"It appears that Officer Lancaster, referred to in the police department as 'Joey' by his peers, is just a good old boy from the Low Country. His family ancestors probably came over on the first ship to dock here in 1685, and he is well-liked by all of his peers, and also by the townsfolk. According to his jacket, he is single, volunteers at the local homeless shelter a couple of times a month, and is a Boy Scout leader. There is nothing in his folder about his being outstanding since he has been on the force, but he doesn't appear to revel in the limelight. And as far as keeping us out of trouble with the locals, he is perfect. I like him for our team, maybe better than Officer Robinson. However, they may complement each other quite well, especially since she appears to be the go-getter, and he appears to be somewhat laid back."

"I think you are correct in your analysis, Jonathan. We need to think of a challenging question for them tomorrow to see how they will react to confrontation."

"Now, with all of that boring stuff done, can we get in the Jacuzzi?"

"Absolutely," she said. "However, since this Jacuzzi is in the public courtyard area, you will have to behave. Do I have your promise?"

"Hmmnn. I guess, if I have to!" And he kissed her convincingly on her lips.

They donned their swimsuits, took a bottle of white wine with plastic-stemmed wine glasses with them, and spent the next hour in the courtyard Jacuzzi before an hour of play in the queen-sized, four poster bed, followed by a great night's sleep.

* * *

They awoke early, got their showers and enjoyed a nice Continental Breakfast on the patio, complete with freshly-squeezed juice, bagels, fresh fruit, and other delights.

"I could get accustomed to this service, Maggie. What say we just move down here, I'll buy this place, and we will live happily ever after!" he teased.

"Right, that would work for you? One hundred degree days with 100% humidity for most of the year?"

"Well, there's that! But you have to admit, in May it is really nice."

"I'll take our six weeks of summer over eight months of this oppressive heat any day!" she said and wiped the small line of perspiration forming above her mouth.

"Remember, Jonathan, we are going to the coroner's office this morning to see if there are any clues that may turn up when she performs the autopsies on our murder victims. If we leave now, we will get there just about on time."

They walked down to Ashley Street to the hospital, got the guard on the desk to key the elevator to go to the basement, and they were on time for Dr. Henshaw's first incision. She was quick, efficient, and worked with excellent precision. Maggie thought she was probably a better coroner than Lonnie Gray, her coroner in Rowlette. In a matter of a few minutes, she pointed out something to them that surprised everyone in the room.

"This man died from toxic poisoning, not from that blow on the head," she said.

"Are you certain, Doctor?" Jonathan asked.

Louise Henshaw just looked at him as if he had two heads.

"Yes, absolutely certain," she said. "See this tissue in his throat lining?" and she pointed to an irritated area in the fleshy part of the larynx. "That only happens if someone has swallowed either poison or acid—which actually is the same thing. I do believe this man was forced to drink liquid drain opener. I don't know if the blow on the head came before or after the poison, but I will know by the end of the day. Why don't you let me finish this autopsy, and the other one as well, and stop by later this afternoon, and I will have a more complete picture for you."

"OK," Maggie replied. "We need to get to the police department anyway, so what time would be best for us to check back this afternoon?"

"Stop by around 4:00 PM—I will probably have finished both autopsies by then."

They left her office and got back on the elevator to go to the first floor of the hospital. Fortunately, they didn't need a key to activate the elevator from the morgue.

"We only have a few minutes until our young officers join us, so I guess we need to head back to the police station."

"It's only three blocks, Jonathan. Of course, we will be dripping wet with sweat by the time we get there!" She gathered her files and notes together, and they headed up Ashley Street in the heat.

Chapter 9

The Investigation

Jonathan and Maggie arrived at Charleston's historic building currently housing the police department, somewhat sweaty, but in good spirits. They both enjoyed exercise, and walking three blocks in this heat was like running a half-marathon! The building looked as if it had been built hundreds of years ago, with plaster frescos and ornate carvings adorning the columns, window sills, and dormers overlooking the streets below. It was truly a work of architectural beauty, but it was only one of the many hundreds of such buildings in the downtown area of Charleston. And although they thought the building was charming and beautiful, they wondered just how efficient it could be having the headquarters of the major policing agency in such antiquated facilities. Oh, well, that wasn't their problem, and once they figured out what had happened with these Piccolo Festival murders, they would be back on a flight to Chicago.

Both young officers were in the conference room waiting on them. Jonathan and Maggie could see them through the hallway windows, and they marveled at how young these officers looked from a distance. She had asked for rookies, and that's who she got. She would be tough, but not insensitive to their lack of experience and knowledge of routine police work. She was looking for a spark of energy and personal confidence, more than she was looking for experience.

"At ease," Maggie said to the young officers as they jumped up at attention when she walked into the room. "My name is Maggie, and this is Jonathan," she said, pointing to him. "I think we need to clear the air, first and foremost, so please don't worry about protocol with me or Jonathan. You will impress us, and your local supervisors, by helping us solve these horrific murders. Do you both understand?"

"Maggie, just what is it you want us to do to help you?" Joey asked.

"Should I call you Joey or Jerome?" Maggie asked.

"Oh, please call me Joey," his winning smile filling his young face from ear to ear. "My folks obviously wanted me to be more formal than I turned out. But everyone, and I mean everyone, calls me Joey."

"OK, Joey it is," she said. "To answer your question, Jonathan and I will be trying to analyze and link all of the data that, hopefully, you and Juliet are able to help us gather at the scene of each crime. We are headed over there now, so make sure you get everything you need for the next few hours, because you will be stationed there until lunchtime. Any questions?"

"No, ma'am," they both answered, and they rose to prepare leaving for the theatres.

"Juliet, do you go by Juliet or Julie?" Maggie inquired.

"Juliet is fine, ma'am."

"OK, Juliet and Joey it is! Juliet, I want you to go with Jonathan to the Strand Theatre. I believe from the street map on the wall here that it is only a few blocks to the east of here. Is that right?"

"Yes, ma'am. What do you want me to do once I get there?"

"Whatever Jonathan asks you to do, but feel free to ask questions of him as well. No one has all the answers or solutions at this point, so your input will be welcomed and appreciated. Joey and I will walk up the street at the Gaillard Theatre if you need me for any reason. By the way, do you think you can check out four handheld police band, two-way radios, so we can all keep in touch?"

"I'll do it now," she said, and she disappeared into the back office. She returned with four identical radios. "Will these be OK?"

"Absolutely. Let's all set our radios to channel 21, instead of 19. I don't particularly want everyone with a CB radio or police radio to know what we are communicating about during this investigation. It's not that it is a secret or anything like that, but even the perpetrator of these crimes may be listening on a CB radio. We don't want to give up any advantage we might have due to carelessness."

They all set their radios to the correct channel, and they set out for their specific areas to investigate. It was hot and steamy, so by the time they got to the two theatres where the murders had been committed, they were perspiring heavily. Since the theatres were not being used currently, the air conditioning had been turned off in both halls. The police officers that Maggie had requested to be posted to prevent contamination of the crime scenes were in place, and they were also suffering from the excessive heat.

"Somebody get the air conditioning turned on," she said when she and Joey arrived at the Gaillard. "Jonathan," she spoke into the hand-held radio, "get someone to turn the air-conditioning on there as well. If anyone complains, tell them to take it up with the mayor!"

"Joey, I am going to give you a specific instruction that I want to make sure you understand, OK?"

"Yes, ma'am, what is that?"

"Do you know what I mean when I say 'Keep this area from further cross-contamination?'"

"I would say you don't want anyone walking or moving around the crime scene. What else do you mean?"

"Do you understand that means you as well?" she asked with a questioning look.

"Of course, I could introduce microscopic evidence that might make the forensic investigator's job a lot harder to determine who might have walked around the body initially. I suggest we mark the area you want totally avoided with police crime tape, and I will assure you no one will walk there until you say it's OK."

"Joey, you and I are going to get along just fine!" she said with satisfaction.

Maggie turned up the house lights and began walking carefully around the theatre to see if anything unusual jumped out at her as to being out of place, or if anything irregular seemed to be visible. She then took the stage area, each section of seats, and then the rear of the theatre where the last known sighting of the suspected murderer was seen by Jonathan as he had slipped out into the alley. This was going to be a difficult task now that over twenty-four hours had elapsed since the first murder, but it just couldn't be helped.

Just when she thought that there were no clues to discover, she saw a piece of cloth with a small speck of blood on it lying on the floor. She had put surgical gloves on when she began her search, so she simply reached into her suit pocket and took a small clear plastic evidence bag from her pocket and placed the small scrap of cloth in it. She would get it to the coroner or a forensic lab technician to see if they could type the blood and find anything unusual about the stain on the cloth. Encouraged with her find, she called back to Joey, "Will you please turn the lights off in the theater—all of them? Don't go anywhere, but stay at the light panel because I will have you turn them back on pretty soon."

"Yes, ma'am," she heard him say and saw him moving toward the stage and the power switches. He was walking carefully, leading his steps with his small flashlight to ensure that he would not destroy any evidence that she might have missed. She was really encouraged with this young officer's common sense and understanding of what needed to be done and thought there was hope for the new recruits that were being turned out by the police academies today.

"OK, Joey, turn the lights off," she said and illuminated her black light, while spraying a fine mist of luminol in the area where she had found the scrap of cloth. Sure enough, there was a track of blood that led down the aisle and out the backdoor of the theatre. She also noticed that the blood trail moved toward the front door, where the body of the victim eventually was discovered. This was very helpful, because the forensic investigator could distinguish the perpetrator's blood from the victim's blood. She told Joey to turn the lights back on in the hall, and she picked up the police band radio and checked in with headquarters.

"This is Lieutenant Maggie Watson. I need to speak to Major Pinckney if he is available," she said to the radio operator and waited for the response.

"I'm sorry, but Major Pinckney is not available right now, Lieutenant. Can someone else help you?"

"No, I will call Dr. Henshaw, the coroner, and maybe she can help."

"Well, Lieutenant, that's actually where the major went. You can probably catch them both there if you call now."

"Thank you." Maggie placed a call to the morgue and was encouraged when Dr. Henshaw answered the telephone and asked, "How may I help you?"

"Dr. Henshaw, this is Lieutenant Watson, and I have a question for either you or Major Pinckney. Do you have a forensic pathologist who can work a crime scene? I have detected two different patterns of blood with luminol at the Gaillard Theatre, and I want someone who has some experience with crime scene collection of pathogen evidence to come and assist me. Do you have someone like that on staff?"

"Unfortunately, you are speaking to our forensic investigator. I will be happy to assist you as soon as I finish the second murdered victim's autopsy. We don't have the funding for a full-time forensic investigator, so it falls under my authority," Dr. Henshaw replied, sounding fatigued.

"That's fine, Dr. Henshaw, anytime will be fine. I do hope we may be able to determine the blood type and other characteristics about the suspect. We should be able to match the blood type with the first murdered victim with one of the blood patterns. And if that's so, then we might be able to isolate the other blood pattern and match it to the murderer."

"Maybe, but we never know these things until the results come back," she said, somewhat skeptical. "When you have seen as much as I have seen of inhumane behavior, you never take anything for granted."

Maggie then called Jonathan on the police band radio and asked how their investigation was proceeding. She was interested to know how efficient Juliet was compared to Joey. Maybe they would get lucky and have two outstanding young investigators.

"Well, I guess you can say it's going about as well as one could expect it to go," Jonathan replied. "Juliet is helpful, but she is not quite as sharp as we thought she might be when we looked at her qualifications on paper. By the way, how is our laid back Joey working out for you?"

"He's quite a breath of fresh air, as young officers go. I don't have to explain everything to him, and he picks up on instruction very quickly. He seems advanced beyond his training and his experience here in Charleston. I haven't gotten into any small talk with him yet, but he has to have some history working in a similar situation in the past. He's just too cool and contained within himself to be a rookie. It's a nice surprise, I have to admit."

"Isn't it amazing how files mislead?"

"How's that?" he asked.

"If I had been a gambler, I would have given you odds that Juliet would have been far superior to Joey in the field, based solely on her personnel jacket. So, have you and Juliet found anything at the crime scene that we can follow up with a forensic investigator?"

"Have you found a forensic investigator here in Charleston?

"Yep, do you want to take a guess who our forensic investigator is going to be?

"Not Dr. Henshaw?"

"Absolutely. In fact, that woman has her dance card full!"

"Oh, crap," he said, totally out of context in the conversation that he and Maggie were having.

"Jonathan, are you OK? What's up? I don't understand your reaction."

"You're probably not going to like what I have to say, so maybe we should talk about it tonight at the hotel."

"Now you really have piqued my interest. Give it up, Jonathan. Is this a 'ghost from Christmas past' coming back to haunt you?"

"More or less," he said in a small voice. "It's not what you think, but it's not good for us if she if going to be a very important cog in our wheel of discovery connected with these murders."

"I've got to tell you, Jonathan, I am totally in the dark here. Why don't you and I let the rookies hold down the fort, and we can get a bite of lunch and discuss what's going on, or what has gone on in the past. I really need to understand how Dr. Henshaw might affect the outcome of this investigation."

"OK," he said reluctantly. "I understand that there is a brewery on E. Bay Street, and we can get some local seafood and a draft beer, and I'll tell you the whole story, as best I remember it."

* * *

"This is a cool place, Jonathan," Maggie said as she looked around at the huge stainless steel containers used in processing the draft beer.

"Since we have a limited time to talk at lunch, I have already ordered us salmon and grits and a draft beer. Is that OK with you?"

"That will be fine," she responded. "I am more interested in the story that has to do with Dr. Louise Henshaw and why it could affect our investigation."

"Do you remember when she asked about the real estate business in New York when we first met her?"

"Yes, and I actually sensed that there was more to that short conversation that anyone was willing to discuss at that time."

"Ironically, I just remembered the story when you mentioned her again earlier this morning on the phone. When I said it wasn't what you thought, I didn't want you to think that I had been involved romantically with Louise Henshaw in the past. That's something we could excuse due to my stupidity as a young man full of piss and vinegar. This could be much worse," and he took a gulp of his draft beer to bolster his courage.

"Worse? How? What could be worse than you playing coy with this young woman and leading her on to think that you were really interested in her? You need to be more specific, Jonathan," she said sternly.

"Do remember what Louise Henshaw asked me specifically yesterday?"

She thought for a minute and tried to recall their conversation with the coroner when they had initially met her at the morgue. She attempted to recall the exact words to Jonathan. "Are you related to someone with the Pembroke Real Estate Company from New York City,' or something to that effect?" she replied. "How can that be problematic? Just the fact that she knows you are related to someone with the agency?"

"What you may not have heard or remembered is that she also asked about my father. Therein lies the possible problem."

"I feel like a taffy puller in the candy store over on Market Street, Jonathan. Help me out here."

"If my memory serves me well, Louise's mother had a fling with my dad about thirty years ago," he replied and said no more.

"You don't think that..." She didn't finish her thought but looked at Jonathan in disbelief. "Could Louise be your half-sister?"

"Who knows, Maggie? All my dad said about that situation was that he had had an affair with a young woman when he was in his mid-thirties and that she told him that she was pregnant. He asked her if she intended to keep the baby, and she stormed out of the restaurant where they were eating lunch, and he never saw her again. That's the last he ever heard from her, and he was never able to find her again. That was about thirty years ago. Wouldn't you say our Dr. Henshaw is about twenty-nine or thirty years old?" and he raised his eyebrows.

"That doesn't mean this coroner is the child of your dad. I mean, what are the odds?"

"One thing that I didn't tell you, Maggie. The woman's name that he was having the affair with was named Marilyn Henshaw!"

"Oh crap, Jonathan. How are we going to work with this woman if she is the same woman who was born out of an affair between her mother and your dad?"

"Beats the hell out of me!" he said, frustrated with the thought of how to even approach her about the subject.

"Maybe if you just get it out on the table, she will work it out with you. I don't know how to advise you, Jonathan. It's not like it's your fault! I've never had anything like this happen before in an investigation."

"Me either," he said disdainfully. "Why don't we just ask her to meet us at 82 Queen for a drink and talk it out over some cocktails? It couldn't hurt."

"That works for me if it works for you. We will be going back to the morgue shortly to get the complete autopsy results on the two murdered victims. Why don't you ask her to join us after work today?"

"That sounds like a good idea. I would be most appreciative if you would join us in that drink," he said.

"Do you think I would volunteer to leave you in a bar with a pretty woman, unlimited alcohol, and your track record?" she asked him, laughing. "Not on your life, Jonathan! Right now, we need to get back to our rookies before they muck up the works at the crime scenes."

They went back to their respective crime scenes and worked for the remaining part of the afternoon. Jonathan and Juliet found some stains in the dressing room where the actor was murdered, but other than that no other evidence was found. Maggie suggested that Jonathan use luminol, as well, to see if there was any blood not clearly visible in the immediate area where the body was discovered. They were trying to make sense of the two murders, but until they received the coroner's report on these two actors, they wouldn't have all the facts from which to draw conclusions.

"Let's keep the police presence at the crime scenes until Dr. Henshaw can do her forensic work at both venues, and let's make both of our rookies responsible for protecting those crime scenes," Maggie said. "Now, we can head toward the morgue to start our venture into something strange," she said with a little laugh.

"It's not funny, Maggie—not funny at all!"

Chapter 10

The Morgue

The walk to the hospital down Ashley Street was uneventful, with the exception of Maggie commenting on how beautiful the colors of the homes were on East Bay Street.

"What a gorgeous sight! It almost looks like these people planned the colors of their homes to give them a rainbow effect," she said.

Jonathan began to laugh, and Maggie asked defensively, "So, what's so damn funny?"

"Funny you should describe the houses before us as looking like a rainbow of color. Actually, this street is referred to officially as 'Rainbow Row,' and they make up the longest cluster of Georgian row houses, thirteen in all, in the United States. Just a little history from my research before we came to Charleston."

"So, I was correct!" She smiled at him. "If you are a good detective, you don't need history books to see things right in front of your face!"

"The Charleston Historical Society suggests that they may have been initially painted that way so drunken sailors would not terrorize the neighborhood when they came home from the local drinking establishments."

"I can see that. Seriously, Jonathan, we need to play this 'potential issue' between you and your sister, if that is the case, carefully so we won't jeopardize our investigation. We will need the coroner's help to make all the pieces of evidence fit together to give us an accurate idea of what really happened."

"I know, I know," he sighed.

As they saw the guard at the hospital, he nodded to them and began approaching the elevator.

"If you two stay here much longer, I should just get you a copy of the special key to the basement elevator button," he kidded as his key turned in the elevator panel to allow the basement button to be activated.

"Gosh, Sergeant. I hope we are not here that long," she said in a light and cheery voice. "You have been most kind to assist us so far," and Jonathan could have sworn that she batted her eyes at the guard. As they were riding down in anticipation of confronting Dr. Henshaw once more, he said, "Were you flirting with that guard to help us gain favor with the staff in the hospital, Maggie?"

"Who, little old me?" she asked and batted her eyes at him in the same manner that she had done with the guard.

"Oh, please!" he said and opened the morgue door for them to enter.

They walked into the autopsy room to a very busy Dr. Henshaw, who was making incisions on the body of a small child. When she saw them approaching, she covered the small body with a white sheet out of respect for the child's life and the parents' grief at his passing.

"Sorry to come unannounced, Dr. Henshaw, but you had invited us back this morning at the end of the day, so we thought it would be a good time to get updated on the results of your two autopsies of our murder victims," Maggie said simply. "How are you able to perform an autopsy on such an innocent child and not become jaded with all of the issues of child abuse, mistreatment, and potential murder of one so young?"

"Who said I'm not jaded?" she said, giving both of them a stern, sorrowful look. "As far as coming unannounced or without an appointment, that's not a problem," she said without fanfare, and invited them into her office, where she had a normal setup, with a nice desk, two chairs facing the desk, and a full-sized plastic skeleton. "You may want to take out your notebooks for this briefing, as I haven't had the opportunity yet to make copies of my reports for you."

"OK," Jonathan answered her cordially, and he and Maggie produced standard black, flip top-lined notebooks to be able to take down her words. She motioned them into the chairs, they took their seats, and she began the summation.

"The first victim, Lester Timmons, was from Cleveland, Ohio, and from some of the papers in his pocket, it appears that he was here to perform in the Spoleto Festival musical, *Porgy and*

Bess. You will want to substantiate that with the Spoleto Festival Office, if that is an important fact." She went to the cooler in the morgue and pulled out a sliding body tray displaying his remains. "According to the identification that we found on his body, he was twenty-nine years old, divorced with two children, ages eight and five years old. He had an active Actor's Guild union card in his possession, and his driver's license address matched his union card address. I have made a notation for you of his address, and I will get you a copy of those documents before you leave the morgue. All the other personal effects are located in this yellow envelope that you can take with you and log as evidence in the case. Now, as to how he died," and she paused to look at the young man with some compassion. "It appeared initially that the contusion on the back of his head was the cause of death," and she rolled his head to the side to show the area to which she was referring. "However, he was dying before the blow was ever struck on his head, having ingested sulfuric acid approximately twenty minutes before he passed out and died on the floor at the entrance of the Gaillard Theatre. Look at the tissue here in his throat," and she tilted his head back, opened his mouth and pointed with a penlight to the discolored tissue on the lining of the throat. "Sulfuric acid reacts with water, and tremendous heat is generated when the two items are mixed together, creating smoke at times, and poisonous and noxious fumes. Eventually, he died of hemorrhaging and sudden circulatory collapse. He didn't have a chance."

"Where would the murderer get sulfuric acid?" Jonathan asked.

She smiled sadly and said, "It is present in most bathrooms, either as a bowl cleaner or a drain-opener. It would be almost impossible to determine the actual origin of the acid, unless the killer used it as a poison of opportunity just because it was present when he decided to kill this man. If he brought it with him, it could have been purchased from more than a dozen stores within five miles of the Gaillard Theatre."

"Was there anything else of note that the autopsy revealed?" Maggie asked.

"Before I answer that question, I want to take a swab of the blood samples that you spotted at the Gaillard and compare them to Mr. Timmons' blood type. We should be able to narrow our facts once we are able to do that. I plan to get by there first thing in the morning, and then I will come back to the lab and run comparisons with the samples of Mr. Timmons' test results."

"Now, on to victim number two," and when she said that she continued with, "I could say the MO was almost identical to the first murder. His name is Terrell Swanson, and he was a local graduate of the College of Charleston, with a Major in Fine Arts. He had been performing with the same theatrical group since his graduation in 1990. According to his papers, he was twenty-seven years old, single, and in the best physical shape possible. He was primarily a dancer."

"Well, we thought the same murderer was responsible for this death as well, especially since it happened almost immediately after the first one—especially since he was an actor who was also starring in a Spoleto play."

"That's not all that bothers me, Lieutenant," she said with worry on her pretty face. "The acid used was almost identical, and the blow to the head was in a similar place as the first murder victim. What concerns me is that we may have a serial murderer on our hands. Fortunately, if we can say that, he's just getting started, and maybe we can find him and get him off the streets before he kills more innocents."

"Do you see any signs indicating that these murders may have been personal in nature?" asked Jonathan.

"Hard to tell from what I have observed so far," she replied. "I will tell you that given the age of both victims, and the fact they were both actors, the crime may very well be a crime of passion or jealousy. However, I guess that conclusion would be more in the area of yours and Lieutenant Watson's area of expertise. It just seems very coincidental that the particulars of each murder are so similar."

"Jonathan and I don't really believe too much in coincidence, especially when it comes to murder victims," Maggie said. "We'll need to make a full report to the mayor and the chief of police, unless you have already done that."

"I will let you fill them in on the details of the autopsies while you are bringing them up to date on your own investigations.

I hope to be able to get out of here in the next half-hour and kick up my feet. It has been a long day!" She grimaced as she began to uncover the small child's body again to resume his autopsy.

"Dr. Henshaw," Jonathan interrupted her concentration on the boy's body, "What plans do you have after work?"

"Nothing much, why do you ask?"

"Maggie and I would like to buy you a drink and chat with you a little about other things than bodies and autopsies, and we were hoping you would let us treat you to dinner at Slightly North of Broad Restaurant this evening."

"S.N.O.B.?"

They looked dumbstruck, and she just laughed. "That's what the locals call it. It is a very nice restaurant, so don't let the name put you off."

"What say we meet you there at 7:00 PM? I will call ahead and make reservations for three, unless you have someone you would like to bring with you," Jonathan said.

"No significant other at this time in my life, and you must make reservations if you want to make sure we get a table before midnight," she said.

"OK, I will that do as soon as we leave the morgue. We look forward to seeing you then."

Chapter 11

Slightly North of Broad

"Can you believe the number of first class restaurants in so close a proximity?" Maggie asked Jonathan as they were being seated at S.N.O.B. They had walked by no less than a dozen unbelievably beautiful restaurants as they made their way over to East Bay Street from the Gaslight Inn. What impressed Maggie was that it was only a couple of blocks from the hotel to this restaurant. Slightly North of Broad Restaurant had the signature "old building look" that most of the restaurants and other permanent buildings had in the downtown area of Charleston. Antique gas lights illuminated the outside of the building welcoming guests to the restaurant, and the decorations inside were as handsome as any governor's mansion. What a beautiful city for such a terrible crime spree to be taking place.

"Only New York City in the theatrical district can rival this place for fancy restaurants. Of course, if this were New York City, these establishments would serve two or three times as many dinners every night. The managers and proprietors would be shooing those who had completed their dinners out with a 'Could you please move on so someone else can take your table' comment," Jonathan said.

"Oh, they really don't do that in NYC, do they?" Maggie asked.

"Yeah, they really do. I was at a delicatessen in Manhattan once when the manager came through, picked up all of the plates of those who had finished their lunches, and I overheard him say, 'Now let's move along so someone else can eat.' No one seemed to care or was offended by his comments."

"They would not only be offended in Charleston, they would probably bring out their ceremonial sword and run you through for questioning their honor!" Maggie laughed heartily. "I don't think I want to see a mob of angry Charlestonians—anyone this calm most of the time doesn't know how to be angry without hurting someone badly."

"You're probably right about that, Maggie. At least we don't have to worry about that tonight. All we have to be concerned about is Louise Henshaw pulling out a 'Saturday Night Special' and blowing me away because my dad mistreated her mother."

"Nice thought, Jonathan. Here comes our girl now," and she nodded at the door where Dr. Louise Henshaw had just arrived and was being ushered over to their table. As the hostess showed her to their table, Jonathan got up and helped her with her chair.

"Sorry I was a little late," she apologized. "I live in Mt. Pleasant, and the traffic coming over the Cooper River Bridge was impossible getting back into the city. Every time we have a festival of any kind in the city, the traffic gets backed up on the bridge. There are plans for the replacement of that bridge in the future, but right now it is two lanes, and it can be scary when the wind is blowing hard or there is bad weather moving into the area. Hurricane Hugo in 1989 almost destroyed it with winds exceeding 140 miles per hour. Piccolo/Spoleto is a very busy time for us here in Charleston every year, and the bridge gets a serious workout from the visitors and locals."

"It must be a busy time, because when I called to make reservations for this restaurant, they said I was in luck because they had had a cancellation. Otherwise, I guess we would have been eating at the Waffle House!" Jonathan laughed.

"Even the Waffle House is overbooked during Piccolo/Spoleto," Louise said with a smile. "So, what have you been able to see and enjoy since you arrived?"

They both looked at each other, smiled, and Maggie replied, "The first day we arrived was the day that Lester Timmons was murdered at the Galliard. As you can imagine, we modified our plans once that happened, so we really haven't had very much time to do any visiting. We have eaten at 82 Queen a couple of times, but other than that it has been all police business."

"I'm so sorry for you, because the Piccolo/Spoleto Festival is a great time to be in Charleston. There are hundreds of performers, and thousands of people visiting from all over the world during the festival. Maybe you will get a chance to enjoy some of the festivities before you return to Illinois."

Their server returned, and they ordered She-crab soup, appetizers all around, and a bottle of Chardonnay. When the server came back with the fresh bread, they ordered their entrees and began settling into the ambiance of the restaurant.

"May I call you Louise?" Jonathan asked the coroner.

"Of course, Jonathan. Charlestonians are not too concerned about formality. We try to concentrate on hospitality and making visitors to our city feel welcome."

The food was delivered to the table by the server, and as they began to eat, Jonathan continued his conversation.

"I think I understand a lot more about the statement you made when I first met you at the morgue the other day. You mentioned my father's company, the Pembroke Real Estate Firm in New York City. He has now retired from the business, and I have taken over the reins, so to speak. I actually have someone running it for me, but I am the one in charge of the business when it comes to the tough and final decisions that have to be made. I am going to tell you what I was told about you and your mother—that is, what my dad told me. Please fill in the blanks for me, because all I have is a broad outline of who your mom is, who you are, and I want to get to know all about you and your family. My dad, Weatherford Winthrop Pembroke, was in his late twenties when he said he met a beautiful cocktail waitress at one of the dinner clubs in New York. One thing led to another, and they began to date.

"After a few months, this young woman told my father that she was pregnant and that he was the father. Her name was Jennifer Henshaw, and she was a student at New York University. She was in her last year at NYU, and she was working at a club to help pay for her tuition and college fees. When she approached my father, he was surprised that she had not told him that she was not using birth control. It was about the time the birth control pill controversy was prevalent in the country. He told me that when she told him she was pregnant, he asked her if she intended to keep the baby. The Roe vs. Wade case was being tried in the courts, and abortion was not some backroom procedure anymore. Anyway, she got the impression that he wanted her to give up her baby, so she just disappeared. He looked for her but never saw her again. He later found out that she had move to a Southern city, and that was the last he ever heard from her. Now whether his version is totally true or not, I cannot tell you. That's what he told me, so that's what I know. What do I not know about my half-sister, Louise?"

She took a long sip of her wine and said, "He was correct about my mother moving south. She had a cousin who lived in Birmingham, Alabama, so she stayed with her until she gave birth to me. She named me Louisa Sinclair Henshaw, after her cousin Louisa from Birmingham, and also from her grandfather on my mother's side of the family, Sinclair. She decided to call me Louise. We lived in the Homewood area of Birmingham while I was in high school. Mother was able to get a decent job at one of the newspaper companies downtown, and when I finished high school at Shades Valley High, I was able to get a full scholarship at the University of Alabama Birmingham, UAB. By living at home and working at a local restaurant in Five Points, I was able to complete my bachelor's degree, and then finish my med school at UAB in about four years after that. Within a year of my graduation from medical school, my mother was diagnosed with an aggressive form of breast cancer. She lived only seven months after the diagnosis. I was heartbroken and could no longer feel comfortable in the Birmingham area, so I applied to several hospitals within a few hundred miles of home to try to start my personal and professional life in a new city. I was hired by the University of South Carolina Hospital in Charleston as their coroner about five years ago, and I've been here ever since. It's not a very exciting story, is it?"

"And your mother's name was Jennifer?" Jonathan asked.

"That's right. However, to make sure she would not be easily discovered, after moving to Birmingham she changed her name to Maria."

"So, you only have this cousin in Birmingham as your nearest relative?"

"Until I met you, that is. Now I have a half-brother from New York, or should I say Illinois?"

"I moved to Rowlette, Illinois, after living in New York City for many years as I began to get involved in my father's business. Rowlette is a city of about 150,000 people, and it is located just fifty miles to the Southwest of Chicago. It is a charming place to live. That is where I met this beautiful and charming woman to my left," he said proudly. "However, now I have a reason to get to know you and do what I can to restore any family ties that I can."

"Jonathan, it really isn't necessary for you to feel guilty about anything that might have happened when you were a baby. Anything that happened between my mother and your father is not your responsibility, nor is it something that I believe needs to be corrected. Just for the record, all of that is in the past, and I hold no hard feelings toward your father, our father, and it is probably history that needs to be left undisturbed," Louise said calmly.

"Louise, you are my half-sister, and that means a lot to me. I have no other siblings other than you. I'm not prepared to let you escape back into the past without getting to know you better. I'm sure my dad would like to know that your mom didn't abandon you or have you aborted. He is really a pretty nice guy now, although I can't tell you anything about how he was in his youth when he and your mother were together. Would you consider letting me tell him that you are alive and doing well? And if it's OK with you, we can all get together and have a belated family reunion."

She began to tear up, and then she said, "Jonathan, as I told you earlier, my mom died of cancer when I was a senior in high school. She didn't suffer too long, but I dedicated my future career to her memory, and that's when I decided to become a physician. I just don't want to dig up old memories that I have conveniently put to rest for the past few years. I'm not sure I can get away to visit our father in New York soon. My only relatives that I am aware of are in Birmingham, Alabama." There's a bunch of cousins, but no other siblings."

"Have you considered moving to New York or another place up North to practice your skills? If you're happy here, I understand why you would want to remain, but my dad could probably pull some strings to help you get a good job in the medical field in New York, assuming you are interested."

"Unfortunately, my only opportunity so far out of medical school and certification for forensic pathology has been as a coroner. I have had a lot of success at this job, and it almost seems as if I was fated to wind up in the morgue and in this city. I really like helping find out why someone may have died or was murdered, so maybe people like you and Maggie can prevent the same thing happening to someone else. I guess I am stuck in the morgue for the rest of my professional career," and she smiled a little. "Is your mother still alive?"

"Yes, and I am sure she would love to know all about you and your mom. She is a saint. Dad was all business and very calculating. He tried to drive me and my wife up the ladder of success into the politically correct power circles in New York City. However, that didn't work out so well, so here I am working as a part-time investigator with one of the most dynamic criminologists in the country. He was so disappointed that I didn't rub enough elbows with the correct people to become a legislator or a senator. However, I am happy and I intend to follow this lady to my left around indefinitely, until she agrees to marry me and have my kids!"

Maggie looked at him like he had two heads. "What? Did you just propose to me?" her face a combination of joy and confusion.

"Would that be a good thing, Maggie?" Jonathan asked her.

"Why don't we discuss this later this evening? I'm sure Louise is not interested in our love life," Maggie said with finality.

"Actually, this is quite a development, isn't it?" and Louise looked at both of them for a sign of acknowledgement. "Are you sure that you don't want to be alone at a time like this? And I thought you said that you were already married, Jonathan? Did you two get a divorce, and now you're contemplating getting back together?"

Jonathan and Maggie began to giggle, leaving Louise with more questions than answers. Before too long, they were laughing out loud, threatening to draw unwanted attention to their table.

"Did I miss the punchline or what?" Louise asked sincerely.

"Louise, Jonathan and I were college friends. He married a high-society girl that his folks thought would be good for him and the business, but Jonathan is not anything like his father. He cares nothing about the trappings of political power or financial exceptionalism. Oh, he likes being independently wealthy, but he and I have been working together as friends and colleagues for the past few months in Rowlette, Illinois, to determine who was murdering people in and around a Catholic cathedral. We are more than friends," and she looked at Jonathan with a wicked smile, "but we have never even talked about engagement or steady dating. So any suggestion of a lifetime commitment, as in marriage, just surprises me. Please forgive us for laughing a minute ago, but it had nothing to do with you. The situation seemed so absurd to me that I couldn't help but giggle," Maggie said and looked at her new friend to make sure Louise was taking in this explanation and processing it rationally.

"I think I understand," Louise said reluctantly. "You and Jonathan are close friends, and he is independently wealthy and has decided to live the good life. Money is not an issue, but happiness is what drives your relationship. How am I doing so far?"

"Pretty damn good," Jonathan said with wonder. "Are you sure you didn't get a degree in psychology, instead of in medicine?"

This time she smiled and said, "Actually, I specialized in Psychiatry, after obtaining my MD, and certification in Forensic Pathology. So, I guess you can say that I both understand matters of the heart— how to surgically repair it, as well as emotionally understand it, not to mention what makes it stop!"

"I am sitting between two great women with the ability to change the world," Jonathan remarked to them. "A toast to beauty and brains!" he exclaimed, raising his glass to toast them both.

"Is he always like this?" Louise joked with Maggie as they clinked their wine glasses together.

"Unfortunately, yes," she said, and she leaned over and gave him a peck on the cheek. "You'll get accustomed to it after a while," she said and smiled at him warmly.

"So Louise, what about that reunion? Do you have other siblings that we might want to include in the party? I am inviting Maggie, so any significant other or siblings are welcome!" Jonathan said.

"You're actually serious about this reunion with your folks, aren't you?" Louise asked.

"Absolutely, Louise. I am so excited that I have a sister. Isn't that just great, Maggie?" he asked her with a huge smile on his face.

"Yes, Jonathan. It is great. However, we need to solve a couple of murders before we go running off to New York to meet the folks," Maggie replied.

"Of course. However, I'm not giving up on the reunion. Both of you need to plan for that to happen as soon as we wrap things up here in Charleston." Both women looked at each other and nodded approval. Jonathan was pretty difficult to dissuade once he made his mind up about something.

They finished their dinners, Jonathan paid the check, and they walked outside into the sultry, humid Charleston evening air.

"May we walk you to your car, Louise?" Jonathan asked as a gentleman from Charleston might do.

"Oh no. I used valet parking, and they are bringing my car up as we speak." She got into a 1967 red corvette. The top was down, and her long raven hair was blowing in the wind as she drove off up East Bay Street toward the Cooper River Bridge.

"Now that scene makes me believe in genetics!" Maggie said and looked at Jonathan and smiled. "What are the odds your half-sister would have a vintage red sports car?" she said, thinking about his classic red Porsche that he had named "Lucy" after the Lucille Ball character on "I Love Lucy."

"Genes don't lie," he said and pulled her close to him as they walked up East Bay Street to Queen Street. They took a left on Queen and then a right turn on Meeting Street, and they were back at the Gaslight Inn within ten minutes.

"I'll meet you in the Jacuzzi," Jonathan told her. He went inside their room, put on his swimsuit, and eased himself into the 106 degree water. The jets were bubbling, and Maggie appeared at the pool's edge with a bottle of white wine and two glasses.

"Now let's talk a little more about the informal proposal you made at dinner!" she said and eased into the Jacuzzi beside him.

Chapter 12

Comparison of Notes

Six o'clock came early the next morning for Maggie and Jonathan. They had stayed out in the Jacuzzi until the desk manager had come and asked them to turn off the jets. With no bubbles in the water, they decided to turn in for the evening. However, either due to the wine or their relaxed states of mind, they spent another hour with an endurance contest in bed. Just as Maggie had expected, she has outlasted Jonathan. He was dead to the world. She kissed him lightly on the forehead, turned over on her side, and went to sleep. When she woke to the sunlight streaming through the windows of their room, she noticed that Jonathan had already risen and was not in the room. She peeked out the door and saw him sipping coffee and eating a croissant on the patio. She stuck her head out the door.

"So, you're an early bird this morning?"

"I guess you can call me that. At least I am earlier to rise than you!" he said and laughed at the ridiculous sight of her talking head peeking outside their hotel room door. "Are you ready to get going? We probably need to sit here first on the patio and compare notes on our investigations of the Strand and the Galliard."

"With what we know now about the deaths of the two actors, along with the timeline that we should be able to put together on each death, we might come up with some kind of profile on the suspected killer," she said.

He agreed, went back to the room, showered, and dressed in very cool, comfortable clothes. When Maggie saw how he had dressed down from yesterday's attire, she couldn't help but tease him.

"Are we going casual today, Mr. Prim and Proper?"

"According to the local news channel, the temperature today is going to be around ninety-five degrees, with a heat index of one-hundred-and-eight. I think that's a good reason to dress comfortably, don't you?"

"Since I didn't bring any official uniforms, my suits will have to do. Fortunately, I'm not as hot-natured as you."

"Except in bed."

"Don't men ever think of anything else?"

"In a word, no. What else is there that is that important?"

"Geez!" Maggie said. "Why do I even try?"

"I guess it's in your genes, Maggie. What other good reason could there be?" and he kissed her on the top of her head.

While they sat at the table in the courtyard, they played back the events of the past few days in their minds, both of them making notes on legal pads that Maggie had brought from the police department.

"So what do we know, and what do we not know so far?" Jonathan asked.

"Well, both victims were actors or dancers who were in plays that are sponsored by the Piccolo/Spoleto Festival. One is from Ohio, and one is local. They both were killed when very few other people were in the venues where they were murdered. Both were poisoned, and both murderers seemed to know the theatres well, escaping the murder scene with no apparent difficulty. What else do we know?"

Jonathan thought again, running all of the recent events through his mind, and then said, "I can't think of anything else, Maggie. Let's get with our rookies and see what they remember. It can't hurt to have a couple more opinions, right?"

"Agreed. We are missing something, Jonathan. Right now, none of this makes a lot of sense to me."

As they were sitting there at the table, a front desk clerk approached them in a hurried manner. She told Maggie that Major Pinckney had left a message that he needed for them to call him immediately. He told the clerk that it was in regards to the murder investigation. They thanked the clerk, tipped her for her trouble, and they both went back into the hotel room to put the final touches on their appearances before they left to walk down to the police department.

When they arrived at the police station, they were ushered into the conference room quickly. The mayor, the chief, and both of their rookies were waiting on them in the room, anticipating some important announcement.

"Maggie, I have some bad news this morning that I need to share with you. It appears from an early report from one of our beat officers, one of the primary directors of the Piccolo/Spoleto Festival plays has been murdered in his hotel room. We have sealed his hotel room, and we have posted officers to protect the crime scene, but we need for you and your team to see if this latest incident is connected to the earlier murders. He was staying at the Magnolia Bed and Breakfast Inn off King Street."

Jonathan gave Maggie a look of concern, and then he said, "Another murder that relates to the festival. Was he local, or was he from another part of the country?"

"All his press office could say was that Lawrence Baker lived in Pittsburgh, Pennsylvania, and was involved in 'Off Broadway' events most of the year. He had been directing plays here at the Piccolo/Spoleto Festival for over ten years. The really interesting finding is that he was a graduate of the College of Charleston some twenty years ago or more. His office is at a loss about who might want to harm him, much less kill him," Major Pinckney answered.

"Where is his body now?" Maggie asked.

"He is still in his room. The maid found him this morning when she was freshening up his quarters at 8:00 AM."

"Jonathan, I need you and Juliet to go back to the Galliard and the Strand and comb over every square inch of those theatres to see if there is anything that we could have missed in our initial investigations yesterday," Maggie instructed him. "Take some luminol and a black light with you to look for any blood splatter that we may have overlooked. Please give Dr. Henshaw a call and ask her to meet me at the Magnolia Bed and Breakfast Inn and to bring her luminol kit with her to the scene. It looks as though there may be a pattern of blood that we can follow that ties all of these murders together. If she can find matching blood samples at Magnolia, then we may have something to begin to help us put this all together."

"Do we want her to visit the other crime scenes today to take samples of the blood patterns there to see if they match the victims' blood? If there is blood splatter at all three scenes that match, we can assume that we have a serial killer on our hands, right?" Jonathan asked Maggie.

"Wait, wait," the mayor said. "Let's not jump to conclusions just yet and start speaking about 'serial killers' until we know for sure that these crimes are all tied together."

Even Major Pinckney looked at the mayor with disdain at his comment, and he said, "Mayor, I know you don't want the press to get hold of this information and project it all over the news outlets, but we do have a responsibility here to act responsibly."

Mayor Anderson looked angrily at Major Pinckney and said, "Gerald, we have one opportunity to get this right. If we are not careful, this murderer will destroy our chances of having a successful Piccolo/Spoleto Festival. You know, as well as I, that we need this event to be successful to help carry us through the lean months of winter when tourism is not a big factor in our city. I just want to be sure that we proceed with caution."

"Mayor," Maggie said with contempt. "If you fail to notify the public about the specifics of this crime spree and more people are murdered, that is on you! Don't get me wrong, but I do believe that is a recallable offense for your voters."

The mayor reacted as Jonathan expected and said, "I don't need a civics lesson from someone who is not even a citizen of this city or state, Maggie. You have been asked to help us solve these murders—not to decide how I run this city."

Major Pinckney could see that this situation was about to blow up in everyone's faces, and he coaxed, "Look, everybody, let's just settle down and think of the proper way to move forward. Mayor, as much as you don't want to admit it, Lieutenant Watson is correct in the notification of the public from a safety point of view. If you don't handle the situation, I will. I am an elected official, just like you, and I can't sit by and let a disturbed individual run around this city on a killing spree and try to keep that knowledge from the public. That's your call, but you need to make that decision now."

It was obvious that the mayor felt defeated, because his shoulders slumped and his demeanor became almost passive. He said he would make a public service announcement after consulting with the detectives and Major Pinckney.

"It is important that we release this statement with care and try not to inflame the general public to panic," the mayor concluded. He got up from the chair in the conference room and silently walked out of their presence into his personal office and closed the door.

"He's taking this pretty hard," Jonathan said to Major Pinckney. "Surely, he doesn't think the local people will blame him for what's happening at the festival, does he?"

"Politics makes strange bedfellows, Jonathan. He will be OK when the dust settles on this situation, but for now he is trying to justify how to notify the public without scaring off the visitors who have come here to party."

"Do you want to go with us to the Blossom B&B, or do you need to stay her to coordinate everything that is going on around you?" Maggie asked Pinckney.

"I trust you and Joey explicitly, so you go on, and I will try to hold down the fort from here. Whoever is perpetuating these crimes is getting more daring with each victim. He's going to make a mistake, and we are going to nab him, but I'm concerned how much damage he will do until we are able to identify who he is and how to stop him."

"I don't mean to complicate your thinking, Major, but it could be a woman and not a man. I am not ruling out anyone as a suspect at this point of the investigation," Maggie said.

"You're right, I guess, but we in Charleston look upon the fairer sex as being less threatening and less crude than their male counterparts. However, I will keep an open mind until we know for certain who has it in for the Piccolo/Spoleto Festival and the City of Charleston."

BOOK II: MOTIVATION FOR MURDER

Chapter 13

And Then There Were Three

When Maggie and Joey arrived at the Blossom Bed and Breakfast Inn, they saw the police had secured the scene and marked off the area with yellow police crime tape. The building had been emptied by notifying the tenants that they needed to vacate the hotel for a few hours while the police conducted an investigation. Everyone seemed to take the situation in stride, much as Charlestonians always seem to do. These were really relaxed people.

The Blossom Bed and Breakfast Inn was as beautiful as any antique space that Maggie had seen in magazines. The chandeliers were crystal, the draperies were heavy brocade, and the stained glass windows that faced the street were magnificent. Dark hardwood floors that could have dated back to the eighteenth century shone like a mirror—the overall ambiance of the inn was overwhelming.

"Who is in charge here?" Maggie asked a uniformed young man who was standing behind the front desk.

"I guess that would be me," he answered. "How can I help you, ma'am?"

"I need to speak to the maid who discovered the body this morning. Can you tell me where I can find her?" Maggie persisted.

"She was really upset and wanted to go home, but I told her that she had to remain here until you had spoken to her. She's lying down in a vacant room." He gave Maggie a key to room 215, instructing her to knock first, and then to let herself into the room if the maid did not respond to her summons.

"The room where the body was discovered is room 116, just down the hall on the right," he indicated. Maggie and Joey could see the yellow police tape marking the door to the room. There was a police officer standing guard over the room, not allowing anyone into the room for any reason.

"I am Lieutenant Maggie Watson, the chief investigator for this case, and this is Officer Joey Lancaster," she told the officer at the door. "And you are?" She looked for his nameplate on his chest.

"Officer Washington?" Maggie asked. "Have you been here since the body was discovered?

"Yes, ma'am. Do you want me to keep guard on this room?"

"Yes, at least until the coroner gets here. I expect her at any time."

The maid was still lying on the bed when Maggie and Jonathan entered the room. They saw another woman sitting in a chair positioned at the foot of the bed. So, they asked her who she was and why she was there.

"My name is Sherry Lafonte, and I was told to watch the lady in this room to ensure she didn't leave the hotel until she was interviewed by someone from headquarters. I am assuming that person is you, Lieutenant," the young woman said to her as he opened the door for Maggie and Joey to enter the maid's room.

The maid was lying very still, watching an Hispanic game show. Although Maggie had taken Spanish in high school and college, she was nowhere near fluent. The girl looked to be no older than in her early 20s, and she appeared very scared. Maggie approached her, showed her the detective badge that she had remembered to include in her luggage, and began to try to converse with her.

"Do you speak English?" Maggie asked the young maid.

"No hablo engles," she muttered in Spanish.

Maggie rolled her eyes and thought to herself, "Is this really the way my day is going to go today?" Suddenly, from out of nowhere Maggie heard a male voice ask, "Hablas espanol?"

"Si," the young girl replied with a quizzical look on her face.

"Que ser, estar tu el nombre?" he asked.

"Wow, Joey, do you speak Spanish? What did you just say to her?"

"I asked her to tell me her name?" he said.

"Meh yah-moh mah-ree-yah," she replied.

"Her name is Maria," he told Maggie.

"What would you like for me to ask her about finding the body?"

Maggie thought for a minute and said, "See if you can get her to tell you what she did when she first found the body. Did she clean up anything, or did she just notify her supervisor?"

Joey spoke to Maria for about five minutes in an exaggerated tone, and she finally seemed to relax. Obviously, Joey was having a calming effect on her. Once he was finished questioning her, he told her in Spanish, "Muchas gracias por tu ayuda!" and he looked at Maggie and said, "That's about all we're going to get from her. Should I let her go for now?"

"Yes, but get an address or telephone number where we can reach her if we have other questions. Was she able to give you any pertinent information that might help us in our investigation?"

He nodded positively at both Maggie and Maria and then told her, "Puede que le devuelva la llamada. Si?"

"Si," she said and nodded again in a positive manner.

"Tu puedes ir," and he smiled at her. She smiled back, got her things together, and headed for the door.

After the young woman had left, Maggie looked at Joey and said, "Boy, am I glad you were here today. I would never have gotten any good information from her. I didn't see anything in your personnel folder that indicated that you are fluent in Spanish. How did that escape the personnel department?"

He chuckled and responded, "No one ever asked if I spoke Spanish, and I didn't want to go tooting my own horn about something that I thought I would never use in Charleston."

"You are an interesting young man, Joey. You could go far in this business." She patted him on the back. "Now, tell me everything that Maria told you about the murder victim."

Joey repeated everything that Maria had told him. The victim had checked into room 116 the day before the Piccolo/Spoleto Festival started, and he had only slept here in the evenings. Maria had not seen much of him in the morning when she cleaned his room. He would hang a "Do Not Disturb" sign on his doorknob until he left every day around 10:00 AM. She would go into the room, clean the bathroom, make the bed, vacuum the floor, and replenish the linens and paper products. However, there was a young woman whom she saw enter and leave his room yesterday morning around 9:00 AM. She didn't think much about it, since all American men seem to have 'amantes de las mujeres," or women lovers, visit them in hotel rooms. She had not seen her this morning, and when she opened his door to clean his room, she found his body. That's really all she knew.

"Again, Joey, I can't thank you enough for being here to help me find out what Maria had seen. Those are clues that we might never have discovered if it hadn't been for you. I will see that a letter of commendation makes it to your file when this investigation is completed."

"Thank you, Lieutenant Watson. I was just doing my job," he said humbly.

Maggie and Joey carefully proceeded into room 116 to survey the situation. It appeared from first glance that the victim had been hit on the head with something heavy, because there was a nasty red gash on the top of his head.

"Does this look like a murder by head trauma? I know we can't be too certain of anything until the coroner makes her declaration, but it looks pretty obvious to me," Joey said.

"Never trust your eyes, nose, or ears when it comes to cause of death. Always wait until the coroner determines the cause of death. What happens is that we can overlook what we need to look for if we don't have a pretty good idea of how it happened."

The room evoked the 18th century, when four-poster beds, coal-burning fireplaces, and very ornate furniture were the order of the day. Nothing in the room seemed to be out of place, with the obvious exception of a dead body. Maggie was carefully walking around the body, moving to the bathroom to see if there were any tell-tell containers of bowl cleaner or drain opener visible. To her dismay, there was nothing there but a plunger and a toilet bowl brush—no chemicals. She thought to herself, "Why would the maid leave instruments to mechanically clean a toilet without the chemicals that had to be applied to make that job possible?" That was something that she should have asked the maid when they interviewed her. She and Joey continued to look for irregularities in the condition of the room, but she didn't see a thing out of place.

They combed over the room as best they could without fingerprinting tools or other forensic items that she wished she had with her. She picked up the telephone and called Louise in the coroner's office.

"Louise," she spoke into the receiver when she recognized her new friend's voice, "Do you think that you can come on over to the Magnolia B&B and get started on the forensic investigation for us? I'm sure Major Pinckney called and told you that we have a third body, right?"

"Yes, he did. I am leaving now, so I should be there in a few minutes. Should I bring all my tools with me?"

"Absolutely. We are looking to see if there is a similar blood splatter pattern as with the other murder scenes. The body is in room 116."

"OK, I'm on my way."

Chapter 14

Potential Suspects

While Maggie and Joey were waiting on the coroner at the Blossom Bed and Breakfast Inn, Maggie began to piece together what information she had acquired and what it might possibly mean. All the victims were considered local, and Lawrence Baker had gone to college at the College of Charleston, the same school that Lester Timmons had attended some twenty years later. He also was currently teaching in the Fine Arts Department there. Was that just coincidental, or was there a possible connection between the local college and these murders?

"Joey," Maggie called him from the other room, "will you please write something down for me?"

"Sure, Lieutenant, and what might that be?" he asked with his pencil on his notepad.

"I want you to go to the College of Charleston personnel office or admissions office, and I want you to ask them for a printout of all graduates who majored or minored in the Fine Arts during the following time periods—from 1986-1990, and again from 1966-1970. I am most interested in anyone who might have been in the same classes with our two victims, assuming they can refine the computer search results that well. If it only takes an hour or so for them to get that done, please wait on the list and take it back to the conference room at the police station. I have a feeling that I will be back over there in the next forty-five minutes to an hour."

"Yes, ma'am," he said courteously. "Do you think they may want a search warrant to get that done for us?"

"Joey, you have been watching too many TV crime shows. For the most part, most institutions want these criminals off the street as much as us. However, if they require a search warrant or try to give you that excuse, simply say, 'OK, but if we get a search warrant, we will ask for more extensive records than these currently requested.'"

"Would we?"

Maggie had already turned and was examining the clothes of the third victim when Joey asked his follow up question.

"Would we what?" she asked, oblivious to the fact that she had not made herself perfectly clear in her instructions to the rookie cop.

"Would we ask for more information?"

"Does it matter if we did or didn't? Look, Joey, there's something you have to understand about getting information in a timely manner. Sometimes the mere threat of more inconvenience to people holding out that information can make them decide to go ahead and get things moving. It's a ploy that we use in the field that is not taught in the textbooks at the academy."

"Oh, I think I understand," he said, and it was as if a lightbulb switched on. "That's cool, Lieutenant. It's not illegal or pushy, just a way to move things along to get the info we need."

"You are a quick study, Joey. Now get over to the college and get my list!" she chided him playfully.

"Will do, Lieutenant. I'm going to miss your insight when this case is over!"

"Oh, I'm sure by then you will have had enough of me to last a lifetime."

* * *

Joey went to the admissions office and spoke to a very friendly and cute undergraduate student who told him she would get him whatever he needed. He thought it might have had something to do with the uniform, but he would use any advantage offered to him. He told her what he needed, and she told him it would take about thirty minutes to get it done. He told her he would be back and left the office grinning from ear to ear. The more he thought about it, the more he thought he might ask this friendly young woman out. It was a sultry day, but there was a pleasant breeze blowing off the water and up the peninsula, so he decided to walk outside, take a seat on a sturdy bench in the shade just outside the door of the building, and rest his eyes for a moment. Since it was still a little warm, he dozed off for what seemed like a moment, only to be awakened by Juliet Robinson, the student worker.

"Are you OK?" she asked him with some concern.

"I'm fine," he said, a little embarrassed that he had nodded off while on duty. "I guess the heat and the gentle breeze lulled me to sleep for a moment. What are you doing out here, anyway?"

"When I finished with the list that you wanted, I looked around but didn't see you. I remember that you had stepped outside for a few minutes, so I thought I would check on you. It's not uncommon at all for people waiting on one of us at the desk to go outside and relax on the bench."

"OK," he said, grinning back at her. "Just don't tell my boss that I'm a slacker!"   "I doubt you're a slacker," she said, and she pointed to two ribbons displayed on his chest. "Looks like you've been rewarded for bravery. My dad is a police officer, and I know how that works."

"Well, if being a perfect shot with one's pistol and rescuing a child from an overheating automobile are valorous, then you've got me."

"Why don't we go for a burger after I get off, and you can tell me all about it, Officer Lancaster? You're not married, are you? I didn't see any rings on your fingers."

"Yes, I mean no," he stammered.

"Yes on the hamburger, and no on the marriage, or yes on the marriage and no on the burger?" she teased him.

"No, I'm not married—not even dating anyone right now. It's a long story. But yes on the burger. There's a great place over on East Bay Street, assuming that is OK with you"

"That would be fine. I am living on campus in a dormitory, as bad as I hate it, but it is cheap and safe. I'm in Dodson Hall, located just off Calhoun Street. You can't miss it. It's the tall building that looks like a dump!" and her smile was enchanting to Joey.

"I'll call on you in the lobby around 7:00 PM?"

"OK," she said, handing him the thick manila folder with the list of university students' names. "Don't forget this, or your boss might remove one of those ribbons." She winked at Joey devilishly.

"Right, right," he stammered again. He had just had his heart stolen by a beautiful woman who he knew absolutely nothing about—except that her dad was a cop.

"Oh, by the way, my name is Jerome Lancaster, but everyone just calls me Joey," and he stuck out his hand for her to shake.

"And mine is Jill Masterson, but everyone just calls me 'Jill,'" She shook his hand and squeezed it a little. He decided to never wash that hand again!

He walked back down King Street to the Magnolia B&B, but it appeared that the crime investigation team had finished their job and had moved back over to the station. He continued to walk down King Street, turned left at Queen Street and then another right on Meeting Street. The entire trip back to headquarters took about fifteen minutes, and he thought about Ms. Jill Masterson the whole way.

Chapter 15

Lawrence Baker

About the time Joey left the Blossom B&B, Dr. Henshaw arrived at the front desk of the hotel. The clerk directed her to go to room 116, where Lieutenant Watson was working.

"Louise, I'm glad you could come right away, because we have some serious similarities with this victim and the other two in your cooler at the morgue. I have restricted the movement around the body, and no one has touched anything in the room, but it appears that our victim has a serious laceration on the back of his head, and there is some blood oozing from his nose and mouth. I don't want to guess, but if I were guessing, I would say that his body resembles the other two who were poisoned. Am I right?"

"The injuries seem the same, but I won't know for sure until I get him on the table in my lab. Blood coming from the mouth of a corpse can definitely mean poisoning, but there are some other tests I will need to perform before I can make a proper diagnosis."

"There's something I just found that may shed some light on our cases," and Maggie produced a note of paper, securely deposited in an evidence bag. Louise could see that there was some writing on it in Roman letters.

"So what does the note say? Does it tie the murders together?"

"Et tu, Brute," Maggie said with a smile.

"Et tu, Brute? What does that mean? Is there no end to this craziness?"

"Well, Louise, if we take the statement at face value, it means 'And you, Brutus,' which of course were the last words supposedly spoken by Julius Caesar in the Roman Senate when he was assassinated by his close friend."

"And how is this significant?"

"We don't know how significant it may be. It's just one more clue in the mix, but it is a famous line from a play, and all three of these recent murder victims are theatrical people."

"I'm just glad you're the investigator, and I'm just a medical examiner."

"Oh, yeah, your job is much easier than mine—not!" and Maggie laughed with her new friend. She and Louise had seemed to bridge the gap between investigator and coroner rather quickly. Sometimes, a coroner and police detectives could be at odds when they most needed to work together closely on serious matters. That would not be the case for them.

Louise proceeded to examine the corpse with temperature devices. She inspected the victim's mouth and his toenails and fingernails. "He most likely died of poisoning, much like the others. I'll know for sure when I do the autopsy. I would put his death around 5:00 AM this morning."

"Thanks, Doc," Maggie said. "Jonathan and I will drop by the morgue when you finish the autopsy later today. While you are here, please take a few swabs of blood evidence for me," and she pointed with her black light where the drops were on the carpet and hardwood flooring. "Can you get the sample in a liquid form again so we can test it?"

"It's a fairly simple task, reconstituting the dried blood to liquid again. The trick is to ensure that the actual blood sample is collected, and not the environment around it. The way we do this is to add three to four drops of water to the dried blood spots, lay a piece of thin, white filter paper over the reconstituted blood, and let it flow onto the sterile paper. It can then be put into a cyclometer, which will let us pull the markers from the blood sample as if it were liquid. It's not a new process, but it is not as widely used as one might think."

"Nice," she said. Maggie was really impressed with Dr. Henshaw and how efficiently she worked a crime scene. Her old buddy back in Rowlette—Coroner Lonnie Gray—could learn a thing or two from Dr. Henshaw.

"When you leave here, could you please go to the Galliard and the Strand Theatres, meet Jonathan there and do the same for the dried blood spots that we were able to detect at those crime scenes?"

"Absolutely. I should have completed the autopsy on this victim and the analysis of blood by late afternoon. If you and

Jonathan want to stop by later today, I should have some information for you."

"That sounds great, Louise. Let me radio Jonathan to make sure he will be there when you arrive at the theatres." After speaking briefly to Jonathan, Maggie told Louise, "He will be waiting on you at the Strand. And, thanks for dropping all of your other work and putting this investigation ahead of your normal work."

"All in a day's work, Maggie," she responded. "We are just fortunate to have you and Jonathan here to help us solve these mysteries." Louise packed up her tools. "With so few murders in Charleston each year, our people are just not experienced enough to work a crime scene as efficiently as you two."

"Believe me, Louise. That's a good thing for Charleston—a very good thing!"

Chapter 16

The Student List

"Joey, bring that list over here," Maggie said to him when he returned to the station. He opened the manila envelope, took the sheets of legal paper out and placed them on the table. She was surprised at how many people were on the list. She had been hoping for a few dozen, not a few hundred names.

They alphabetized the names and created a chronological list that could be put into another alphabetized order, so it would make it much easier to look for specific names. Maggie picked up the radio, activated the talk button, and called Jonathan.

"This is Jonathan. Who is this?"

"This is your superior," she said with a laugh.

"That's no secret to anyone who has met us both."

"Is Louise still there?"

"No, she just left, so I imagine you will be able to contact her in the morgue pretty soon. What's up?"

"Was she able to get any blood samples from the Galliard and the Strand?"

"I think so. She seemed pleased with the results of her work. She works so quietly that if you don't ask her, she doesn't share what she's doing. Have you ever noticed that about her?"

"It's called being an introvert, Jonathan. You're used to a mouthy woman like me, so you think I'm normal, and she's not!"

"I wouldn't touch that statement with a ten-foot pole," he laughed.

"Being introverted is not unusual for physicians and other analytical types. It's important for them to spend a lot of quiet time thinking on their research. But it is important for us to get people talking—just the opposite skill set."

"How did you get so smart?"

"I guess by hanging around you!"

"Yeah, and I have some land in Florida I want to sell you."

"Hey, I need to visit the coroner's office. Do you want to meet me there? I have Joey working on a project that will keep him busy for the rest of the day. Why don't you send Juliet over to work with Joey while we visit Louise?"

"OK. Are you leaving for the morgue now?"

"Yes."

"I have to walk by the station on my way to the morgue. If you will wait a few minutes, Juliet and I will be there, and I will walk with you to see Louise."

"Come into the conference room, and we can put the rookies to work productively while we follow up on the autopsy."

* * *

When Jonathan arrived with Juliet, Maggie put Juliet to work with Joey coordinating the names with the dates of attendance for the two College of Charleston alumni victims. She figured it would take them a couple of hours to get that done, so she told them to take the rest of the day off once they finished that assignment. That was music to Joey's ears, because he had big plans.

As Jonathan and Maggie walked down Ashley Street toward the morgue, she asked him what his impression of Juliet was after spending a couple of days with her.

"How can I say this nicely?"

"So, 'Bless her heart' sounds appropriate to say at this point," Maggie said and laughed.

"Huh?" he asked, totally clueless to the Southern phrase that women might use right before saying something "catty" about one of their friends.

"I didn't mean to distract you. What were you going to say about Juliet?"

"I just am amazed that her personnel jacket was so impressive, and her actual work is not."

"Well, the good news is that Joey is just the opposite. He has far exceeded his ability 'on paper' numerous times. I guess we should stop putting people in categories and just take the recommendations from their supervisors," she said with resolve.

"No, let's not change anything with our selection process. You have chosen four young officers, two of whom have been satisfactory, and two of whom have been outstanding. I like our odds." He leaned down and kissed her lightly on the top of her head.

They were about to enter the hospital when Maggie stopped him.

"Jonathan, I want us to befriend Louise as much as possible while we are in Charleston. She is your half-sister, and you need to get to know her better. I don't think your father and Louise will be able to transcend all those years quickly, and she needs family. She's lost her mother to a terrible disease, and the only other family members she mentioned are in Birmingham, Alabama. Maybe after all of this is behind us, you and I can take a little time and go with her to Birmingham. We could visit with her cousins and whoever else she is related to there and try to get to know her on a more personal level."

"That sounds nice, but do you think you will ever take a few days to do something unrelated to work?"

"I deserve that," she said, "but for you and for Louise Henshaw, I would make an exception."

He nodded, hugged her, and opened the door for her to enter the hospital.

Chapter 17

Blood's Lessons

The guard saw them coming, smiled broadly at Maggie, and said, "You've been gone so long that I thought you had completed your investigation and left the city." He put his key in the elevator panel, tuned the key, and pressed the basement button.

"Yeah," she smiled back at him. "Geez, it's been almost an entire day since I was here!" and they all laughed heartily.

As they were descending toward the basement, Jonathan said, "You probably just made his day. The other physicians and lab assistants here probably don't even see him anymore—he's just an ornament required by the hospital administration and the security company who employs him."

"I actually like Butch," she said enthusiastically.

"Butch?" he looked at her, surprised that she knew his first name. "What else do you know about our guard extraordinaire?" guessing that his name was probably the extent of her knowledge about Butch.

She scratched her head, thought a minute, and then said, "Butch has been married to Mary for forty-five years, he has two kids—a boy and a girl, two grandchildren, three and four, and he likes to go crabbing in the sloughs of the Cooper and Ashley Rivers."

"No shit?" he said, simply amazed at her knowledge about such a common worker.

"Jonathan, I have been at this detective business for almost ten years, and one thing that I have learned, the hard way, is that you never know who may wind up being useful during your investigation. My motto these past few years has been, 'Treat people as you would like to be treated—they might be important to you down the road.' I promise you that if I need Butch to do something special for me, he would do it, and he would do it without question."

"And I thought I was the one who took the extra psychology classes after graduation."

"Unfortunately, I had to learn that lesson the hard way. It wasn't as if I purposely went out of my way to snub people in the past, but I didn't go out of my way to make them feel important either. I was on a case in Rowlette requiring a lot of research outside the investigation time, and I asked one of the staff secretaries to help me with the laborious research. She just looked at me and said, 'Do you even know my name, Lieutenant?' And, you know, Jonathan, I didn't know her name or anything else about her. The good news is that she was a hell-of-a-lot nicer to me than I had been to her. She stayed beyond normal office hours, and we knocked out the research in half the time it would have taken me to do it solo. I have never made that mistake again. So yes, I get to know the 'little people' every chance I get."

"When I grow up, I want to be like you!" Jonathan said and kissed her as the elevator door was opening. Standing directly in front of them as the door opened was Dr. Henshaw. She was as surprised as they, and they all giggled a little and moved toward the morgue. No one said a word about "the kiss," although it remained the white elephant in the room for a few minutes until the seriousness of the situation made them all forget about it.

"What have you got for us, Doc?"

"Some interesting things, Maggie, that's for sure," she said, and she pulled all three trays of bodies out so she could point to the autopsied bodies as she talked with a long, cylindrical stick. "Let's look at Lester Timmons and Terrell Swanson first," and she used a long, cylindrical stick, much like a wooden dowel, to point out the areas she was discussing. "On Mr. Timmons, we have a gash in the back of his head—same with Terrell Swanson. They are almost identical in their placement on the skull and the severity of the wound. However, now look at Mr. Baker's skull—it's a similar wound, but look at the depth and length of the gash. It is almost twice as long and twice as deep as that of the other two victims. Since they were all dying of sulfuric acid poisoning, the whacks on the head were symbolic in nature only. These blows were totally unnecessary, and the killer probably knew it. So, you have to ask yourself, 'Why did the killer hit the director more than the other two?' Once you have figured that out, you may find who did this."

"Jonathan, let's put this lady on the street, and I will do the autopsies," Maggie was totally surprised at the detail that Louise had been able to tie to the potential criminal motive for the murders.

Laughing, Jonathan said, "I'm sure she would have a better first day as a detective than you would have as a medical examiner!"

They all burst out laughing, letting the pressure out that had been building over the past few days. Even with so many dead bodies around them, they just couldn't help themselves.

"It's pretty obvious to me that all three of these people were murdered by the same person or persons. The sulfuric acid was introduced the same way, which makes me think that none of these people suspected anything until it was too late. Maybe—and this is just a guess--it was someone they all trusted. Maybe a friend. I know I'm not a detective, but the repetitive pattern of poisoning can't be explained any other way. Other than that, I don't have much more info on these bodies, but the dry blood spots turned up some interesting results."

"What?" Maggie asked with anticipation.

"One of them was HIV-positive, and each of the three murder scenes had a characteristic that one does not see often."

"What was that?" Jonathan asked her.

"Sickle cell anemia," she said, looking at them with concern.

"So we're looking for an African-American with sickle-cells, correct?"

"Not necessarily, Maggie. The odds are that we are looking for a black person, but they are not the only people with sickle cell anemia. Anyone, and I mean anyone, can have sickle cell anemia and never know it until special blood tests reveal it."

"You mean Caucasians carry the gene, too?" she said with amazement.

"They can carry it, but it is very rare. However, it is passed from generation to generation through the DNA of one or the other parent of the offspring. The fact that almost ten percent of all black people from all over the world carry that gene tells us that your murderer is probably black. However, some of the common mistakes often made by those researching the spreading of the disease are made out of ignorance of the nature of the disease. For instance, people is born with sickle cell. They can't contract it, and it's not contagious. One out of about four hundred African-American babies are born with a recognizable case of it every year. There are millions of people affected with the gene throughout the world, but what is not generally known about the sickness is that it tends to follow outbreaks of malaria in countries where proper control of the mosquitos spreading the disease is not under control. Once it is in the bloodstream of a person, it is there forever, and it is usually passed along to their children. So, to answer your question, 'Is it a black man or woman?', I would say probably, but not definitely. Is that helpful?"

"If I'm understanding your previous description, while the murderer may not be black, he or she is most probably carrying the sickle cell traits."

"Exactly. The murderers may be African-American, Haitians, Ethiopians, Sudanese—you get the picture?"

"OK, I think I have it now. The odds are the person or persons are black, possibly from an African nation state, or even a Caucasian whose parent genetically passed that gene on to them. How am I doing, Doc?"

"I think you've got it, Maggie."

"Now, our problem is how to extract a blood sample from any and all suspects without infringing upon their Fourth Amendment and Fourteenth Amendment rights under the U.S. Constitution," Jonathan said.

"You are precisely correct," Maggie stated to them both. "We will need corroborating evidence that puts the suspect at the scene of the crime before any judge is going to give us the right to seize DNA that could possibly lead to arrest and imprisonment. Otherwise, the Fifth Amendment keeps us in the dark on the potential sickle cell markers that the murderer possesses."

"No one said this was going to be easy, Maggie," Jonathan said seriously.

"No one was correct," Maggie said, and she began to gather up her notes so she could go back to the Gaslight Inn and put a plan together to figure out how to nail this person, without stepping on their Fourth, Fifth, and Fourteenth Amendment rights. It would be a long evening.

They excused themselves from Louise, took the elevator to the main floor, where Maggie made a parting wave to Butch. Once outside, they moved up Ashley Street, chatting about the recent visit to the morgue.

"You know, Jonathan, I seem to learn more every day that I spend around you. Why, if it were not for your good-for-nothing father, I would never have met one of the most interesting and intelligent coroners in the world!"

"Let's go back to the hotel, get in the Jacuzzi and relax a little, and then we can drink in style to that good-for-nothing man," and he kissed her again on the top of her head.

"I want a steak to beat all steaks tonight, and I saw where there was a Ruth's Chris Steak House on Market Street. How do you feel about spending several hundred dollars on me for dinner and drinks?" she asked him seductively.

"I guess it matters what I get in return for my kindness and good taste," he said, matching her devilish grin.

"Well, just what do you want, Jonathan."

"Let's get that special steak dinner, and then we'll see what comes up."

Chapter 18

Jacuzzi Consultations

It had been a very long day for Maggie and Jonathan. It seemed hard to believe that only this morning they had learned of the third murder. With diligent police work and a very gifted coroner, they now had a few clues to chase in their attempt to find the murderer.

"What do you make of the sickle cell nature of the murderer's blood? How can that help us discover who the prime suspects might be? How will we go about obtaining a warrant for a DNA sample, or other items that could tie that person to these crimes?" Jonathan popped questions so non-stop that Maggie couldn't begin to answer them.

"Which one do you want me to answer first?"

"I just don't see how this new information is going to help us that much. In fact, it may cloud the picture even more if we assume that just because the perpetrator had sickle cell anemia that he is African-American."

"You heard Louise, Jonathan. There is a possibility that this person with sickle cell anemia is not black, or that he could be black and from Nigeria or another foreign country. Let's detail what we know and what we think we know," she said, sipping her wine. Sitting in the Jacuzzi in the courtyard of the Gaslight Inn, enjoying the soothing, bubbling water, they reviewed the facts.

"What we know is that two of the three murder victims had a history with the College of Charleston. That is a fact. We also know that these two men were involved in the Fine Arts Department. Second, we know that someone left a quotation from *Julius Caesar* at the last murder scene. Third, the MO for all three murders is the same, with the only deviation being a much more severe blow to the head of the last victim, a director in the Piccolo/Spoleto Festival. Perhaps the murderer has some reason to discredit the College of Charleston, the artists who performed, or the director, who was the last victim. What did I miss?"

"Well, as far as facts are concerned, you probably covered most of them. However, the first thing we both learned in criminology class was the most common motives for murder. Number one is war. I think we can rule that out, since the last war fought in Charleston was in 1865. Reason number two is cheating. Again, it's possible, but probably not the reason these three theatrical people were killed. Number three, safety—absolutely not applicable here. Number four, humiliation, and number five, greed. What monetary benefits does the murderer get from killing these actors? It doesn't fit the crimes. So, I would boldly say, the motive for these murders is humiliation. How's that for a quick analysis?" Jonathan looked at Maggie for approval.

"Dead on, Mr. Pembroke. Dead on. Now what we need to do is go through the list of names from the College of Charleston that Joey brought me today and narrow down the suspect pool. I think we may be on to something here," and she raised her wine glass to his for a toast.

"Won't the pages get wet if we review the list in the Jacuzzi?" he asked.

"Oh, you are a clever one, Jonathan. Now, why didn't I think of that?" and she kissed him on the mouth. "Now get your skinny butt out of the Jacuzzi and let's get cleaned up, so we can review the names."

As he got out of the pool in his wet bathing trunks, he asked Maggie mischievously, "Do you think these trunks make my butt look big?"

Maggie just shook her head and went into their room, only a few feet from the Jacuzzi. She wondered if Jonathan had anything to do with the room selection, but since she had "bigger fish to fry," she let that thought pass. They showered, dressed casually for dinner, and decided to have dinner at the steak house before they got too bogged down with the details of the students at the College of Charleston. Jonathan called for reservations, but they were booked solid for the evening.

"Where should we go for dinner tonight, Alan?" Maggie asked the hotel manager. "We had planned to eat at a steak house, but we can't get a reservation." According to the information guide that was available at the desk, Alan had been managing this hotel for many years.

"Have you tried Eli's Table, just down the street a couple of blocks?" Alan asked.

"No."

"I have recommended Eli's often, and I can't remember anyone coming back to me telling me that it wasn't a good place to eat. Actually, just about any restaurant in the Historic Charleston peninsula is going to be good. Most of the chefs in this district were trained at Johnson and Wales University on East Bay Street. They have been in business in various locations in the United States since about 1910. We are lucky to have them here in Charleston."

"It sounds wonderful, Alan. Thanks for the recommendation!" Maggie said and winked at him. "Do we need reservations since it is a very busy weekend?"

"I would be happy to secure a reservation for you. Can you wait a minute, so I can make sure they are not overbooked for tonight? You can help yourself to our complimentary wine and snacks while you wait."

"That would be great," Jonathan said, picking up a wine stem and pouring Maggie a glass of Chardonnay. In less than five minutes, Alan gave them a "thumbs-up" signal.

"Your reservations are in the next thirty minutes, and the restaurant is located on the right side in the next block down Meeting Street. Tell them that I sent you, and they may offer you a free dessert or a glass of their house wine!"

"Thanks, Alan!" Maggie said, winking.

As they were walking down the two blocks to the restaurant, Jonathan asked her, "Do you flirt with every man you talk to?"

"No, but now that you mention it, it may be a good idea," she said coyly. "I think Alan is handsome!"

"Oh, behave."

Chapter 19

Out on the Town

"What will you have to start?" the handsome, articulate waiter asked Jonathan and Maggie after they had been seated at Eli's Table. Since they asked for a discrete and quiet table, the maître'd seated them in a small nook just beyond the front door. There was a large, plate-glass window that gave them a wonderful view of the countless number of visitors walking down Meeting Street in front of Eli's toward venues and toward other restaurants and venues toward Battery Park.

"We will have a bottle of your finest Chardonnay, with some bread and cheese to start. Then we will both have the ribeye steak and fresh vegetables. Make the steak medium-well."

"Very good, sir," he said and left the table with their order.

"They should charge more for this table," Jonathan said as he pointed out several couples, made personal comments about them, and then focused on the next group of pedestrians.

"They probably do, Jonathan. Don't be surprised if there is an 'entertainment charge' on the bill when we leave."

"Just about every view in this city is 'entertainment' and well worth any charge they add for it. I can see how this city can grow on a person—not that I don't like the freezing cold, snow, ice, and temperatures below zero several times a year. Nothing like good old 'home sweet home!'"

"There she is again!" Jonathan said. "Do you recognize who is with Officer Robinson? Is that one of the suspects?"

"I can't tell from this distance, but the woman is Juliet."

"What are the odds we would see them walking in the evening in a city the size of Charleston?"

"I have no idea, but I think we should ask her about her date tonight when we get the opportunity. It has to be subtle, though, because we don't want to spook him—or her."

"You think she is involved with a potential murderer?" Jonathan asked.

"Stranger things have happened. We need to make sure we know as much about him as possible—it could be a coincidence."

They both looked at each other and said in unison, "No way!"

"We have a few days before we confront the suspects—let's not move too hastily. However, we need to keep both of them on our radar!"

The waiter brought the wine, bread and cheese, and Jonathan lifted his glass and toasted Maggie's glass of wine: "To the brightest and most beautiful crime solver in Charleston!"

She smiled, "Did you see my competition? I don't think Major Pinckney is going to win any beauty contests! Although I have to admit, he has been very kind to both of us through all of this craziness."

"That's true, but I'm sure there are more beautiful women in the police department that we haven't met yet. You exceed them all!"

"If you say so," she said and returned the toast. "At least we are taking a little time to ourselves to enjoy some of the local cuisine before we jump back into the craziness of this investigation."

"Did you bring the names on the list from the college? While we are waiting on our food, we might read through them."

"Excellent idea, Jonathan," and she gave him about half of the sheets of names that Joey had brought back from his visit that afternoon with Jill Masterson.

Joey had requested name, age, ethnicity, major concentration of study, social clubs, and other pertinent information that might help narrow the suspect pool. Maggie had brought a couple of yellow markers and a couple of red ballpoint pens to mark the lists if they saw something they might want to reconsider once they had read through the many pages of names.

They worked silently, with an occasional nod of the head to one another, until Maggie said, "You know, Jonathan, I have looked through my names, and I have narrowed the possible students to only eight who attended during the time of either victim's time at the university. How many did you find?"

"Only three."

"That gives us eleven. We should be able to check that many names out tomorrow, especially with our rookies doing some of the footwork. Do you think that Juliet is capable of working on her own, or do we need to supervise her activities to make sure she doesn't take shortcuts?"

"Don't get me wrong, I'm sure she is a nice girl," Jonathan tried to soften his answer, "and she will probably be a decent officer once she gets some experience. However, right now she appears to be more concerned how things look to other people, rather than just getting the work done and letting the credit for the research fall where it should. Also, I could swear the guy she was with tonight appeared to be one of those students we looked at earlier. Joey's initial list had lots of pictures, and I can't remember names to match the photographs, but that gives me more reason to keep a close eye on Juliet."

"I agree. We can't have anything left to chance with this investigation. We probably need to have someone keep an eye on her for now. I think that Joey might be capable of that task, assuming that I coach him on what I want him to do. He's nice enough to get the job done without lording it over her. What do you think?"

"I don't see how it can hurt anything, because right now anything that we give her to do will have to be followed up on by one of us. I say go for it!"

Their dinner came and was absolutely wonderful. They chatted about other options that they might have, but they made no specific plans. They wanted to get back to the hotel and put everything down on paper before their meeting in the morning with their rookies. It was important to make sure that their plan was clear and concise.

"Let's do something daring, Maggie."

"Like what?"

"There is a candlelight, champagne cruise that hovers along the coast of Charleston, with the highlight being a brief visit to Fort Sumter, where the first battle of the Civil War was fought."

"OK, my historian. Tell me all you know about Fort Sumter—I'm sure you have gone to a lot of trouble researching the subject. I don't want all of your efforts to go unappreciated."

"Truly a tragic and useless war, in my opinion. Only one soldier died in the first battle of the war—the attack on Fort Sumter—and that was a Union soldier during the evacuation after the surrender of the facility to the Confederate States Army. However, by the end of the war in 1865, 750,000 soldiers from both sides were dead. It remains the largest loss of life in the history of the United States from war. In addition to the military deaths, an estimated 50,000 civilians also lost their lives. Historians estimate that over 3 million families of soldiers were adversely affected by the four-year war. About 2.5% of the entire U.S. population at the time of the Civil War died over that four-year time. It makes us wonder today how insane the hatred between the nation's two opposing sides could have gotten so out of hand."

"I understand from my readings, the second and third generations of Southern women thought of General Sherman as the Devil himself! Even the gentlewomen of Charleston refer to him as an S.O.B. That's pretty strong for these normally kind and welcoming women."

"It appears there are still some 'hurt feelings' between the people of the South and the U.S. Government. So, let's keep the origin of our permanent residence to ourselves as much as possible," Jonathan suggested.

"Let's just say if I planned to live here on a permanent basis, I would have to acquire a Southern accent."

* * *

As they entered the pier where the tickets were being sold for the evening cruise, Maggie turned to Jonathan and said, "It's a shame that this beautiful city was racked by such a terrible war those many years ago. It does appear, however, that they have risen from the ashes, like the Phoenix."

Out of the corner of his eye, Jonathan saw Officer Juliet Robinson with a young man, or at least he thought he had seen her.

Her incidental appearance was not unusual, but the young man's face looked very familiar. He couldn't place it immediately, but he believed it was one of the suspects they had been investigating.

"Maggie, did you see Juliet over there?" pointing to the area of the dock where he saw her earlier.

"Juliet? Juliet Robinson?"

"Yes."

"No, but why do you ask? It is not beyond reason that she might be out in the evening during this festive time in Charleston. What is your point?"

"I can't swear to it, but I think I saw her again with one of the suspects we have been investigating. Should we try to find her and see if I was correct?"

"And do what? Arrest him for dating Juliet? Right now we have nothing in evidence on any of the suspects that will let us hold them for suspicion of murder. We would be showing our cards before the game was in a critical situation—no, let's bide our time until we get something more concrete in evidence before we begin bringing these people in for questioning. If you are correct, maybe she's doing some undercover work."

"Undercover work? Can we do some of that?"

"Really, Jonathan? You are oversexed!"

"Maybe. How can I disagree when you're the boss?"

"I don't know about that, but we decided to tour the city and relax tonight. Let's get back to our original plan—unless you want to go back to the Gaslight Inn."

"For fun and games?"

"For rest and sleep!"

"I think a moonlight cruise is a better idea."

* * *

As they were preparing to board the ship, Jonathan looked over the skyline of the city, marveled at its beautiful cathedrals and historic buildings, and the hustle and bustle of the visitors to the city. He turned to Maggie and said, "It's always a nice thing to see life return to normal, or what appears normal, after such a bad experience. However, I'm not sure the wounds the South suffered will ever be forgotten totally."

The small cruise ship called for boarding, so they purchased their tickets, walked up the stairs to the entrance to the deck and stepped aboard. They immediately decided to go to the top of the ship to ensure their views were the best possible. Since it was May, it was still very warm after dark, and the humidity was somewhat oppressive, but there was a cool breeze blowing up the peninsula that seemed to counter the sticky weather.

They pulled out of the harbor and immediately noticed a school of dolphins moving in rhythm alongside the ship. They were chattering, and everyone on the boat was charmed by their presence.

"I wonder if we are permitted to feed them?" Maggie asked.

"From the looks of the signs over there, 'Fresh fish for the dolphins $2.50 per bucket,' I would say yes."

"Oh Jonathan, please indulge me and get a couple of buckets. I think that would be a fun thing to do. We can go back to Rowlette and tell all our friends how spectacular the event was. Look how they jump up and flip to get the fish thrown to them."

"You are such a 'softie' when it comes to animals and small children. I'll indulge you."

Maggie just smiled at him, and for a minute he forgot all about the murder investigation that they had to tackle soon. They fed the dolphins, took pictures of Fort Hood when they passed slowly by, and then more photos when they began returning to the harbor. The beautifully lighted pastel homes in the Battery area were absolutely stunning. The ship docked, they disembarked, and as they walked down the plank and steps to the dock, the reality of why they were remaining in Charleston hit them once more like a ton of bricks.

* * *

They walked back to the hotel, got undressed and put their swimsuits on for the Jacuzzi. As they were slipping into the hot, bubbly water, Jonathan said to Maggie, "I guess you know we have to get one of these when we go home."

"My thinking exactly," she said and planted a big kiss on his lips.

"Except in ours, we can play 'watersports' nude as long as we wish!"

"It never gets old to you, does it?"

"Does what?"

"Really? I have to spell it out for you?"

He just grinned from ear to ear and slid down into the 106-degree water.

They spent about thirty minutes in the water, splashing each other, and generally acting like teenagers. Jonathan told her that she was acting silly, and then he dunked her under the water. She retaliated by pouring cold wine down his swimsuit. It was clearly time to take their activities into the room.

Chapter 20

The Mayor

Jonathan and Maggie arrived at the police station the next morning at 9:00 AM, ready to begin the task of narrowing down potential suspects for the three murders. It was becoming apparent to everyone that the murderer was someone connected to the Piccolo/Spoleto Festival, the artists performing in the plays, or someone closely affiliated with the activities of the festival. The logical conclusion was that since two of the three murder victims had had close ties with the College of Charleston, there was more than a casual connection possible between the murderer, school, and its fine arts department. However, before they could get started on their analysis, the mayor's office had called Major Pinckney and had requested that he and his investigative crew appear at his office immediately. Maggie, Jonathan, and Pinckney walked across Meeting Street to the City Hall building. They were ushered into the mayor's chambers, seated at the conference table, and immediately joined by Mayor Anderson.

"I am increasingly concerned about how this investigation might damage the tranquility and appeal that we have here in Charleston every year for the Piccolo/Spoleto Festival."

"I understand," Maggie said to Mayor Anderson, "but we have to follow the leads wherever they take us."

"I'm not trying to tell you how to do your job, Lieutenant. I'm just trying to tell you that when you begin to attack the very institutions that support and sustain our city, you are getting close to agitating the entire community. We don't want the city and its visitors up in arms about this situation. We have to approach these murders in a way as not to damage the credibility of the city or its entertainment industry. You see what I mean, don't you?" He looked at Maggie and Jonathan with hopeful reassurance to his point.

"Mayor, let me be blunt with you. There is someone who is roaming your city streets with one goal, and that is to do harm to innocent people who appear to be performing in this annual festival. The only way to find this person or persons is to follow every lead to its roots, discern if that lead is viable, and then move on to the next one. What we have discovered is that there is a good probability that the victims were associated with someone who also attended or was influenced by the College of Charleston. The investigation will take us wherever the leads and threads of evidence take us. We can't arbitrarily decide whom to investigate for politically correct reasons. The only way we can go forward with this murder investigation is to do what we are currently doing. If that doesn't work for you, we will simply give our statement on the status of the investigation to the local newspaper, and then we will return to Illinois. It's your choice," she said irritably.

"Oh, don't get me wrong, Lieutenant. We want you to continue your investigation into these murders, but we just want you to tread softly, when possible," he said apologetically.

"Mayor Anderson, the facts are the facts. We will not go out of our way to fan the flames of rumors or to introduce drama into our investigation. We have kept most of the facts of this situation from the reporters, and we have referred the press to your office for comment. You, sir, can control what is shared with the media and the public. We, however, will deal only with the facts."

"Mayor," Major Pinckney added, "I can tell you that these two investigators have accomplished more than my entire department could have done, and in much less time as well. My department will continue to work this matter as quietly as we can without compromising the investigation. I do believe that everyone, even these detectives, understand the importance of keeping the facts of this investigation under wraps until we have a clear picture of who our murderer might be."

"OK, Major Pinckney. Just don't forget that this festival is very, very important to our local economy and we don't want to see it damaged in any way."

"You have our word, Mayor, that we will keep that in mind," Pinckney said.

The mayor stood up, indicating that the meeting was over. Maggie and Jonathan couldn't be happier. Now, perhaps, they might be able to get back to work. On the walk back to the police station, Maggie asked Pinckney, "Pardon my directness, Major, but does your mayor always keep his head up his butt when something that might hurt the economy or damage the good name of Charleston arises?"

Pinckney just laughed a little and said, "Lieutenant, you would have to have lived in the Deep South all your life, be a third or fourth generation Charlestonian, and become totally immersed in the Southern culture to understand where the mayor is coming from on his request. Let's just say he is steeped in old Southern traditions."

"That's something I won't miss when I get back to Rowlette," she said emphatically. "Black and white in Illinois seem more like shades of gray in Charleston."

"Now, Maggie, you're beginning to understand Charleston's culture," and he grinned as he opened the door to the headquarters building for them.

They had just cleared the City Hall building when a trove of news people with cameras and flash bulbs began to blind them. Maggie had seen this type of thing on the news in places like Chicago, New York, and cities with major network headquarters, but she never thought it would happen in "sleepy Charleston."

"What can you tell us about the murders that are going on in Charleston, Lieutenant? Are you close to figuring out who is doing this? Is this a serial killer? Are our citizens safe to walk the streets at night during the Piccolo/Spoleto Festival?"

"We will address what we know soon," the major told the reporters, and he attempted to evade the large gathering of those with tape recorders and cameras.

Maggie turned to Major Pinckney and said, "Major, you really can't ignore the throng of reporters trying to get feedback. What will happen is that they will 'fill in' the missing information with their imaginations. If you know anything about the press, you know reporters will always imagine things worse than they really are. We are going to have to stop, address their questions, and generally 'baffle them with bullshit' to make this work. Do you trust me?"

"Sure, Lieutenant Watson. What do you have in mind?"

"Just let me handle this, and they will not bother us anymore today or in the near future—I can almost guarantee it."

"You're on!"

Maggie stopped her forward progress, turned to the reporters, and began to speak. When she made the abrupt change in attitude, it caught many of them off guard, and the questions she had to negotiate were less than Pinckney had feared.

"Look," she said in a quiet, patient tone. "We are a special team of investigators that the mayor has brought into this case to make sure everything possible is done in a timely manner to ensure the safety of all citizens of Charleston, as well as the many visitors from around the world who are here to enjoy and celebrate the Piccolo/Spoleto Festival. To ensure that no incomplete information is released prematurely, all communications and responses have been directed to be gathered directly from the mayor's office. We, as special investigators, are bound by our oath to him and his office to preserve the integrity of the investigation until he deems it proper to release that information to you. So, please direct all future questions directly to his communication's spokesman. Thank you." Maggie turned on her heel and proceeded toward the Charleston Police Department.

As the three of them moved toward the police department, Major Pinckney looked at Maggie. "Where did you learn to speak like that? That was simply genius."

"Why do you think that was so smart?" she asked.

"Well, the mayor has insisted that the information released has to be done in a sensitive and calculating way, right? You have simply put the responsibility of dealing with the press back on his office. He actually got what he wanted—you and Jonathan investigating the crimes, and his office releasing what information he deems necessary and non-inflammatory."

Maggie just smiled and continued to walk toward the station. Jonathan was doing his best impression of holding back a giggle but then said to the major, "Isn't she something?!"

Chapter 21

The College of Charleston

"Tell us, Joey, about your new girlfriend." Jonathan was picking at him at the lunch meeting, where they were enjoying some takeout lunches from Poogan's Porch, a restaurant a few blocks down the street from the police station.

"She's not really my 'girlfriend,' Jonathan. We just seemed to hit it off when I went to the library to search the records for the College of Charleston. She recommended that I pick up lunch for you from Poogan's—it's her favorite restaurant."

"So what's so special about this 'Poogan's' place?"

"Well, according to my new friend, Poogan's had a colorful history in the Historic Downtown Charleston area, because it was in a 'haunted house' built in 1888. The ghost of a spinster, who had lived there for many years, was often 'reportedly' seen by diners in the evenings as she walked the upstairs balcony overlooking Queen Street. The restaurant had acquired its name in an unusual manner as well. It seems in the late 1970s, a small dog named 'Poogan' lived in the house with his owners until they sold the house and moved out of the area. Poogan refused to leave his porch, and he stayed at the residence until he died in 1979. When the restaurant was opened a few years later, the owner named it in his honor."

"That's a nice story. Wait until Maggie hears how much I know about this local restaurant!"

Partly because of the Johnson and Wales Chef University, and partly because Charleston boasted of having over one hundred of the best restaurants in America, Poogan's was considered good, but not the best restaurant in the famous Low-Country City. Anson's, Peninsula, 82 Queen, and an exhaustive list of other restaurants competed on a daily basis to be deemed the "Best of Charleston!" Each of the restaurants had exotic or eccentric stories of their origination like Poogan's—many claiming to be the favorite dining spot of the pirates who lived just outside of Charleston proper some 250 years ago!. The pirates would plunder and steal, and then go to a local restaurant to celebrate their new found wealth. Although many of the city's fathers knew the rumors held only a kernel of truth in them, no one was confident enough to confront the restaurant's marketing ploys while they were partaking of the wonderful ambiance of Charleston's finest eateries.

So, sitting in the police station, chowing down on wonderful delights from Poogan's was a pretty common experience for the locals like Joey and the other officers in the Charleston Police Department. And since continually talking about the wonderful food of the Low Country seemed to bore most Charlestonians, Jonathan took this opportunity to raze his young apprentice investigator.

"I wouldn't say she was my girlfriend," Joey said and blushed a little. "I just met her—she was the person who helped me get the list of fine arts people from the College of Charleston. She was a very nice young woman who seemed to see it as her community duty to help us find the perpetrator behind these murders."

"And from what I hear, you have already had a date with her!" Jonathan continued to tease the young officer. "Was it the uniform that made you so attractive to her?"

"Jonathan, knock it off," Maggie said and gave him a stern look. "Joey did very well yesterday securing the info for us, and we are most appreciative of his efforts."

Jonathan looked at Joey and winked. Jonathan might have slowed down in his pursuit of the ladies, but he admired Joey for his opportunistic moves. "Hey, I'm just kidding, Joey. I'm sure she's a nice girl."

Joey blushed bright red. He tried to ignore the attention that had landed on him unexpectedly, but it wasn't working very well.

"Can we please get back to the subject of the students who may have come in contact with our victims?" Maggie asked. "What we do know is that eleven students on the list that Joey was able to secure for us were in classes in or around the time that the two victims were in attendance or involved with the College of Charleston. I want Joey and Juliet to take a name each and perform background investigations on these individuals. I want to know when they left the College of Charleston, if they married, had kids, where they worked, and everything that has gone on in their lives through yesterday. If they are no longer local, could they have come back to Charleston long enough to be involved with these crimes? Jonathan and I will take the next two names, and we will do the same research. Major Pinckney said that the library has a couple of computers that we can use, so I'm sending you two over there. Jonathan and I will work from here. If anyone gets a legitimate hit on any information that seems pertinent to these murders, I want to hear about it immediately. If there aren't any questions, let do it."

Joey and Juliet walked up Meeting Street, took a right turn on Calhoun Street and found the Charleston County Public Library. By the time they had walked the seven or eight blocks to the building, the chief had called ahead, and the library staff had restricted a small area of the library research area for their use. They would be able to use the computers and reference materials without worrying about competing with other library patrons. They got settled in, turned on the computers, and dove into the massive task of following a person's life from day to day for several years. It was boring, but it was a necessary task that someone had to do. Surprisingly, Juliet was really good at research, so Joey didn't have to carry the project by himself. Although the library was open to the public until 4:00 PM, the head librarian told them they could stay until 6:00 PM if they wanted.

Back at the station, Maggie and Jonathan had taken a name each and had begun the same procedure. Before they could get too far along in their research, the telephone rang and the chief called Maggie to the phone.

"Louise, is that you?"

"Yes, and I think that you and Jonathan need to come here as soon as possible. I have found something that may change your approach to this entire investigation."

"Do you want to share that information on the phone?"

"Absolutely not. This is so sensitive that I'm not sure how you're going to be able to use it, but I need to speak to you in person."

"OK, we are on our way."

"Jonathan, mark your place in your research. You and I are going on a field trip," Maggie said without further explanation.

"Huh?" he asked, looking up from the computer screen. "Field trip? Where?"

"The morgue. Let's go." When she got him out the door on their way down to Ashley Street and the hospital, she said, "It appears that Louise has come up with some information that she thinks could alter the way we are looking at these murders."

"Like what?"

"She wouldn't say on the telephone, but knowing Louise, it is probably something really big. She is the master of the understatement, so when she says she has something that will blow the roof off this investigation, I'm all for hearing it!" Maggie said excitedly.

"I wonder what it could be? I mean, she is dealing with tissue, blood, guts, injuries, and stuff like that. What could she have discovered that is so important?"

"Look, all I know is that Louise is one smart lady. She is head and shoulders above any medical examiner I've ever known, so if she says she has something 'big,' she probably has something huge!"

They continued to walk down Ashley until they arrived at the hospital. Maggie waved at Butch Blakeley, who came to the elevator and turned his passkey into the panel for them. "How are your grandkids?" she asked him.

"Just fine. I'm taking the boys fishing tomorrow, or should I say gigging. We will be looking for flounder. They love to watch me gig some flounder, clean them, and fry them up for dinner."

"That sounds great. Watch out for the snakes!" she said as the elevator door closed to take them down to the morgue.

"Snakes?"

"There are thirty-eight species of snakes in the Charleston area, but only six are poisonous. You should keep up, Jonathan," and she lightly kissed him on the cheek.

"Uh huh," he sighed and the door opened. They walked to the door of the morgue, where she stopped for a moment. "Let's give Louise a chance to tell us what she's concerned about before we start questioning her information."

"Of course, don't you think I would do that anyway?" he asked somewhat offended.

"You are a man of action, Jonathan. That's good most of the time. However, sometimes you have to let the info come to you. I don't want to put any damper on Louise's energy to help us solve these murders, even if her new information is not helpful. OK?"

"OK. Man of action, huh?"

They stepped into Louise's lab. She was working on a small child, and she covered the body with a sheet quickly when they came into the morgue. Louise had the utmost respect for the dead who were left in her charge. She invited them into her office, motioned to the two chairs in front of her desk, and sat down behind it. She opened a manila folder, lifting a chart that appeared to have a DNA pattern displayed.

"So, Dr. Hensley, what is so exciting that we needed to come in person to see it?" Maggie asked.

"I'm glad you're sitting down, because it is really revealing stuff. It appears that the director of the play has sickle cell markers in his blood. He doesn't have a full-blown case of it, but he is definitely a carrier. And, as you already know, he is Caucasian and not African-American."

"So what does that mean?" Jonathan asked, anticipating more information from Louise.

"Since it was such a coincidence, I decided to run a DNA test on both him and the one other victim that had sickle cell—Lester Timmons. They are related." She disclosed this bombshell of information matter of factly.

"They what?" Maggie asked with total astonishment.

"They are either father and son, brother and brother, or uncle and nephew. Since the DNA is so close, it appears they are no more than one link away from being the same person."

"And you are pretty sure about this?" Maggie asked.

"Absolutely certain. In fact, look at these DNA panels and tell me if you are able to tell one from the other." Louise held up the two panels for them to view. When she held them side-by-side, Maggie and Jonathan looked at each other and just nodded their heads at her.

"Now it's your turn to tell me what that means," Louise told them. "I can define and explain the genetics of these victims, but I can't tell you how or why this all happened."

"We are working on it, but what you have just shared with us might help us narrow the field even more. I don't guess you can perform a DNA test on the third victim to see if he was related to the other two, or is that too expensive to request?"

"I can do that, if you think it would help in the investigation."

"The worst thing it can do is eliminate them as all being related. That alone would help us narrow the field of suspects," Jonathan replied.

"Then consider it done," Louise said and stood to get back to her lab.

Louise reminded them that DNA testing was a relatively new concept that gave local police departments a way to go back to 'cold cases' and revive their research. Many of the cases that could not be solved without blood and other body fluid analysis in the past were now being reopened using this new technical approach to evidence. Louise was hopeful that her extensive DNA research in this case would prove helpful providing some definite leads for her new friends.

Maggie was familiar with the story of the first successful conviction of a cold case in 1986 when a lab in England provided the DNA evidence that helped convict a serial rapist and murderer of three counts in a small village in Leicestershire. Louise could only hope she could help generate the same results in this murder case. The major drawback was that convictions were not always a result of the expensive process, and with limited budgets for such things, each police department across the country had to decide how much of their budget could be dedicated to this new procedure. Other important factors that had to be determined was whether or not the statute of limitations had expired for the particular crime in question, or whether the person was a minor at the time of the offense. So, it wasn't just a cut-and-dried procedure always performed at the whim of the coroner or an over-eager investigator. Maggie was eager, too, but also took care of the details which made her a better detective. Even though many times the upper management of the policing authority had to check budgetary constraints before authorizing DNA testing, in this situation, Louise knew the mayor well enough to feel confident that moving the DNA testing along without seeking special authorization would be acceptable. She would push the limits of authority to order the extra tests and anticipate that her efforts could lead to a breakthrough—otherwise, she might get a less than friendly call from the city manager citing budgetary concerns.

They all said their goodbyes, and both Jonathan and Maggie chatted on the way back to the main floor. As they were walking back up Ashley Street toward the police department, Jonathan said, "I think you're 100% correct about Louise. I think we need to be supportive of her on a personal level. We'll have to think about how we can get that done."

"Well, knowing that her few relatives live in the Birmingham, Alabama, area, we should definitely plan to visit her when things slow down. Since they are her cousins and you are blood-kin with her, you could have a 'family reunion' of sorts that will help her feel special and at the same time introduce me to some of your distant relatives. The only issue I see in such a plan is finding the off-time to take a weekend to ourselves. We'll have to look into the possibility one day."

"I like the sound of that plan—I really want to get to know her better. I hate that our only connection is my dad, who had a disastrous relationship with her mother. Then to lose her mother to a debilitating disease with no other close family to help her overcome her insecurities—it's just not fair."

"Fair? Right. Like we have any say over what's fair and what's not. I do like that quality in you, Jonathan."

"What quality is that?"
"Eternal optimism!"

*   *   *

They arrived back at the police station, called the library where Joey and Juliet were working, and decided that the four of them should reassemble in the conference room to merge their results of the investigation.

"We need to invite Major Pinckney to meet with us as well, and let him decide how much he wants to share with the mayor. I personally don't think we should tell the mayor too much, but since we are here because Pinckney trusts us to do the right thing, we should leave the decision of relating the inside information to the mayor up to him. Do you agree?"

"I don't see where you have a choice. It's not like back in Rowlette, where you could control what the mayor and chief leaked to the local press. We are here in an unknown city, working with people who are trying to help us, but they have other people to whom they have to answer. I think you should be forthcoming with Major Pinckney and hope he uses some discretion with the mayor."

When the rookies returned to the police station, the four of them called Major Pinckney's office, requesting that he join them in the conference room if he had time. In just a few minutes, he appeared at the door.

"Yes, Lieutenant Watson, what can I do for you?"

"It's more what we can do for you, Major," she replied.

"And how is that?"

"We have a summary of the investigation that we would like to share with you, and we will let you decide how much of it you will want to share with Mayor Anderson. I have to tell you up front, if he shares all of the information that we are going to share with you with the press, he may damage the ability for us to determine who the murderer is and prevent us from being able to catch him or her. However, that will be your decision once you have heard what we now know."

"Gee, thanks for putting me on the hot seat."

"Here's what we have so far. The three murder victims are somewhat related. We are not exactly sure how related at this time, but there is a familial connection between two of them."

"Familial? What do you mean by that?"

"We are almost 100% sure that Lester Timmons and Lawrence Baker both carry much of the same DNA. That would make them father and son, or brother and brother, or something akin to that. With that information in mind, we have to believe that the College of Charleston connection is somehow tied into all of this madness. We aren't exactly sure just why or how, but the coroner is certain that these two victims were closely related."

"Crap!" he said, and then blushed a little at his outburst. "Sorry about that, but it just gets better and better, doesn't it?"

"I'm afraid so. We have asked the coroner to run a DNA test on the third victim, Terrell Swanson, to see if he is related somehow to the other two victims."

"And if he is, what does that say?"

"I'm not sure, but it might tell us that he murdered Swanson to throw us off the real reason for his other two crimes."

"I'm afraid I'm not following you on this point. How can that muddy the water?"

"If it is a crime of passion, and if it has something to do with a familial situation, then a random murder of a similar nature keeps us from narrowing down the motive. If he was out to get these two men because they are related, the third murder doesn't fit, especially since it occurred between the other two murders."

"Hmmnn. Yes, I can see how that might muddy the water a lot to a jury. And if it comes back that all three are related, then what does that tell us?"

"I'm not sure, but we should know sometime later today or early tomorrow, once the coroner completes the DNA testing of Swanson's body. At this point, I would place the odds against their all being related, but it's just a guess."

"What do you think the odds are you are correct?"

"Probably ten-to-one. But again, that's just a guess. From a statistical point of view, the odds are probably greater than that. However, we can't move too far forward until we have that answer. It will totally change how we go about flushing out the murderer."

"What else do you know that I may need to know?"

"We have narrowed the probable suspects down to eleven people who attended the college during the periods that Lester Timmons attended as a student and Lawrence Baker taught there. Since both X and Y chromosomes showed up in the special blood tests, we are pretty sure that the murderer is a male. The dried blood sample shows two things in particular. First, the murderer had a Y chromosome in his blood panel."

"And the second?" The major looked at them as they hesitated to continue.

"The second unusual finding in the blood type was that both Timmons and Baker, the ones with similar DNA, also both have markers for sickle cell anemia. It appears that Timmons actually had a full blown case of sickle cell anemia. The odds of those two things happening without their being related are infinitesimal. You may know, or you may not know, but the most common way sickle cell is acquired by an individual is from a parent. It is almost always from genetic transfer."

"Crap, crap, crap!" he said again, and this time without an apology.

"So you see, Major, those factors help us in a way, and they harm our process going forward in another way."

"How can it be a problem if it lets you narrow down the suspects for murder?"

"Jonathan is a lawyer, as well as a first class investigator," and she smiled at him when she gave Jonathan the compliment. "He will explain succinctly why we have a problem."

"Major, to delve far into the personal lives of sickle cell victims puts us on the cusp of violating the First, Fourth, and Fourteenth Amendments to the U.S. Constitution. If that were not enough, the recently passed EEOC laws prohibit discrimination or exploitation of those with diseases like sickle cell anemia. Although the two murder victims, Timmons and Baker, won't object to anything, their families might determine that their rights had been violated and come after the city for discrimination. That's something you need to talk over with the mayor to determine how the city wants to approach the potential liability. Again, we not only want to move forward with the investigation, but we need to pursue whatever avenue it leads us down if we are going to solve these murders. After the mayor's earlier warning, I thought you might want to get his approval for us to go forward. I can imagine that he cannot keep a lid on that kind of information too long and still maintain control of the investigation."

"It appears that I get to be the messenger who is killed because of this message," he said reluctantly.

"Oh, but you have big, broad shoulders Major, and I'm sure you can pull it off if anyone can!" Maggie told him confidently.

"Yeah, right. Well, he has to know. I will speak with him after lunch, and I will let you know his decision about going forward or letting things cool off. However, don't pack your things just yet. I know Mayor Anderson seems a little hesitant to pull the trigger at times, but he has been in the same hot seat many times over the past thirty years, so he might just surprise us all!"

Chapter 22

Full Speed Ahead

"I have good news and bad news," the major reported to Maggie after a long meeting with Mayor Anderson.

"OK," she played along. "Give me the good news first."

"The mayor is in agreement that we have no choice but to move forward with this investigation."

"That's really good news. So, what is the bad news?"

"He feels like he needs to come clean with the press and the public. I tried to suggest a moderate approach of feeding a little information to them along, but he is leaning toward sharing everything with them at once."

"That would be bad, Major. We will lose total control of the investigation if he does that. The suspects will know what we know and can simply leave the area until the heat of the investigation is off," Jonathan added.

"I don't know what to tell you, other than I suggested that he minimize the details when he breaks the news. He is holding a press conference in about an hour, so I guess we will all know soon."

* * *

Maggie, Jonathan, and the rookies were glued to the TV monitor in the conference room when the mayor appeared in front of the cameras to begin his press conference. This could be a big mistake, but evidently this chief of police had complete confidence in his mayor. Major Pinckney was sitting in the conference room with them, so they couldn't use foul language as a reaction to the mayor's address. Mayor Anderson stepped to the microphone.

"Citizens and friends of Charleston, as your duly elected mayor for many years, I have tried to do my best to keep you informed on the positive and negative events that have great potential to help or damage the image of our fair city. As we all know, this is a wonderful city in which to live, work, and play. We have one of the lowest violent crime rates for any major city in the United States—five to six times lower than other major cities within a few hundred miles radius of our beloved Battery. It is a rare and infrequent situation over these past 16+ years that I have had to tell you difficult information about crime in Charleston, but that is what I am having to do this morning. It appears that we have had three similar murders in the past days. We are currently investigating them, and all I can tell you specifically about these unfortunate happenings is that we have acquired a special investigation team from another state to help us sort through the clues so we can solve these crimes more efficiently. These don't appear to be random acts of violence, and we are treating them with the utmost urgency. When there is more information to share, we will do that through an announcement on the local news stations. Thank you for your understanding. Good day."

Maggie looked at Jonathan and Pinckney and asked, "What the hell did he just say?" and she burst out laughing.

Pinckney looked at Maggie and grinned. "I told you not to underestimate him. He's a pro, and he has been doing this kind of thing for many, many years."

"If I were the average person listening to that press conference, I wouldn't have any idea what he was talking about," Joey said. "That's good for us, isn't it?" and he directed that question to Maggie.

"Oh, yes, Joey. No harm, no foul, as far as I am concerned," she added.

The conversation about Mayor Anderson's address continued for about ten minutes, until Jonathan suggested that they get back to analyzing their available information on the suspect list. First, though, they decided to walk down to Poogan's Porch for some shrimp and grits. Maggie reminded Jonathan that her size six clothes might not fit if they didn't solve these murders pretty soon.

* * *

"Let's all report back on the names that we were given to research yesterday," Maggie said after lunch. "By the way, if anyone had a female name, we will simply disregard those names, since the coroner has determined that the suspect's blood had a Y chromosome. And as I'm sure all of us know in this room, only males carry the Y chromosome."

"That eliminates my suspect," Juliet said. "Do you want to give me another one to research?" she asked halfheartedly.

"All in good time, Juliet. You and Joey are probably going to make another appearance at the library. There are eight more males, so we will divide up the other five names and do some more research. I want to meet back here tomorrow morning at 9:00 AM with all eight people of interest researched as much as possible." She gave Joey two more names, Juliet one, and she and Jonathan took the remaining two.

They would work as efficiently as possible to get that information before the business day ended, if possible. Jonathan and Maggie had begun to find that Charleston at night was a fine place to be, and if they could free up another evening to enjoy Low Country Cuisine, that would be a bonus. After the champagne cruise and the time spent looking at the pastel-painted homes on Rainbow Row, she was beginning to believe that she might just be able to adjust to this slower-paced city atmosphere.

Tonight, they decided to go to the FIG Restaurant on Meeting Street, just up from their hotel at the Gaslight Inn. Although the restaurant had come highly recommended by Major Pinckney, for some reason they expected to find something with figs listed on the menu as an entree or a dessert. There was nothing on the menu that even mentioned figs, so they settled for fried frog legs with rice pilaf. Jonathan looked at his pretty associate and said, "I think you are correct. My thirty-four waist pants are crying out in distress. I think I have gained ten pounds this week!"

"All the more reason to get these murders solved, so we can get back to Rowlette with its dull food!"

They got up from the table slowly and walked back toward their hotel across from the city market.

Suddenly, there was the sound of breaking glass at the bank on the corner of Meeting Street and Market Street. They looked at the ground at their feet and saw a pile of safety glass around their feet and on their shoes. Jonathan was somewhat oblivious to what was happening, but Maggie had been fired at before from a moving vehicle, so she pulled him down into a crouching position just in time for a couple of bullets to go whizzing over his head. If he had still been standing, he would have been hit in the chest or head.

"What the hell?" he said as she pushed him to the sidewalk.

"Someone is taking shots at us, Jonathan," and she pulled him into a sandwich shop storefront that was next to the bank.

"What kind of sandwich would you like?" the clerk answered, oblivious that they were seeking refuge and a safe temporary hiding place until the shooter moved on. Once she showed him her badge and told him to call 911, he got the message. Just as quickly as it started, it was over. The clerk turned white and seemed paralyzed in place behind the counter. Maggie figured he might even need to take a break to change his underwear. Despite her heightened sense of danger, she chuckled to herself about the clerk. He was a wreck! Fortunately, they only had to wait about ten minutes for a police cruiser to show up with its lights flashing and the siren blaring.

"What's going on here?" the young patrolman asked Maggie and Jonathan.

Maggie showed her badge and reported to the officer what had happened. He radioed back to the station to get a forensic team out to perform a follow-up investigation, hoping to collect some information on the caliber of the ammunition used in the shooting attempt, spent cartridges, or anything that might help them determine the identity of the shooter. After questioning Maggie, Jonathan, and the store clerk, he released them and they made their way back to the Gaslight Inn.

Once they were back on the street, they realized that they were only a storefront or two from their hotel. They decided to go to their room and properly report the incident by phone to Major Pinckney and his men. Jonathan opened the door to their room very carefully, just in case the gunman had set another trap for them.

Maggie immediately called Major Pinckney on his private cell phone number. When he answered, he said. "What's up, Maggie? Did you and Jonathan have a nice dinner at FIG? I hope my recommendation was a good one."

"Dinner was great, but that's not why I am calling," she said with some trembling still in her voice. "Something happened that surprised us, and I thought you might want to know about it before we see you in the morning." She described in detail about the shooting attempt and the official report that was taken by the patrolman. Maggie said she felt as though they must be getting closer to the killer if he felt that he needed to either kill them or scare them away from the investigation.

Pinckney was at a loss for words. He couldn't imagine what kind of madman would try to take out the leading investigator of a crime spree. This guy was either brazenly cold, or he was simply an idiot, but the drive by shooting simply reinforced what Maggie had speculated about the murderer's traits and probable motivation for the murders. Pinckney was sure that Lieutenant Watson would be more driven than ever now to solve these murders.

It was only 11 PM, but the major was wide awake and began to dress to return back to the police department to follow up on the events of the evening. Events like this just didn't happen in Charleston, much less on Meeting Street in the historic portion of the city. He wanted to take all of the information that had been compiled to this point on this case, sift through it again, and see if he could put more pieces together, so that he could be more helpful to Maggie and Jonathan when they reported to the office in the morning. In fact, he thought it might be better to get their statements while the facts were still fresh in their minds. He placed a telephone call to the hotel and asked for Maggie's room.

"Do you mind coming into the station now and giving us a fuller statement in person about the events of the evening?"

"We don't mind at all, Major. What time do you think you will be there?"

"It's 11 PM now, so I would think I can be there by 11:30 PM, if that's not too late for you two."

"11:30 PM is fine," she said. "I really can't tell you much more than I have already shared with you, but I understand about paperwork and required reports. See you soon."

"Jonathan, since we have half an hour to kill before Pinckney arrives at the police station, and since it is only a five-minute walk there from the hotel, why don't we try Kaminski's on Market Street for a late dessert while we wait?"

He looked at her as if she had two heads and asked, "Doesn't anything rattle you? We were almost shot and killed a few minutes ago! Doesn't that bother you?"

"Sure, but he missed us," she said calmly.

They headed out for ice cream and chocolate squares.

* * *

"Tell me exactly what happened, and don't omit any details," Pinckney told them when they met him at the station.

"Like I said on the telephone, we were simply walking down the street when someone took some shots at us. Either he just wanted to warn us off the investigation or he is a bad shot with a pistol. Even though the vehicle was moving, we were no more than ten feet from the shooter, so it wasn't a difficult shot to make."

"I don't like people shooting up my city and using out-of-town guests for target practice. Did you see the vehicle or anyone's face from the vehicle?"

"We were too busy kissing the street," Jonathan responded to his question before Maggie could do so. "It scared the crap out of me, but Maggie decided that we would celebrate not getting shot by going to Kaminski's and getting ice cream cones."

"You should try their hot fudge sundaes," he told her. "They are to die for! Oops, didn't mean it quite that way," he apologized.

"Think nothing of it," she said calmly. "Do they use white chocolate or dark chocolate to make the sundaes?"

"What's wrong with you two?" Jonathan looked at both of them in wonder. "If I didn't know before tonight that long-term police work was not my strong suit, I would definitely understand that now."

Both Pinckney and Maggie just looked at each other and laughed at Jonathan's expense. He finally figured out that they were teasing him and joined in laughing with them. However, in his own mind he knew that police officers were cut from a very different cloth than he was.

"Since no one got hurt, let's keep this little incident to ourselves. I don't want to have the rookies overreact, nor do I want the mayor to change how we are moving forward. Agreed? I guess his press conference may have made you a target tonight. I apologize for that if, indeed, that is the case."

"In for a penny, in for a pound," Jonathan said.

"Well, aren't you the philosopher tonight Mr. Pembroke?" Maggie said with a smile. "Just for the record, Major, we are both in this to the end." Maggie nodded at Jonathan, who also nodded, but not as convincingly as Maggie did!

Chapter 23

Suspects

"I want everyone on this task force to wear a bulletproof safety vest at all times when in public, at least until the murderer or murderers are identified and taken off the street," Major Pinckney told Maggie and her crew, who were busy at work around the conference table. "Statistics tell us that an officer is three to four times less likely to die of a gunshot wound wearing a vest, versus not wearing one."

"Really, Major? Do you think that it's necessary for us to suit up in those impossibly hot outfits in this Charleston heat and humidity?" Jonathan asked. He had never worn one, but of course the rookies and Maggie were familiar with them.

"Jonathan, I am responsible for the safety of all of you, and I would feel much better knowing that you all had another layer of protection around you with this crazy nut out there taking shots at you while you're simply walking down the street, like last night."

"What happened last night, Lieutenant?" Joey asked and looked at Juliet to see if she knew what the major was speaking about. He could tell that she was clueless.

"It really wasn't anything much to talk about," she said and gave the major a stern look. She didn't want to spook her rookies and have them looking at everyone who approached them on the streets as a potential suspect.

"I really don't care if you think it is nothing to worry about or not. The mayor and I both agree that everyone working in the police department, including guest detectives, will wear these safety vests, with no exceptions," and he glared back at Maggie.

"OK, OK," she relented. "But just on the streets, right?"

"That will be fine, Lieutenant."

"Now, back to the matter at hand. Let's talk about our research yesterday on the eight remaining potential suspects from the College of Charleston. Joey, you had two names, so what did you discover?" Maggie asked him.

"I had two of the more recent students to research, that is, those who attended the university the same times that Lester Timmons and Terrell Swanson were there. It appears that Andy Brownlee was from Atlanta, Georgia, and that he graduated, with honors, in 1988. He moved back to the City of Atlanta and started his own business as an art critic for the local newspaper. As far as we can determine, he has never come back to the Charleston area since graduation, even as a visitor or for any alumni functions. There is nothing in his school records to indicate any interface with the other two young victims, and he only attended one class that was taught by Lawrence Baker. He made some of the highest scores on the exams that Mr. Baker gave during that time. Nothing else jumped out at me about him that is even noteworthy to mention."

"Could you determine if he had the highest grades in Mr. Baker's class that semester?"

"He did not. Actually, Terrell Swanson, our second victim, had the highest scores that semester that Mr. Baker gave any student. On a scale of one to ten, I would say Brownlee would rate about a one on the scale as someone I would suspect of murdering these men. There's just nothing in his past to indicate that might even be a threat."

"So, you would not consider him a suspect in any way?" Jonathan asked.

"Nope. I just don't see it," Joey repeated.

"That leaves seven potential suspects. Tell us about Lewis Milton, your other potential suspect," Maggie requested.

"He attended classes in 1988-1990, and he actually majored in Theatre. He had Mr. Baker for several classes, but I saw no evidence in the records that indicates he had any conflicts with the professor. Since he had taken so many of Mr. Baker's classes, I thought we might consider him a potential threat, just out of extreme caution. Again, there was no apparent conflict with Baker, but he did have a lot of exposure to the man. Still, he would be low on my suspect list. He didn't stay around this area once he graduated. It appears that his last known address of record was in Miami. Again, there is no evidence he is an alumnus who regularly returns to the campus for any alumni functions."

"Did any of the other people on our list of eight potential suspects have classes with Lewis Milton?" asked Maggie.

"Yes, in fact, two other names appeared on some of the rosters with Lewis' name, as well—both Andy Brownlee, whom we have pretty much eliminated as a suspect, and Michael Hanson, who was a Theatre Major."

"Who had Michael Hanson on their list of potential suspects?" Maggie asked, looking at both Juliet and Jonathan.

"I have him, Maggie," Jonathan replied. "His personnel jacket is a bit more interesting than the first two people we have discussed. He had a beef with Mr. Baker. In fact, he had threatened him, according to a police report that was filed back in 1989. No charges were ever brought against Hanson, and it appears that the complaint was eventually dismissed by the local D.A. However, he would be pretty high on my list of having a motive. I don't know about his means and opportunity, but he sure fits the motive part of the crime."

"Hmmnn. Maybe we should follow up on the potential means and whereabouts of Mr. Hanson for the past few days. If he has been somewhere other than Charleston since these deaths have occurred, then he probably won't be our killer. Joey, why don't you follow up for us on him and let me know what you find?"

"Yes, ma'am. I will do that the first thing tomorrow morning."

"That covers three of the eight people on our initial list, but only one of them might have a real motive, to our knowledge, for wanting to do harm to Mr. Baker. Since it is getting close to quitting time, let's pick up here tomorrow morning. I'll meet you all in here at 9:00 AM tomorrow morning."

She dismissed the rookies, and she and Jonathan decided to pay another call on Louise. The research on the possible suspects was going along pretty well, but Maggie thought that Louise might have more to share on the autopsies. Maggie also determined that she needed to get out in the fresh, afternoon air that was blowing over the peninsula from the bay. She took Jonathan's arm, led him out onto Market Street and pointed him in the direction of the morgue.

"You really know how to make a guy feel special," he kidded her since he knew she wanted to go back to the morgue.

"You'll feel special enough before you go to bed tonight, Jonathan. Trust me!" and she reached up and planted a huge kiss on the mouth.

He put his arm around her firmly as they walked in the direction of Ashley Street.

Chapter 24

A Veiled Threat

The walk to the coroner's office took about fifteen minutes, but the breeze coming off the bay was so pleasant, they hardly noticed the time. When the breeze was blowing across the peninsula from the bay, the temperature seemed to drop twenty degrees. The actual temperature was still in the high eighties or low nineties, but the cool sea breeze made it very pleasant and nice to be outside in the elements.

They arrived at the morgue, saw that Louise was sitting at her desk going through papers, let themselves into the room, and pulled up chairs in front of her desk.

"Are you OK?" Maggie asked Louise when they sat down.

"Why do you ask?" Louise tried to hide the tension in her face from Maggie. She should have known that a great investigator missed nothing obvious, and it was more than obvious that Louise was flustered about something.

Jonathan glanced at Maggie, then looked directly in the face of the coroner. "Louise, is there something wrong? What's going on?"

She looked skeptically at both of them, handed them a note that appeared to have been triple folded to fit into an envelope, and gave them a minute to read it. They both looked up with concerned expressions on their faces.

"Where did you get this note?" Maggie asked.

"It was delivered to my home through the U.S. Mail. I opened it, read it, and brought it here."

"Did you keep the envelope?" Maggie asked, hoping that she might have an opportunity to inspect it for fingerprints or other DNA.

"Yes, I have it over there by the electron microscope. I have already checked for fingerprints, but the only fingerprints are the postman's. The postal service fingerprints the mail carriers because it is a federal government job, and they are required to perform background investigations on all of their employees. His prints are the only ones present, with the exception of my own."

"What do you think the message means? 'You're going to wish you weren't so smart'—is that a direct threat to me or to my profession as the coroner?"

They looked at each other skeptically, and then Jonathan said, "It could mean a lot of things, Louise, but we should probably get you some protection to and from the morgue until we figure all this out."

"I agree, Louise. It probably is an empty threat, but you can't be too careful."

"The person doing all of this is about to piss me off!" Louise said dramatically. "I'm getting tired of all of this violence."

"Yes, we know," Maggie comforted her new friend. "We'll take care of it. Just keep doing your job, and we will find the person responsible for these crimes and put him behind bars."

"OK," she said suddenly in a quiet voice. "I just want it to be over."

"Do you want Maggie or me to camp out at your place until these crimes are solved? Do you think you need added protection?"

She laughed so hard that they thought she might be having a hysterical reaction to their question until she said, "I have a 200 pound St. Bernard that will eat anyone who comes near me without my approval. I think I'm safe at home."

"OK, but just keep an eye out for anything unusual happening around you," Jonathan continued. "Maggie and I were walking down Meeting Street last evening, returning to our hotel after dinner, when someone took a couple of shots at us. He missed, of course, but if you look closely, you will see that we are now wearing body armor, thanks to the mayor and Major Pinckney."

"Is it that serious?"

"Well, we were fitted for the vests the first day on the job, but until now no one thought it was absolutely essential that we wear them out in public. That has now changed, thanks to the incident last night," Maggie responded.

"Do you think I should be wearing one, too?"

"Would you like us to get the major to get one issued to you until all of this is over? I'm sure he would be happy to do so," Jonathan asked.

She thought a minute and then said, "No, I'm only in my car from the house to the parking lot here at the morgue, so I doubt it would be necessary. Thanks anyway."

"So what can I help you with this morning?" Louise asked.

"Is there anything, even something that seems insignificant—something you think is too small to make a difference—that might indicate the identity of the perpetrator? We have narrowed our suspect list down to some possible students who were attending the College of Charleston at the same time the victims were also there. We are about to begin the second half of our list, dismissing those who have little probability to harm the students or the professor, but we were hoping there might be some latent prints or some other evidence that has appeared since our last conversation with you," Maggie said.

"Not so far, but I will continue to study the results of the tests that we have performed to see if I have missed anything."

"That would be great," Jonathan said, and they got up from their chairs to leave her office.

"What I don't understand," Louise said with concern written all over her face, "is how did the murderer know 'how smart I was', as he stated in his threatening note to me? There has been no publication of facts about our findings with the blood tests in the press. Is he talking about the sickle cell indicators, and if not, what is he referring to in his note? Doesn't it seem a bit strange to you, unless he may be somehow connected with the police department?"

Jonathan looked at Maggie, and they both recognized a much more potential threat to Louise than a leak in the police department. Without Jonathan saying anything to Maggie, she nodded to him in acknowledgement of the potential danger, and she spoke calmly to Louise.

"I don't want to scare you, Louise, but the biggest potential threat is not from the police department. It could be from someone here at the hospital that might have had access to your files. Can you think of anyone who might have been down here and who could have seen your records?"

Looking totally baffled, Louise answered, "I can't think of anyone, other than you, the major, and myself who has had any disclosure of the facts in this case that I generated here in my lab. You know how restricted the access to this floor is."

"It could be nothing, or it could be that someone is employing a strategy of fear to knock you off your game and intimidate you into not cooperating with the police department with your findings. Unless we get a more direct threat, we will consider that it is exactly that—an attempt to intimidate you. Just let us know if anything else like this letter is directed your way," Maggie said.

"Oh, don't worry. You'll be the first people I call."

PART III: IT ALWAYS ENDS IN THE MORGUE

Chapter 25

An AWOL Rookie

Maggie and Jonathan spent a good bit of the morning speaking to the coroner, so they hoped that Juliet and Joey were continuing to work on the profiles of the remaining potential suspects. When they arrived in the conference room, Joey was there, but Juliet was not.

"Where's Juliet?" Jonathan asked Joey.

"I don't know. She just didn't come into work today."

"Did the duty officer call her home to see why she is absent?"

"I don't know, Lieutenant. I have been trying to work on these files, as you instructed us to do when you left yesterday."

"OK, let me check things out, and we will get back with you. Keep going over the files that you have, and we will resume in earnest after lunch," Maggie told him.

Maggie knocked lightly Major Pinckney's office door. When he saw Jonathan and her standing outside his office, he motioned them inside.

"What can I do for you two?"

"Did you know that Officer Robinson hasn't reported for duty today? I hate to ask," Maggie said, "but who is her supervisor?"

"SGT Lawton, our usual desk sergeant, is her immediate supervisor. Let me see what she has to say," he replied. He got up from his desk, strolled into the lobby area of the station, and was surprised to see SGT Brian Black, another of his officers, sitting at the desk.

"Brian, where is SGT Lawton today?"

"She called in sick this morning. Why? What's up, Major?"

"Did Officer Robinson call in absent today?"

"Nope. I just assumed that she was here. We didn't take roll call, but we haven't been doing that since this investigation began last week. Should I call her at home?"

"Absolutely, and I want her butt in here pronto, unless she has a very good excuse—and I mean very good!" issuing the orders loudly.

"Yes, sir." The sergeant picked up the phone to call the rookie cop.

"Has she had a problem reporting to work in the past?" asked Jonathan.

"Never missed a day until today, and that's unusual in itself," the major replied. One thing that I have noticed, however, is that she has been less than enthusiastic about her work since the first murder occurred. She was late arriving some days, she had some attitude when asked to do things that she had not complained about in the past, and she seemed to want to leave early many days. That is a complete turnaround from her earlier attitude and actions in the past. Have you noticed anything unusual in her attitude since she had been working with your team? I never like to beat up on rookie cops, but she was not competent in her duties. We didn't say anything, because some of her duties were just being a flunky for me at the crime scenes. However, the results of her research on the individual suspects were less than satisfactory. In fact, she said one of the suspects was not involved in any way, but she didn't have any evidence to that effect. She just wanted us to take her word for it."

"What is his name?" Maggie broke into the conversation.

"Juliet had two names—Clayton Huntsman and Samuel Hogdon. We didn't get to Huntsman or Hogdon before we stopped yesterday. I see from the notes that she left on the conference table that she had done some pretty good research on Huntsman, but there is simply nothing on Hogdon."

"Is he the one who she said there was no reason to pursue?" the major asked Joey.

"Yes, sir. That's what she told me. She seemed miffed that I challenged her on her opinion, but I thought we were all going to look at the research on each suspect before we declared someone not of interest."

"You are totally correct, Joey. I want you to get Juliet's home address and discreetly go by her place. See what's going on, if anything, and report back to us as soon as you have anything. Do it now," Pinckney said with concern.

Joey put his safety vest on over his uniform shirt, slid his police-issued handgun in the holster, and checked his utility belt for everything he was required to have with him on the street. He then waved at Jonathan, Maggie, and Major Pinckney before walking to his cruiser.

"What are you thinking, Major? Do you think we may have a problem here?" Maggie asked.

"Let's don't jump to conclusions just yet," Pinckney replied. "Let's see what Officer Lancaster finds before we read too much into her unexcused absence."

Jonathan and Maggie nodded positively, but they both had an instinctive concern that Juliet might have been the source of the leak of information about the autopsies. It all made too much sense to be dismissed easily. They would, however, give her the benefit of the doubt until it was obvious that she was complicit in these criminal activities.

While they waited to hear back from Joey's reconnaissance trip to Juliet's place, they went over the remaining three potential suspects. Clayton Huntsman, Stephen Wittier, and Robert Gurkey were all less likely to have been involved in the murders than the other five who had been researched as suspects. Arthur Burton, one of Jonathan's names, came up totally empty. It appeared from the college records that he had dropped out of school and moved back to the West Coast before the end of his first semester. None of them were in the Charleston area this past week. They had all graduated from the college, moved to faraway places, and resumed lives not affected by anything to do with Charleston or the current festival. That left Lewis Milton, Michael Hanson, and Samuel Hogdon as the most likely suspects from the university. They would have to explore these three people in detail to decide who might possibly be the murderer of these three innocent men. As soon as Joey returned, they would make that happen.

In about an hour they heard from Joey, and the news was confusing. Joey had initially knocked on her apartment door, and since the unit was a ground floor unit, he peeked into the windows to see if he could determine anything amiss about the premises. He reported back what he had seen.

"Nothing. Absolutely nothing was in her unit. No furniture, no food, no clothes—nothing at all!"

"Are you sure she hasn't just moved stuff around so it can't be seen from the windows?" Jonathan asked him.

"The apartment manager was very nice, and when she saw that I was a police officer, she told me that if we needed to check on Juliet's safety that she would let me in with her pass key. I said, 'Sure, that would be great,' and she opened the door to the unit, and you should have seen her face. Her jaw dropped, and her mouth flew open like she was going to swallow a fly. Then she said, 'That little bitch beat me out of the last month's rent,' and she stormed off back to the office. I kind of felt sorry for her. She seemed like a really nice lady," he said, finishing his story.

"Did the manager have a forwarding address for her?" Maggie asked.

"Yes, but she figured it was bogus, especially since she stiffed her on the last month's rent. Should I get that for us?"

"Absolutely," Maggie said. "Don't call her on the phone. Go back to the complex and snoop around and see if Juliet left any clues about where she might be going. Sometimes you can find clues in the garbage cans, dumpsters, and places like that. You would be surprised how many people don't think that they are leaving all of those clues around when they discard stuff in the trash or in nearby waste containers. See what you can find, and thank the manager for her help," she instructed him. "Now, get going before the manager cools off and is afraid to share everything she may know about Juliet."

"Yes, ma'am." Maggie thought this young man was going to be an outstanding detective one day.

Maggie and Jonathan knocked on Major Pinckney's office door again and observed that he was not as calm as the last time. He appeared to be very concerned about Juliet Robinson and her disappearance into thin air without any explanation. Pinkney had been an officer of the law for many years, had seen a lot of weird stuff, but he was all but speechless over this rookie officer's behavior.

"I'm at a loss for words, Maggie. I would never have approved of your selection of her if I had known she was so flaky. Why in the world would she just disappear now that we are closing in on the real suspect in these murders? It doesn't make sense to me," Pinckney lamented.

"I'm afraid it may be a lot more than irresponsibility on her part, Major," Maggie said.

"What do you mean? Is there some other indication of wrongdoing that I am not aware of with her?" He looked at both Jonathan and Maggie, trying his best to understand this new twist in the investigation.

"What we have seen in the past, in some investigations similar to this one, is that the person who simply disappears when the heat is turned up on a suspect may actually be complicit with the criminal in some way. We sent Joey back to the scene to see what he might discover in and around her apartment—you know, anything that she may have left in the trash or clues that she might have inadvertently left for us. He will also talk to her neighbors to get a more complete picture of her personal life outside of work. I told him to report back here at the end of the day to share what he has discovered, if anything, so we can add that information to our overall research folder. Hopefully, she is just an irresponsible young woman who used poor judgement. Unfortunately, she has most of the information about the suspect, including the DNA that we know the murderer possesses. If she is in alliance with him, that could hurt us in our search for him. The element of surprise will be gone. However, there is another way to get him to react, but it might be dangerous. This is a man who has already murdered three people, taken shots at me and Jonathan, and threatened the coroner," Maggie said.

"The coroner? What did he do to Louise?"

"Threatened her with a note delivered to her home address. This guy is out of control, and we need to corner him before he flips out altogether and hurts or kills more people," Jonathan chimed in.

"Let's just hope Joey finds something useful to help us find Juliet. That way, we can either clear her in this investigation, or we will know that she is working against us," Maggie said.

"We hope for the first result—and that she is just immature—but knowing where we stand with her will clarify which way we will need to move this investigation. We can actually use her actions against him if she is, indeed, his girlfriend or partner in crime," Jonathan said confidently.

Major Pinckney just looked at both of them and said, "You two constantly amaze me. You always see a way out of our situation, even if things are going against us. Now that is the kind of experience that we figured you brought to the table when we persuaded your boss to let you help us down here. The mayor and I will be in your debt if we get out of this with our jobs!"

"You'll be fine, Major. We are in this to the end," Maggie said and patted him on the back. "We police officers need to stick together in times like these. We don't intend to leave Charleston until this case is settled. You have our word on it."

Pinckney nodded his approval of her last statement, and just then his desk phone rang, disturbing his thoughts and jolting him back into the present reality.

"Hello, Major Pinckney here," he said formally.

"Major, this is Joey. I wanted to report my finding back to you as soon as possible, and I am on my way back to the station now. I couldn't find anything written or printed on paper that gave me any clues to Juliet's possible reason for leaving so abruptly, but I was able to speak to a couple of her neighbors. One of them told me that she had been dating a young man, about twenty-five years old, and that they had moved her out of her unit yesterday. I think if we ask that neighbor to come down to the office and get with a sketch artist, she may be able to give us a pretty good likeness of Juliet's boyfriend. It could wind up being a dead end, but maybe not," he said, and then he paused to see what his commanding officer would suggest that he do.

"Bring her in, and I will get the artist to sketch what she saw. It surely can't hurt us," he said and hung up the phone.

Chapter 26

Discerning the Real Suspect

"The three suspects remaining, Milton, Hogdon, and Hanson, should be pretty easy to research, as we already have a start on all of them," Jonathan said to Maggie when they resumed their coordinated assembly of files into a probability curve. "Anyone is certainly capable of murder, under certain conditions. However, crimes of passion usually happen only once, and never three times in such a short period of time. Since Juliet is missing, should we include her on our list of probable suspects?"

"I don't think so. Something is definitely up with her, but we've been around her too many times when things were happening that surprised her as well as us. There could be some connection, and I can't place my finger on it just now, but there's no way in my mind that she is a murderer or an accomplice to such. We will just have to sort that out once we locate her."

When they were able to see the artist's rendition of Juliet's boyfriend, they might be able to recognize one of the suspects without much more research. They were hoping to have that picture soon. And as they delved further into the pasts of these three potential murder suspects, they noticed that one in particular stood out, and not in a good way. Hanson and Milton had had the opportunity and, in Hanson's case, the potential motive, but Hogdon was the real question mark in the investigation. Just why did Juliet rule Hogdon out without sharing her findings with the team?

"Why did Juliet not think that Hogdon was even capable of being a suspect, and where was the initial research she found about his past and current situation?" Maggie asked Jonathan and Joey, actually looking for an answer from one of them. "Something stinks to high heaven about Juliet and this Hogdon character."

"When I asked her how she was able to determine that Hogdon had no value as a suspect, she said that he was just a local boy, trying to keep his nose clean. I have no idea what that means. Do either of you?"

Juliet's neighbor had been with the graphic artist for about thirty minutes, and when she emerged from their session, she looked a little harried.

"Are you OK?" Joey asked the young lady who had volunteered to work with the sketch artist.

"Yes. This is just so unnerving for me and for all of the other residents of the complex. We actually thought that we were getting a little special protection by having a police officer live in our building, but now I'm not so sure. Do you think that the guy I described to the artist is a criminal?"

"We actually don't know who he is or what his relationship is to Officer Robinson. As soon as we know something for sure, we will let you know. It's probably not anything for you to be concerned about at this time," Joey assured her.

Once the girl had left the station, they went down to the artist's office and inquired about the likeness he was able to draw from the description he had been given. The suspect had a slight build, brown hair, brown eyes, shoulder-length hair, and a scar above his left eye that could be easily seen from several feet away. According to the witness, he was about five-feet-eight inches in height and weighed approximately one hundred seventy pounds. None of them recognized the likeness, but they would be putting posters up on campus and around the immediate area to see if anyone else did.

"What do we know about Juliet Robinson—about her history prior to joining the police academy?" Maggie asked Joey.

"You would need to ask Major Pinckney, since I haven't had the authorization to search her files until now."

Maggie sent Jonathan to Pinckney's office with the request for Juliet's personnel file and any impressions that the major might have had of her when he was hiring her for his department.

"Well, there wasn't much outstanding about her. Of course, we are now just getting into the quota system with our hiring of personnel, and she scored high on the exit examination from the academy. She is above average in intelligence, and until very recently she appeared to be a team player. About six months ago she became argumentative, and she would push the limits of insubordination, backing down just about the time I was going to write her up. I just credited it to personal issues not connected with the job, but to tell you the truth, I have no idea why the personality change came over her."

Jonathan showed the major the artist's sketch of the man whom Juliet Robinson had been seeing at her apartment recently and who appeared to have helped her disappear.

"Have you ever seen this guy hanging around here or near Juliet Robinson?" he asked Pinckney.

The major placed his face in his right hand and contemplated the picture. He then said, "Yes, that's the young man she brought with her to the spring picnic that we had in March of this year. They stayed off to themselves most of the time, but I do remember asking him what he did for a living, and he told me that he worked for a theatrical company that did the setups for plays in the city. I didn't think anything about it at the time, but now that you mention it, the company he works for may have the contract for both the Gaillard and the Strand Theatres."

"Thanks, Major," Jonathan replied and hurried back to share the information with Maggie. They were discussing the photo of Juliet's secret boyfriend when Jonathan walked into the conference room.

"Do you think we should put out an APB on him, Lieutenant?" Joey asked.

"Not at this time, because right now he thinks that he is flying under the radar. That means he is more apt to make mistakes because he probably doesn't suspect that we know about him and his possible relationship with Juliet. We need to find her, or him, or both of them as soon as possible. Maybe this is all just a misunderstanding, and it is an innocent set of coincidences," she smiled at Joey, but she looked at Jonathan with a more serious expression. Jonathan knew what she thought about the probability of coincidence.

"I just spoke with the major, and he said that he remembers this guy. They had a department spring party, and he was Juliet Robinson's date. Pinckney was trying to be friendly, so he struck up a little conversation with the young man that day. According to his memory, he thinks that this guy works for one of the local theatrical support companies. Major Pinckney said that he remembers that the company who supplies the staffing for these outside shows that come to town might have a contract with the Strand and the Gaillard Theatres. Now, that cannot be just a coincidence."

"Joey, get on the phone and locate the owner of the theatrical company that employs the setup crews for outside shows. I want a list of their employees, but I want that information to be kept confidential to anyone but the owner and us. OK?"

"Yes, ma'am. I will get right on it. If it is available today and the company has a local business office, I will go by and pick it up to expedite things," Joey said.

"Excellent. And Joey, take a copy of the picture of the suspect with you to show to the owner to see if he recognizes the young man. If he does, I want every bit of information the company has on the suspect—home address, telephone numbers—the works!" she said. "Now, we are getting somewhere," Maggie sighed and looked with some satisfaction at Jonathan.

* * *

Joey called on the manager of the Low Country Staging Company, located on Church Street in the heart of the Historic District. They had a storied past in the history of Charleston, dating back to the first years of the Strand Theatre, which was built in the mid-1700s. The Strand was the first theatre built in America for the sole purpose of the performance of plays. People would come to Charleston from hundreds of miles away in their buckboards, carriages, and on horseback to experience the excitement of the playhouse. Shortly after the construction of the theatre, someone decided that it would be profitable for a permanent crew to be made available to change out the scenes on the stage. John Hallow of the fledgling Low Country Stage Company made that happen. He had two young men whom he paid two pence a day to work as needed in the playhouse.

Although the company had had many managers and owners throughout the years, it bragged that they were the oldest company continually existing in Charleston, South Carolina. The company was probably correct in that assumption.

"May I help you?" the man at the stage door of the Strand asked Joey. It had been about an hour since he had spoken to the manager at the theatre about stopping by to chat with him concerning one of his employees.

"Yes." Showing the stagehand his credentials, Joey said, "I have an appointment to see Winfred Tutwiler."

"Just a moment." The stagehand shut the door in the face of the young investigator while he checked the validity of Joey's claim. After a few minutes, the same worker opened the door, invited Joey into the theatre, and asked him to sit in the lobby while the manager made his way down from his living quarters in the building. According to legend, the first manager of the theatre learned that he needed to stay at the theatre overnight to ensure that the pirates that frequented the city at night did not run off with the oil lamps, chairs, and anything else not securely fastened to the building. From the humble beginnings of that manager standing guard with his American long rifle, to the current situation that boasted of an electronic security system that automatically notified the police of a potential break-in, the theatre had learned to protect its assets. All current managers of the Strand had to live on the premises as a security measure.

"May I help you, Officer?" the middle-aged man asked as he came walking down to the lobby from the winding staircase. "I'm sorry you had to wait for me, but this old building is two hundred and fifty years old, and it is not equipped with an elevator. I would love to have one installed that would make my trips to the main level more pleasant a journey, but the Charleston Historic Preservation Society will have none of it!" and he laughed at the ludicrous suggestion of altering such a historic site.

Winfred Tutwiler appeared to be a no-nonsense, silver-haired man about sixty. He had a stocky build, was about five-feet-eight inches in height, and he was dressed as if he were preparing to perform in an elegant, cutaway, pinstriped suit, tailored to perfection. Joey could see his own reflection in Winfred's black patent leather slippers.

"Yes, sir. My name is Officer Joey Lancaster, and I called earlier about one of your employees."

"Yes, I remember, Officer. What's his name?"

"Well, that's one of the problems that we have, sir. We have a name, but we don't want to prejudice you in your answer."

"So from what you're telling me, you don't have a name for this gentleman?" the manager asked with a smile. "How do you expect me to identify whether he works for me or not without his name?"

"Here is the picture of him that was created by a sketch artist. We think it may look very much like him." Joey showed the manager the sketch, and Winfred immediately replied.

"Samuel Hogdon—Yes, I do remember that young man. He was most disagreeable, as well as being very opinionated. We had to let him go after a short tenure with our company. He offended guest artists, and we just cannot have that!" Tutwiler stated with emphasis.

"When did he last work for you?"

"Let me think a minute," he said, pondering his answer carefully. "I want to say that his last day was about six weeks ago. We were anticipating a lot of guest performers with the Piccolo/Spoleto Festival, and we just couldn't take a chance on his being rude and unprofessional with them."

The manager looked again at the sketch and called his secretary. "Mrs. Castleberry, will you please bring the folder for Samuel Hogdon down to the lobby for me? Thank you," he said and hung up his cell phone.

Joey's spirits received a huge lift when he heard the manager ask for the personnel folder of one of their suspects. Now all they had to do was get the face with the name out to the officers on the street and start looking for him and Juliet. The secretary showed up with the folder, the manager opened it, placed the sketch by the license photo that they had on file and said, "Yes, I think this man is Samuel Hogdon. By the way, what is Mr. Hogdon suspected of doing, Officer?"

"He is under suspicion of being involved to some extent with the murders of the actors and the director of the plays in the Piccolo/Spoleto Festival events this past week. That information is not for publication, but I think it is only fair for you to know what this is all about," Joey confided in the manager. "By the way, did he leave a forwarding address or telephone number?"

"I will check my files, but I would doubt that whatever he told us was truthful. We caught him in many lies while he was working for our company. However, whatever information that we have will be provided to the police department without delay."

"Thank you, sir. While you are looking for that file, can you tell me if you ever saw this young lady with Mr. Hogdon?" He showed the manager a picture of Juliet.

The manager studied her picture for a few minutes and then said, "I think so, but I'm a bit confused. When I saw this young lady with your suspect, she was wearing a police uniform. Is she being sought in connection with these recent crimes as well?"

"We don't know, sir. What I can tell you is that she may have befriended Hogdon, and we just need to speak to her. If you will call me when you have anything else that you think might help us, I will come by and pick it up personally. Also, the chief investigator was hoping that you might agree to keep everything about this investigation confidential for the time being," and he looked at Tutwiler for his assurance.

"Absolutely," he said quickly. "We would not want to sully the Strand's name in any way with this criminal. Anything that we can do to put all of this to rest is fine with us."

Joey felt good about his visit to the Strand, and he was organizing everything in his mind to share with Maggie and Jonathan as he walked the few blocks west on Queen Street to return to Meeting Street and the police department. He caught the image of Juliet in civilian clothes in his peripheral vision, but wisely, he didn't turn his head to confront her directly. He figured that she had not seen him, or she would probably have tried to explain her absence to him. As soon as he turned left at Meeting Street, he stepped inside the doorway of the bank on the corner and called the police department.

"May I speak to Lieutenant Watson or Mr. Pembroke?" he asked the booking officer.

"Just a moment. Who should I say is calling?"

"Officer Joey Lancaster."

After a few minutes, Maggie answered, "This is Lieutenant Watson. Is that you, Joey?"

A very excitable voice answered her, "Maggie, you won't believe who I just saw on Queen Street." Joey exclaimed. "I saw Juliet momentarily out of the corner of my eye when I was leaving the Strand Theatre just a few minutes ago. What do you want me to do?"

"Nothing," she responded back calmly. "We don't want her to know that we are looking for her, and we definitely don't want to spook her. I will put some plainclothes police officers on the street to pick up her trail and follow her. Good job on spotting her. Now come back and let's look at the information that you have secured from the Strand Theatre manager."

Joey hung up the phone, just a little disappointed that he couldn't go after Juliet himself. Of course, he knew that the Lieutenant had done this type of investigation many more times than he, so he complied without objection. Since he was only a few blocks away from the station, he was at the office and in the conference room in less than ten minutes.

"Let me see that folder," Maggie said to Joey when he got settled into his chair. "Did the theatre manager have anything to say that is not in these files?" she asked him.

"I got the impression that the manager and Samuel Hogdon did not get along at all. He said that Hogdon was irresponsible, rude, and insulting to the people associated with the plays that came to the Strand during the Piccolo/Spoleto Festival. He seemed glad that Samuel was no longer in his employment. By the way, he fired him. Do you think we should let him know that we think that Hogdon is a potential threat, for his safety's sake?"

"We don't know that he is totally pathological, and his anger may just be focused on actors and directors—in other words, theatrical people and not the management of the theatres. Let's not whip this up into more than it is already. It is already scary for the local people, for the visitors to the city, and for the performers of the festivals."

Jonathan stepped into Major Pinckney's office and requested a couple of plainclothed policemen to find and track Juliet while she was in the immediate Charleston area. They figured if they hung out near the corner of Church Street and Queen Street, they would pick her trail up again.

"OK," Pinckney said. "I think we need to give them some type of 'job' to be doing while they are hanging out there. Any ideas?"

"We definitely need to watch the actual streets, so maybe one of them can be a street sweeper or sanitary worker for the city. The other can be a street vendor, especially now that there are so many vendors on the street during the festival. Does that work for you?"

"Those both work for me, if Maggie thinks that is the best way to utilize them. The street vendors work from about 10:00 AM until 6:00 PM or 7:00 PM. The street crew normally works from 7:00 AM until about 4:00 PM. If we keep these people working normal hours of their job description, they will probably pull it off. Let's make sure they have a portable radio to report into the station on a routine basis."

Jonathan told Maggie the details he and Pinckney had discussed, and she agreed that the two undercover people would be the best way to surveil Juliet for the present time. The big question was whether or not she would lead them to Hogdon. They would have to play the hand they were dealt at the present time and then regroup and reassess the situation as actual events happen.

Maggie had opened the folder on Samuel Hogdon that the manager of the Strand had released, and she found that there was a lot of personal information present that she hoped she could use. Whether or not the forwarding information was accurate, there were references to his family, friends, and prior work history.

"Jonathan, let's divide up the personal information in his folder and call Hogdon's family contacts, friends, and anyone who may have a clue where he could have disappeared to in the past couple of days. I don't get a feeling that he has left the city altogether, but that he is hiding out until some of the heat of the investigation has cooled. I'll take the parents and the people in his immediate circle of friends who are mentioned in the file, and you can work with the prior employers."

"OK," Jonathan answered, and he took the three previous employer files out and began to organize this research into a chronological order. He figured that since all the employers appeared to be local businesses, he could run down the information pretty quickly. He began to call them and realized something quickly about all of the past employers. No one had a really good report to share about Samuel. The best reference that he received was that the employee wasn't available for rehire, but that his work was satisfactory. The worst report came from a local radio station. The employer stated that they had to let Hogdon go because of threats that he had made on the owner's son. Although the report was sketchy, the personnel manager said that Samuel had appeared to react negatively when he felt that the owner was showing favoritism toward his son and accused the son of trying to show him up in his duties to get him fired.

"Look," the personnel manager stated flatly, "the owner probably did show favoritism with his son, but he is grooming him to eventually take over the business. As far as I know, there is no crime in favoring your family in a family-owned business," he concluded with a laugh. "Samuel was out of line, and we had to get him out of the office and off our employment rolls. He was overheard threatening other employees and customers."

Jonathan thanked the personnel manager for being so forthcoming and then called the last reference. The story went pretty much the same, with threatening behavior, anger, and eventual dismissal from the company. This young man obviously had an anger management problem.

* * *

Maggie thought the first person she should call was Hogdon's mother. The contact information was a few years old, but since Charlestonians seemed to move like molasses in most of their decisions, she hoped the folks still lived in the area.

"Mrs. Hogdon?" Maggie asked when the person listed as Samuel's mother picked up the telephone. Maggie had found the permanent telephone number in Samuel's folder.

"No, you must have the wrong number," the woman said and hung up the telephone before Maggie could question her at length. Maggie redialed. "Yes." The same woman picked up the receiver and before she could protest again that Maggie had reached the wrong number, Maggie asked, "Are you related to Samuel Hogdon, or is anyone at this number related to him?"

"Who's calling?"

"This is Lieutenant Maggie Watson, calling on behalf of the City of Charleston Police Department," she answered with authority.

"Oh, so what has the boy-wonder done now?" was the sarcastic reply.

"I will be happy to discuss Samuel's situation with his mother or guardian. Would that be you?"

"I'm his mother, but my name is not Hogdon," the woman answered, almost angrily.

"To whom am I speaking?" Maggie asked in her most official sounding tone.

"Joan Shilling."

"Mrs. Shilling, we need to get in touch with your son immediately. It is imperative that we reach him to clarify whether or not he is involved in a matter of interest to the police department," she said, trying to remain somewhat vague about the real reason she wanted to talk to him.

"So, is the little bastard involved in the murders that have been going on in the city these past two weeks?"

Maggie was so surprised that his mother assumed the worst for her son that she asked, "Why would you think that, Ms. Shilling? Is there something in his past that might indicate his involvement?"

"Samuel is a troubled young man, Lieutenant. I tried to get him some counseling help several years ago, but he would not stay on the medications that were prescribed for him. When he is on his meds, he is almost normal—almost. However, when he doesn't take his medications for his bipolar disorder, he gets very angry. When he is angry, he is totally uncontrollable. I can't do anything with him anymore, so I just don't have anything to do with him."

"When is the last time you spoke to him?"

"I don't know—a couple of years ago, I would estimate," she said unemotionally. "Look, he was in and out of JUVY for about five years. Once he turned eighteen, he was released, and I haven't kept up with him too well since then."

"Those records are sealed. In fact, there is no evidence in the police files here that he has ever been involved in anything illegal or been charged with any crimes. What did he do to get sent to JUVY?"

"You would have to ask him, because I don't want to know what all he's been doing. When he was a juvenile and being detained, he was involved in fires, burglary, manslaughter—you name it. He's probably been mixed up in everything! He's not a good man, Lieutenant. Whatever he is suspected of doing, he probably did it!"

"Do you have any idea of where we might locate him? Is there possibly a friend that he hangs out with, or maybe an old girlfriend?"

"He's very abusive to women, so I doubt he's got a steady girl. It seems that he takes his hatred for me out on other women. At least, that's what the child psychiatrist told me when he was sixteen. I have been married three times, and his step-dads have been abusive to him. Naturally, he blames me since I married them. I will tell you this, though. If there is a woman involved with him, he is probably abusing and manipulating her. That's his pattern."

"Thank you, Ms. Shilling. You have been a great help to us. Would you like for us to tell him anything if we are able to locate him?"

"Yeah," she said with a snarl. "Tell him to drop dead and go straight to hell!" and she hung up the phone.

Maggie looked down at the legal pad where she had been taking notes about Samuel Hogdon. Unconsciously, she had scribbled, circled, and underlined many expressions that Joan Schilling had shared with her. She knew instinctively that she should hate this young man, and she did have a great distaste for many of the things that he represented and had done, but she also felt somewhat sorry for him. She only hoped that this disturbed suspect in the murder of three people associated with the Piccolo/Spoleto Festival did not wind up like the pathological murderer that she and Jonathan finally had stopped in Rowlette earlier in the year. She walked into the conference room and saw Jonathan and Joey compiling information on the suspects. She noticed that the only folder that they were concentrating on was the one for Samuel Hogdon.

"So, what did you find out from the employers, Jonathan?"

"Joey and I have pretty much decided that Samuel Hogdon is the person who is the most likely suspect in the three murders here in Charleston. The other two potential suspects just don't have the indicators that he does. Every one of them said that he was hostile, disagreeable, insubordinate, and jealous. If you add to that the connection to the theatrical people from the College of Charleston, I think we may be seeing more of a pattern here than just a crime of passion or hate."

"There's one more thing that we need to figure into the mix. I agree with you about Hogdon being the most likely candidate for 'murderer of the week'," she said wryly, "but according to the psychiatrist that his mother took him to when he was sixteen, he is also bipolar. He has this pathological hatred for women, probably intensified by his mother's marriage to three abusive men. To say that Samuel and his mother have an estranged relationship would be the understatement of the year! They apparently hate each other."

"That's good to know, but how does that affect how we go forward with the investigation? I don't see the connection," Joey said.

Jonathan looked knowingly at Maggie and said without further explanation, "You're thinking that Juliet is codependent, aren't you?"

"Co-what?" Joey asked.

"Co-dependent is a term that is used usually when someone becomes an enabler to an addict. For instance, if you had a girlfriend who liked to drink too much, got drunk regularly, and couldn't hold down a job, you would be co-dependent to a degree if you somehow enabled her to drink by taking care of her. Understand?" Maggie asked.

"Yeah, I understand. So, does that give her a pass on all of these things that she might have witnessed or helped him commit?"

"Absolutely not!" Maggie raised her voice in reply. "Many times, people don't really understand the codependence factor for alcoholics or food addicts—committing murder and revenge killings is not the same thing. And given the fact that Juliet is a trained peace officer, there is no excuse for that kind of co-dependence. However, we need to consider that possibility and that maybe we can negotiate with her to help us bring him to justice. It also depends on whether or not she is infatuated with him or involved with him sexually."

"Wow, Maggie! How did you and Jonathan figure all of that out from the limited amount of information that we have been able to get on them as a couple?"

"Let's just say that we have life experiences that help us, along with profiles that we have seen and studied for several years relating to criminal behavior. What we need to do now," she said, looking at both of them, "is to bring Major Pinckney up to speed, along with the mayor, and come up with a plan to get control of the situation. I think it goes without saying, that Hogdon is most likely the murderer. Now all we have to do is prove it!"

Chapter 27

Finding Juliet

"Has anyone seen the 'Sparrow' on the street today?" Maggie spoke into the handheld radio, and then waited for a report from the two undercover officers who were working the area where Juliet was spotted briefly by Joey the day before. Maggie had decided to use code names for all of those officers in the field searching for Juliet. Juliet was "Sparrow"; Maggie was "Mama Bear."

"Ghost One, reporting in, Mama Bear. No sightings of the Sparrow today so far," the "Street Sweeper" said.

"OK, Ghost One," she answered. "Ghost Two, do you have anything for us?"

"No, ma'am," Ghost Two also replied. "What do you want us to do if we spot the Sparrow?"

"Do not approach—repeat, do not approach!" she emphasized. "We will decide what to do once we have a fix on her location."

Maggie had decided to use code names with her undercover officers to ensure that Juliet wouldn't know who they were, in case she had been smart enough to get a list of officers' names before she disappeared from the precinct.

"10-4," came the reply from both officers. What Maggie really wanted was to get close enough to her to plant an electronic bug on her person or in her car somewhere. Even though Juliet was only a rookie cop, she had been schooled in the art of giving a tail the slip. To add to her elusiveness, Juliet was also as smart as they came. According to Juliet's personnel file, she finished with high marks in evasive training, and Maggie assumed that she would be alert to any potential unmarked vehicle following her. No, they would have to play this one close to the vest to get anything over on her.

"Joey, look in the files on both Julie and Samuel and see if you see any parallels or similar activity in the past three or four months. There has to be something that we're not noticing that ties them together," she told him.

"Like what?" He looked puzzled.

"I don't know, but there has to be something," a frustrated Lieutenant Watson replied. "It might be something as simple as Samuel having a concealed weapons carry license, and her identifying with that; or, it could be that she took music lessons in college and she was attracted to him because of her interest in the arts."

After a few minutes, Joey said that he had noticed that Juliet's minor field of study in college was art. He looked at her college transcript and saw that she had taken a dance course and a beginner's public speaking course, both at the College of Charleston.

"Could she be a closet actor, maybe moonlighting at night at one of the theatres when she wasn't working for the CPD? Maybe she met him at the theatre, and one thing led to another, and they got involved romantically. It could have happened," he said and looked to Maggie and Jonathan for approval of his idea.

Maggie and Jonathan both thought that not only was it possible, but that it might be probable. After all, that's how Maggie and Jonathan wound up getting together finally after college.

"If we assume that, perhaps that is why she was on Queen Street yesterday. Several theatres are located in the near vicinity of Church, East Bay, and Queen Streets. Good call, Joey. We're probably going to make an investigator out of you yet," Jonathan congratulated him.

"OK, let's get the word out to the undercover guys, so they can expand their search for her," Maggie said.

"Mama Bear to Ghosts One and Two," Maggie called over the two-way radio. "Please see if our Sparrow might be sneaking into the back of one of the theatres in your immediate area. Be discreet, but let me know as soon as possible if you spot her."

"10-4, Mama Bear."

Within twenty minutes, Maggie heard the reply on the radio, "Mother Bear, this is Ghost Two. I have spotted the Sparrow entering the rear of the Rex Theatre on East Bay Street. I don't think she saw me, but I will get to some cover and watch from this position until she reappears. Any other suggestions, or do you want me to hold my position?"

"Thanks for the update, Ghost Two. Hold your position, and do not approach. We will be there in a few minutes. Please let me know if you spot her leaving before we arrive," Maggie instructed him.

"10-4."

Maggie grabbed Jonathan and Joey, and they all walked toward the theatre. She had Jonathan approach the theatre from Broad Street, Joey approached from Market Street, and Maggie continued to walk east on Queen Street. She had coached them both to act nonchalantly as they approached East Bay Street and the Rex Theatre. Joey had been wearing plainclothes for the past few days, a precaution in case a situation like this presented itself. Maggie whispered into her handheld police radio, "Papa Bear and Baby Bear—what's your 10-20?" Maggie had assigned undercover names for them when they left the station and headed for East Bay Street. Jonathan was 'Papa Bear'; Joey was 'Baby Bear'; Major Pinckney was the 'Zoo Keeper', and the station house was the 'Zoo.' She thought it was pretty imaginative and cute at the same time.

"Zoo Keeper?" she whispered again into the police radio, "The bears are headed east in a possible open-net configuration. I will keep you informed," she said. "Please remain 10-23."

"10-4, Mama Bear. We're 10-23, as requested," Pinckney whispered.

Of course, everyone knew that "10-4" meant "OK," and a lot of people knew "10-20" meant location. But "standing by" and other messages in police code might confuse non-police personnel, assuming they might have secured a police radio. Maggie had no idea whether or not Juliet had pilfered a police-band radio when she disappeared, and she knew that Juliet could possibly be listening in on the conversation. Although Juliet was very bright, it was beginning to appear to Maggie that Juliet's judgement was flawed. In any case, Maggie would have to assume that Juliet was aware of many techniques that Maggie and her team might use to locate and seize her.

"Mama Bear?" the voice came over the police radios. "The Sparrow has just left the Rex Theatre and is headed toward north on East Bay Street toward the market. I'm going to sneak inside and see if I can detect anything going on in the theatre," Ghost Two spoke quietly.

Before Maggie could respond and tell the undercover officer to stand down, there was a huge explosion that rocked the pavement under Maggie's feet. The sound came from the direction of East Bay Street and the Rex Theatre.

"Ghost Two, report in. Ghost Two!" Maggie yelled into the radio. There was no response.

Maggie went to channel 2, the radio channel that was used by the Charleston Police Department, to broadcast an alert. "Mayday, Mayday, Mayday," she screamed into the radio. "We have a 10-80, I repeat, a 10-80 on East Bay Street. It is possibly the Rex Theatre. Notify all rescue units and armed officers in the immediate area of East Bay Street and Queen Streets to proceed with caution. Possible injuries and explosive damage," she finished her instructions. "Papa Bear and Baby Bear, meet Mama Bear at Rex Theatre immediately. Proceed with caution!" Putting her radio in her coat pocket, Maggie ran toward the Rex Theatre.

Maggie rounded the corner of Queen and East Bay Streets and saw heavy black smoke billowing out of the rear of the Rex Theatre. She had arrived before the firemen arrived, and she was hesitant to enter the building without a respirator. She knew how quickly something like this could go bad, and she had no intention of winding up in the hospital for a week in the middle of this investigation.

"Papa Bear and Baby Bear, where are you?" she asked into the radio.

"I'm right behind you," Jonathan said to her as he came running up East Bay Street from Broad. "What have we got?"

"I don't know yet, but according to the last transmission from one of our undercover officers, Juliet was seen leaving this theatre from the area where the smoke is now pouring out into the alley. As I was speaking to Ghost Two over the radio, I heard a loud explosion and the transmission went dead. I'm afraid he may have tried to check things out, so when he went inside he tripped a bomb or similar explosion. I just don't know yet."

"Do you think that we should check it out—he may still be alive, and he might be hurt?"

"No, Jonathan, let's not complicate this situation with one of us getting hurt, or even worse, possibly killed. The paramedics are on the way and will be here momentarily. They and the fire department will have the proper breathing equipment to go into the building."

Joey came running up from the direction of Market Street, and the fire department and paramedics all arrived at the same time. As they were getting their respirators strapped onto their backs, the fire chief asked, "Do we know if anyone may be in the building?"

"Yes," Maggie interrupted his questions and said, "We have an undercover police officer missing, and we are assuming that he went inside the building, possibly triggering the explosion. Right now a lot of that is conjecture, but the fact that the officer is missing is not in question. Please get someone inside and see if you can help him," she pleaded.

"Yes, ma'am," the chief responded. He put on his oxygen tank and headed into the building.

It took about thirty minutes for the fire to be extinguished, and eventually the chief declared the building safe enough for Maggie and her team to enter to check out what they had found inside. The remains of a human being were still smoldering, and the entire interior of the building was burned beyond recognition.

"What happened, Chief?" Maggie asked.

He escorted her around the first level of the theatre, pointing out the visible damage to the interior of the building. The once beautiful, historic lobby of the Rex Theatre was devastated. It was totally gone, with no resemblance of what it had been just a few minutes before the blast.

"How soon can I get the coroner here to see if she can get any DNA samples from the scene?" Maggie asked the fire chief.

"We have completed our initial investigation, so you can have her come at any time. She is a professional, and she has worked these kinds of scenes in the past, so she will not disturb any evidence that needs preserving," the Chief added. "I would trust Dr. Henshaw at any crime scene, and this is definitely not an accident. There was accelerant used in multiple places in the lobby, and it appears that this poor, unfortunate soul tripped some type of fuse that set off the explosion. He didn't have a chance of surviving."

"OK, thanks, Chief. I will give the coroner a call and get her up here as soon as possible. I have a pretty good idea whose body this is," and she pointed to the burned man on the floor of the lobby, "but I want to see if Dr. Henshaw can find any DNA from anyone else, as well."

Maggie called Louise, explained the task at hand, and hung up the phone as soon as her message was delivered. She had no doubt that the coroner would come as soon as she could.

"Jonathan and Joey, I want you to look around the area for signs of anything that may be missing or items that are present that shouldn't be here. I know that much of the area is burned, but there still may be some clues we can salvage from the scene that can help us in our search for Samuel and Juliet."

"Mama Bear?" a voice on the handheld radio spoke softly. "This is Ghost
One. I have the Sparrow still under surveillance. She appears to be just sitting in the park at the Battery, with no one near her and no communications attempted on her cell phone. I followed her here from the Rex Theatre after an explosion there. What would you like for me to do?"

Maggie motioned to Jonathan and Joey to join her outside on the street. She wanted to respond to Juliet's vulnerability of apparently being alone presently, but she did not want anyone else to get hurt or killed.

"Our second undercover officer followed Juliet to the park on the Battery and is currently observing her. She appears to be just sitting there, making no attempt to go anywhere or telephone anyone. We need to catch her, but we need to make sure she is alive so we can question her. If you have to pull your service weapon, try to shoot to wound her and not kill her. We need to know where Samuel Hogdon is hiding and what his plans are for the future. Maybe she will help us and try and save her own skin by cooperating with the investigation. It's worth a try, but not at the expense of taking a bullet. If she draws down on you, shoot to kill!"

Chapter 28

Interrogation

The undercover officer began walking toward Juliet, who was sitting calmly on a park bench some thirty feet from him. Although he had permission to draw his service weapon and shoot to defend himself at any time he felt threatened by her, he really didn't want to move against anyone he didn't absolutely have to shoot. With that going through his mind, he approached Juliet and said calmly, "Juliet Robinson, you are under arrest. Do not make any quick or questionable moves. I don't want to hurt you, so let's just take things really slow and careful."

Juliet did not respond to the officer. She just sat on the bench, looking out on the water that surrounded the park at the Battery. She appeared to be calm, or maybe sad, but she definitely did not appear to be a threat to anyone. Maggie, Jonathan, and Joey appeared on the fringe of the park, and all three had removed the safety strap from their holsters and had their hands on their weapons.

"Juliet," Maggie called to her when she was within speaking range of the bench. "We just want to talk to you—nothing else. Do you have your service weapon or any other weapon on your person?"

Juliet slowly turned her head to look at Maggie and said, "No, I am not armed. I am just tired of all of this crap. I want everything to be back like it was before I got involved with Samuel Hogdon. Otherwise, life is not worth living!" she said and started crying.

Maggie moved slowly toward Juliet, reaching her and cautiously sitting down on the bench beside her. She motioned to Jonathan and Joey to stay back until she had determined if the immediate threat was over. Observing Juliet from a closer perspective, Maggie decided that there was no immediate threat of violence from her.

"Juliet, we need to go back to the police station and debrief you on what has happened since we last saw you a few days ago. What I need for you to do is to stand up, place your hands behind your back, and we will use some restraints on your wrists. We will not intentionally hurt you in any way, but we need to follow procedure. Do you understand?"

"Yes."

"Juliet Robinson, you have the right to remain silent. Anything you say can and will be used against you in a court of law. You have the right to an attorney. If you cannot afford an attorney, one will be provided for you. Do you understand these rights?" Maggie asked her.

"Yes."

"OK, let's get you to the station and work this out to everyone's benefit," Maggie told her calmly.

* * *

Since they were only a few blocks from the police station, they walked Juliet up Meeting Street until they arrived at the police station. They entered the station, Maggie turned Juliet over to the booking officer and then asked Jonathan and Joey to join her in the conference room. On the way to the conference room, she knocked on Major Pinckney's door and found him inside, sitting at his desk.

"Major, will you please join Jonathan, Joey, and me in the conference room? We have a possible break in the murder case, and we want you in the loop on what is about to go down."

"Sure," he said. "This is really good news, Maggie. I have just heard from the mayor, wanting to know where we were on the investigation and why no one had been arrested or detained who might have been complicit in the crimes."

"Well, now you will have some good news to share with him. We have just arrested Juliet Robinson, read the Miranda Rights to her, and we have her in the conference room. We are getting ready to put her in the interrogation room. Jonathan and I will conduct the debriefing session. I think it will be good for Joey to observe that interview, and I thought you might want to observe it as well."

"Absolutely," he said. "Do you think that we should invite the mayor to also observe?" Pinckney asked.

"I don't think that is a good idea, Major. You are a trained peace officer, and you have the experience of running criminals to ground in more than one instance. And, although the mayor has a lot of experience in city management business, he is not a peace officer. Once we get the scoop on whatever involvement Juliet had with the probable killer, we will make sure the mayor's office is brought up to date. Having him present in the interrogation room for observation could compromise our case," and she looked at the major to make sure he understood her concerns.

"You're probably correct, Maggie. So, what can I tell him that will not compromise our case at this point?"

"You can tell him that the police officer that had gone AWOL and that was implicated in the activities of our main suspect has been arrested and is cooperating with those questioning her. That should be sufficient, but if he asks you for more details, I think you know how to answer that, right?" she asked him and smiled.

Major Pinckney reached Mayor Anderson in his office and briefed him on what was known presently about the break in the murder case. As the major sat there listening to the mayor pontificate on the other end of the telephone call, everyone listening to Major Pinckney's response could pretty much guess the kind of questions that Anderson was asking.

"Of course. 'That's all we know at this time, Mayor, but we will let your office know as soon as we have anything else of substance to share with you'," he answered and returned Maggie's smile.

"Yep, you've got it, Major. That answer was perfect!"

"Do you have a specific approach to the interrogation process, or do you just let it develop as you go along? I have seen this kind of thing done on TV crime shows, but I've never seen it done in real situations. We rarely have murders in Charleston, and when we do, it usually is pretty evident who did what to whom."

"Are you asking me if there is a technique that we use, or are you just curious about the process?"

"Both, I guess," he replied. "It would be useful for me to know how the 'big city' cops do things like this, in case we have something like this happen again."

"Well, first of all, I'm not a big city cop. Our city is about the size of Charleston. However, we are close enough to Chicago that we occasionally have crime issues that seem to bleed over from one of the largest, vilest cities in the country into our little town. Unfortunately, we tend to have murders every year that require some interrogation of the witnesses or the perpetrators. In eight years in Rowlette, I have probably done what I am about to do here at least twenty-five or thirty times. I'm not proud of that record, but it has given me a lot of experience when it comes to debriefing a witness or interrogating a suspect."

Juliet had been moved into the interrogation room, outfitted with a one-way mirror that permitted those observing on the opposite side of that mirror to listen and view the process going on in the examination room where the debriefing was being carried out. The observation room was also soundproofed to ensure that no comments from those observing could be heard in the interrogation portion of the room. A remote speaker was available for the observers so they could keep up with the dialogue.

"Jonathan has just taken Juliet into the room, and I need to join him. If you have questions or thoughts that you think I should know in our process of questioning Juliet, please come outside to the door leading into the interrogation room and gently knock on the door. Don't, for any reason, knock on the glass window. Any questions?"

"Nope," the major answered, and Maggie left the observation room to enter the interrogation room.

Maggie knocked on the interrogation room door, Jonathan opened it for her, and she motioned him outside the room, where they could talk without Juliet hearing their conversation.

"Do you think we can do this as an interview, or do we need to proceed with it as an interrogation?" Jonathan asked Maggie.

"Since she basically came in willingly, I think we may get more of the truth from her if we soften our approach with her. Let's start with the interview protocol, and if she is not forthcoming with her answers to our inquiries, then we can move the conversation to more of an interrogation. Do you agree, or do you have some other approach you think we should take with Juliet? I do think that we need to get the D.A. over here, or at least an A.D.A., to hear her explain the circumstances. That way, we will know how strong a case we have against her."

"Good idea, Maggie," and Jonathan had the desk sergeant call the D.A.'s office to see if they could send someone to observe.

"She's on her way over, Lieutenant," the desk sergeant said. "She said to give her ten minutes." Within ten minutes A.D.A. Lorene Dowling was standing at the booking sergeant's desk. She was directed to the observation room, and they were now ready to begin questioning Juliet Robinson.

Maggie and Jonathan sat on the opposite side of the table from Juliet as they questioned her. They had not required that Juliet be handcuffed to the table, nor were her feet shackled to the floor. It was almost like a simple conversation between friends. Maggie and Jonathan planned to follow the steps of an interview protocol with Juliet, rather than those of a more confrontational interrogation. There were distinct differences in the two techniques in acquiring information. An interview used non-accusatory language, and question-and-answer dialogue. An interrogation began with accusatory language, with a strong monologue from the detective to discourage the suspect from speaking until he or she was ready to tell the truth. The main difference in the two techniques was that while trying to elicit the truth from the suspect in both situations, interviewing was more gathering investigative and behavioral information, while interrogating a suspect was designed to obtain a confession of guilt for the purported crime committed. Also, there was no notetaking during an interrogation until the suspect told the truth; notetaking was customary in an interview.

"Juliet, why don't you start from the beginning and just tell us how you got involved with Samuel Hogdon," Maggie suggested. "Go back to the very beginning of your encounter or relationship with him and bring us up to date through today's activities at the Rex Theatre."

Juliet looked tired, breathed in heavily, and began telling of her relationship with Hogdon.

"I actually met him when I first moved to Charleston back in 1994, before I applied and entered the Police Academy. We were introduced by a classmate of mine at the academy, went out on a couple of dates, and became lovers. He was very sweet, smart, and seemingly ambitious. He wanted to own a theatrical company that catered to outside groups coming into Charleston for festivals and other special events. He had just been hired by the Low Country Staging Company, and he thought that he would learn the business from them and then open his own company. What I learned pretty quickly was that Samuel was an irrational and emotional hothead. If he disagreed with someone, he would argue until he made the person see things his way. That didn't work too well for him in Charleston, however, and he got fired from the staging company pretty quickly. I later found out that he had been fired from several other companies because he would argue with the employees, customers, and even the owners. He had a really sweet side to his personality, but his anger would always betray him. I actually became afraid that he might hit me, or do something worse, if I disagreed with him. So, I pretty much went along with what he wanted to do. I didn't know that he was involved in the festival murders until after the second performer was killed. He told me that it was an accident and that the dancer hit his head when they were arguing, and he had nothing to do with his death. I wanted to believe him, and I stood by him until the murder of the director and the coroner's information that all of the victims had been poisoned. I might not be the smartest person in town, but the odds that three people died suspiciously around Samuel, all in accidental circumstances, just didn't add up. I told him I was through defending him and that I had left the police department. I said I would not turn him in to you if he could explain things to me in a way that I could believe him. He got so mad that he slapped me across the face. I almost fell down, but I was smart enough to step back and tell him that we were through. He begged me to forgive him, and I was tempted to be sympathetic, but I had seen my mother knocked around by my father, and I was having none of it!" Juliet took a breath, drank some water and continued.

"Yesterday, Samuel told me that he needed for me to do one more thing for him, and after that he would let me go and not continue to try to persuade me to work with him. He wanted me to go to the Rex Theatre and pick up a box of some kind and deliver it to him at the park on the Battery. When I went into the theatre, I saw Samuel standing there with a pistol. He had tricked me into going into a vacant, dark theatre, and I had the impression that he intended to kill me. Just about the time that I thought that I would be shot by Samuel, someone came into the back door of the theatre. It caught Samuel off guard, and he panicked. He had some kind of button in his hand, and he pressed it. The entire back of the theatre blew up, and a fire began to roar through the lobby area. Fortunately, the debris blew the other way, and I was not injured by the explosion. I was in shock, and when I looked back up to question Samuel about why he would detonate a bomb, he had disappeared. I decided that things had gotten out of hand to the point that I could not control anything about my life or our relationship. That's when I walked down East Bay Street to the Battery and took a seat on the park bench. I had observed the same city workers earlier doing absolutely nothing in the area, so I figured they were surveilling me." Juliet looked at Maggie and Jonathan and said, "I knew if I walked away from the area and appeared to be unarmed and a non-threat that I could give myself up peacefully. That's all I know," and she put her head down on the table and began to weep.

Maggie looked at Jonathan and motioned him outside of the interrogation room. They went into the observation room and asked the A.D.A. what she thought of the story, and if there was anything in there that they could use to convict Samuel Hogdon, assuming they were fortunate enough to find and arrest him.

A.D.A. Dowling thought for a moment and replied, "Unfortunately, everything that Juliet spoke about is hearsay, unless we can corroborate some of the actions of the suspect with physical evidence. Opinions will not hold up in court, nor will a jury of his peers find him guilty just because Juliet, a fugitive from her own police department and profession, has accused him of illegal activities. Based on what I heard from this young lady, we don't have enough to arrest Samuel Hogdon, much less prosecute him. The other question I have is whether or not you believe her story?" She looked at the four officers of the law to see if they would commit to her story.

"Major Pinckney is her boss, even though she had an immediate supervisor who was responsible for her training and progression with the department. What do you think, Major? Is Juliet credible? I think I remember you said that she had changed dramatically not too long ago. Maybe that was the influence of this Samuel Hogdon character. Any thoughts on that?" Maggie fired those questions at Pinckney in rapid succession—so rapidly that it took the major by surprise and left him stuttering.

Regaining his composure somewhat, Pinckney replied, "Juliet began acting reclusively about six weeks ago, so that lines up with her story about meeting Samuel before all of this murder business began. If he was trying to get information about what the police department was doing behind the scenes, Juliet was simply a vehicle for finding out those answers. He obviously used her, and then may have been preparing to tie up loose ends with her at the theatre before our undercover officer stumbled in and was killed in the explosion. The fire and the distraction afterward gave him an opportunity to slip away to strike again another day. I think Julie is telling the truth. I know she needs to be punished, but I don't believe she is complicit in any of the murders or the explosion at the Rex Theatre."

The ADA nodded along with Major Pinckney and then said, "Actually, this young lady is guilty of using bad judgement and being insubordinate—nothing more. It's up to you and the Police Department to determine her punishment, but as far as the DA is concerned, she is in the clear."

"You're probably correct about her innocence, Major, so now we need to pick her brain and find out where Hogdon may be hiding and if he has a plan to continue the violence and murders," Maggie said. "We need a way to sweeten the pot for her if she is instrumental in helping us find this murderer and get him off the street."

"As I said," the A.D.A spoke up with a smile, "if poor judgement were a crime, we would all have to serve time!" She laughed. "Has anyone seen her with the suspect? Has she admitted to helping him murder or endanger anyone?" and she looked around at the puzzled faces. "Look, she obviously used bad judgement. She may have even known about some of the things that he intended to do, but she is not responsible for 'what he might do' or for anything she herself did not commit. I couldn't arrest her and hold her on anything I have heard so far."

"Major," Jonathan spoke up, "I have an idea. Based on what Juliet said in the park at the Battery, and based on her voluntary description of all of her dealings with Samuel Hogdon, she might be motivated to go out of her way to remember things to help us corner this killer—that is, if you offered to take her back as an officer. It would be strictly your call, and I don't think you should consider it if you're not really willing to forgive her and bring her back into the fold."

"It's totally your call, Major," the A.D.A. agreed with Jonathan. "Currently, I can't charge her with anything that will stick, and if you let her go, you may be letting the best lead to finding this murderer walk away. I would give it some serious consideration."

"What do you think, Maggie? You, more than anyone in this city, know what I am struggling with when I consider reinstating someone who has betrayed us already. What would you do if the same thing happened in Rowlette, Illinois?"

"I can't tell you what to do, Major, but what I can do is tell you that Juliet will probably be the best behaved police officer you will have going forward. She will know that you will have your eye on her at all times and that she has to earn her way back into your good graces. She will want to succeed more than ever, if only to show you that you were right to give her a second chance," Maggie said.

"You didn't answer my question, Maggie," and he laughed at her evasiveness.

"I can tell you that I would want to shoot her," she laughed as well, "but the smart thing to do is to learn from your mistakes and hope that Juliet learns from her mistakes as well."

"So, how do you think I should handle the reinstatement?"

"Juliet needs to know that this is not going to be swept under the rug, but that you will give her a legitimate chance to redeem herself. The discussion should probably include my team, since she abandoned us in our time of need, and the A.D.A. might sit in as well. Even though Juliet is a smart young woman, she may not know that what she did was not a crime punishable by law. With the A.D.A. there to tell her that she will not be prosecuted, that may be the motivation she needs to get fully on board with this plan."

"OK, let's do it now. Can we use the interrogation room, or should we move the discussion to the conference room?" Pinckney asked.

"I think you should use the conference room, Major, because it is less threatening. In other words, she has gone from the point of possibly being charged with a crime to a position of helping us solve the crime. That's a healthy approach to mind manipulation," Jonathan smiled as he finished his point.

"Does Jonathan also have a Ph.D. in Psychology, as well?" Pinckney asked with a smile.

"No," Maggie said and gave Jonathan a pat on the back, "he's just smart as the dickens!"

Chapter 29

Deal Making

"Normally, Juliet, we don't make deals with people who are still actively involved in a criminal act. Can you swear to me, under oath, that you are no longer involved with Samuel Hogdon in any way in regards to this murder investigation?" A.D.A. Dowling asked her.

"Yes, ma'am," she said quietly.

"What I need for you to do is to start at the beginning. When and how did you meet Hogdon? When did you get romantically involved with him, and when did you realize that he was the probable murderer? We need to know everything that you can remember. Can you do that for us?"

"I think so, ma'am. Some of it just happened innocently, that is, until he began trying to indoctrinate me on the bad things that had happened to him. He wanted me to help him get justice, and I became overwhelmed with his cause for justice. Looking back on it now, I see that it was stupid and childish to believe him. However, at the time he was telling me everything, he seemed to have a just cause."

"When did you know, or suspect him of being the murderer?" the A.D.A. asked. The answer to this particular question was critical, because depending on how Juliet answered, she could become an accomplice in the murders and other crimes Hogdon had committed recently. If she honestly did not know that Hogdon was the murderer and intended to commit the crimes, she could probably be rehabilitated, and possibly even rehired by the police department.

"I swear I didn't know or even suspect him of the murders until after he had killed the music director. He acted normally when I was around him in the evenings after work. Looking back, I realized that he was very interested, maybe too much so, in what we were doing at the police department to investigate and prosecute the crimes associated with the Piccolo/Spoleto Festival murders. When I asked him why he wanted to know so much about those cases, he got mad at me and accused me of not loving him. He said that if I loved him, I would tell him everything that went on at the station. After the shooting that night on Meeting Street, when he apparently attempted to kill Lieutenant Watson and Jonathan, I put it all together that he must be somehow involved in the crimes. I didn't confront him, because I had seen him get really nasty with people when his integrity was called into question. So, that's when I decided to hide out until things were over—I was really scared of him. I didn't show up for work, I changed all of my routines, and I just hoped that he would eventually be arrested or that he would go away." Observing the A.D.A. question Juliet, Maggie saw that Juliet was really fearful of her life.

"OK, Juliet," the A.D.A. continued. "Was Samuel staying with you at your apartment anytime during the period of time when this was happening?" Dowling had been told by Joey that Hogdon had been spotted at the complex on multiple occasions, and that was how they were able to get a composite sketch of his face from a witness.

"No, there's no way I was living with him. He came over from time to time, and we were having an affair, but he was not living with me, or I with him," and Juliet was adamant about those facts.

"OK, that's good to know. However, did you ever go to his place, instead of his always coming to your apartment? We really need to know where he lives, or at least where he might be staying. We need to get him off the street, Juliet. Can you help us find where he is?" Dowling continued to probe.

"No, he insisted that he keep his hideout a secret—in case I was captured and might be tempted to give him up to the police."

"Many times, a person forgets the details of an incident in their active minds, but much can be retrieved by a psychologist trained in hypnotism. Would you be willing to submit yourself to hypnotism to help us catch this killer?"

Thinking a little and fearing all her personal secrets would be exposed to strangers, Juliet asked, "Can you show me the questions that will be asked while I am under hypnotism? As long as I know that you are not going on a witch hunt, trying to dig up all sorts of dirt on me and my past, I will agree to the hypnotist."

"Sure, Juliet. That's only fair to you. The psychologist performing the hypnotism and only the detectives working this case will have knowledge of your results—and I will observe. If you tell us other things not associated with this murder investigation, unsolicited facts that may be incriminating, we will disregard them and not make them part of your permanent record. Is that fair?"

Reluctantly, Juliet agreed. They would have her stay in the station tonight, and she would begin the hypnotism session at 9:00 AM in the morning. They convinced her to stay overnight in a cell, just for her protection. She didn't seem to have a problem with the arrangements.

"Before we dismiss you for the day, Juliet, can you tell us one more time exactly when you first suspected Samuel of the murders and the other crimes associated with this case?"

"Like I said before, after the professor was found dead and when I heard about the shooting on Meeting Street, I began to put two and two together. I wasn't certain that he was the killer, but I was pretty sure that he was somehow involved."

"OK, tell me again how you wound up on Queen and East Bay Streets today, and what part you played in the explosion of the Rex Theatre."

Juliet rose from her seat quickly and adamantly protested that she had had nothing to do with any of that. She said that Samuel had convinced her that he wanted to protect her against the police department and any possible prosecution and that if she met him at the theatre that he would tell her all about his plan for them both.

"I was reluctant to meet him there, but I thought that there might be one more chance for us and that he could explain how he was not involved with the murders that had recently taken place. When I got there, I entered in the rear of the theatre and saw Samuel standing in the lobby area. He had some type of device in his hand that had blinking red and green lights on the panel. When I asked him about it, he said he would explain and for me to come over to where he was standing. I didn't move from my position, because I sensed that he had been lying all along and that my life was in danger. We heard someone enter the theatre from the rear as I had done, and Samuel cursed, pressed one of the red buttons, and everything began to explode around me. I saw Samuel running out the other entrance to the building, but I was in shock and just wandered out into the alley and began to walk toward the Battery. I sat on the bench, and that's where Maggie and her team found me."

"Did you know that Samuel's explosion at the Rex Theatre took the life of an undercover police officer?" A.D.A. Dowling asked.

"No, I didn't know that anyone else was in the theatre, or I would have tried to help him. I basically could not believe that Samuel would lure me to the theatre and try to kill me. If the officer had not come into the office when he did, I'm convinced Samuel would have killed me and used the explosion to cover up the murder. That's when I decided that I had been wrong about everything and that I would do whatever I could to help catch and prosecute him."

The A.D.A. and the other detectives left Juliet in the conference room. They reassembled in Major Pinckney's office and had a general discussion about whether they thought her testimony was honest and forthcoming, compared to the facts that they had to that point.

"She appears to be telling the truth, as far as I can determine, based on the facts that we have about the Rex Theatre bombing. Does anyone think she may be lying?" Maggie asked the group.

"No, I think she is telling the truth," Joey agreed. "In my opinion, I think she was scared, got sucked more and more into Samuel's plot until she finally saw that he was simply evil and that she couldn't deal with him."

"It almost seems as if Juliet experienced some features of Stockholm Syndrome during her infatuation with Samuel Hogdon. She wasn't a captive, so her situation does not fit the actual definition of Stockholm Syndrome, but the bonding part is there. In her own words, she identified with Hogdon, and she was a willing accomplice to a point in some of his actions," Jonathan offered.

"Maybe," Maggie said. "However, at some point she determined that what Samuel was doing was wrong, and she no longer wanted to have anything to do with him. At any rate, she was never alienated from the police, another feature of Stockholm Syndrome. I think she may be a link to helping us locate Samuel, even if she has forgotten specific information that could lead us to him. Perhaps hypnotism will enable her to remember more that will help us find his hideout."

Maggie addressed Major Pinckney, "From all we can determine, Juliet was not a voluntary participant in any of Samuel's crimes. As best we can determine, when she concluded that Hogdon was in violation of the law and the possible murderer of the festival participants, she went into seclusion and hid from him. That's why she disappeared from the precinct house and her apartment. She feared for her life."

"I thought you said you had heard that Hogdon was helping her move?"

"That does complicate things a bit, doesn't it?"

"So, the explanation of her encounter with Hogdon at the Rex Theatre situation, where she was seen leaving a burning building after the explosion and murder of our undercover officer, adds up to you?" Pinckney asked.

"She told us that she was going to break it off with him, and she went to the theatre to confront him. You know, Major, it makes a lot of sense. I believe Juliet is telling the truth."

"So, Maggie, what would you recommend I do with her?"

"She's young, impressionable, and was very susceptible to Hogdon's strong personality. However, she came in without any resistance and is willing to work to help us find and capture Samuel Hogdon. I don't know what your policy is, but I think if she thought that she had an option for some type of redemption and reinstatement into the department, she might be one of the most loyal employees you could ever find—just my opinion."

Dowling said, "I have a few more questions for her, and then she's all yours. As far as I can determine from what she has told us, she was duped by this guy. She may have had a crush on him, and she may have had a romantic fling with him, but she definitely was not complicit in any of his illegal actions."

Dowling and the others went back into the conference room where Juliet was sitting quietly pondering her fate. "I have a few more questions, but other than that we will be through with the questioning today."

"OK," Juliet replied. "What else can I tell you? I have tried to tell you everything I can remember."

"Tell me again why you just disappeared from work, your apartment, and everywhere else."

"The last day I was here in the conference room, we were going over the research and files of the suspects. I went home with the material that I had gathered on Samuel and began to look deeper into the possibility that he might be the killer. I felt sorry for him, because he had told me that he was just a local boy trying to make his way in the world, and everyone was out to get him. He seemed so sad and helpless that I wanted to help him, assuming he was telling the truth. I needed to find substantial proof that he wasn't involved, so I could return the next day to defend him. However, I went to the library later that evening and discovered irregularities in the stories that he had told me about his history in the city and his involvement at the College of Charleston. There were documented instances where he had had altercations with his fellow classmates, as well as with Lawrence Baker, his teacher. The real history of Samuel Hogdon read nothing like what he had told me. His story that he was just a good, local boy who had had bad luck and was being persecuted for no substantial reason—I know now it was a complete lie. I was devastated, and then I began to worry about him coming after me. In retrospect, I should have confided in Major Pinckney or at least spoken to Maggie and the other team members about what I had discovered about him."

"Why didn't you go to one of them and confide in them? Did you not trust them, or was it something else?"

"I should have done exactly that, but I was afraid that Samuel would find me and kill me, as he had the other people who he felt had harmed him in the past. I thought that if I just disappeared until he was caught and arrested, I could come forward and explain my story to whoever would listen."

"Is there anything, anything at all that you remember that may help us locate him?"

"I remember he said that his maternal grandmother lived in Mt. Pleasant and that he could always hide out with her if things got bad for him in Charleston. I think her last name was Copeland, or Coppell, or something like that."

When Maggie heard that comment, she looked at Jonathan and indicated for him to begin following up that lead while she and Joey remained viewing Juliet's disclosures. He slipped out of the observation room quietly and logged on to a desktop computer. Maggie, Joey and Major Pinckney continued to listen to the exchange between the A.D.A and Juliet.

"Juliet, would you like for us to consider reinstating you to the police force once all of this is cleared up?" Pinckney asked. "I think you have definitely learned your lesson with this little caper. What I would like for you to do is to talk to me, one-on-one, after this current session ends, and see if you can convince me that you want another chance. You must know that you will be on probation for a year and that we will be very observant of your every action if you decide to stay. But if you keep your nose clean and do well, we will expunge your record of all of this after a year. Do you feel comfortable with that offer?

"I will be forever grateful to have another chance, Major. What time do you want me here for the hypnotist in the morning?"

"Let's make it 9:00 AM. I will get the coroner to set that up for us. She has many physicians she can call on at the hospital, and she has helped us in the past with referrals when we needed them. I will make that call, and as soon as the appointment is confirmed, I will let you know. I think we may be getting close to nabbing this demented criminal, and it's not a minute too soon for me! Your cooperation in aiding us in this endeavor will go a long way to restoring our confidence in you," he said. The major was looking very tired and old. This whole matter had taken quite a toll on him.

Jonathan spoke up and said, "Major, we are all ready for this guy to be stopped—one way or the other."

"Unless he forces us, I would like to take him alive, but if he presses his luck, that final decision will be on him," Pinckney replied.

They broke up the meeting, but before Maggie and Jonathan left for the day, they sat down with Juliet, covered the details of the opportunity that Major Pinckney had offered her, and had the major's secretary write up a binding agreement for her participation in the operation.

"This is more than I imagined could happen, Lieutenant. I know I don't deserve any consideration, but if I'm given another chance, I will not screw it up next time!" Juliet said confidently.

"OK, I will let you work out the details with Major Pinckney after all of this settles down. Now, however, I want you to go back to the cell and get a good's night's rest. Tomorrow could be very helpful to us and to you."

"Yes, ma'am," Juliet said and gave Maggie an unexpected hug.

Maggie just smiled at her, patted her hand, and said, "You'll be fine, Juliet. Just remember that very few people get a 'do-over' when they screw up really bad. Major Pinckney is a first class guy, and just don't let him down next time."

"No way, ma'am. I will be the best rookie he's ever had," she said as she rose and went to the door to exit the interrogation room. "And thank you, Joey. I'm sure you had some influence with the lieutenant and this decision."

Joey just nodded sympathetically and opened the door for Juliet to exit the room and go back to her cell for the evening. It took courage to face one's errors, pledge to do better the next time, and then execute that promise. He hoped that Juliet was on her way to a successful police officer's career—albeit a little delayed.

"Jonathan, let's go back to the Gaslight Inn and relax a bit. I would like for you to take me to Anson's and buy me a big old steak with all the trimmings," Maggie said to him in front of the Major and Joey.

"It sounds like you two are celebrating something—want to let me in on it?" the major asked.

"It's not every day you see a soul rescued from falling off a cliff into oblivion. In my opinion, that's the path that Juliet

Robinson was treading. I think what you do can be therapeutic for her, and an excellent decision for the Charleston Police Department. I will follow up once we are back in Rowlette, but I would lay odds that she will develop into a fine officer for your police department and city."

"I agree with Maggie, Major. It would have been a lot easier for you to just start over with another rookie than to try to straighten out a flawed one. However, she now has something to prove to you, the other officers on the force, and herself. We know she is bright and that she finished close to the top of her class at the academy. I think the chance you are taking by bringing her back into the fold is miniscule, compared to the possible upside of what she could mean to this department. I think it takes a pretty big man to overlook some errors as serious as Juliet has displayed these past few days and weeks. However, I do believe you have her attention at this point in her career."

Joey had left for the day, so it was only Maggie, Jonathan, and the major standing in the conference room talking about Juliet and where she might fit into the scheme of things. Maggie had a suggestion that she was going to make, even if the subject matter wasn't any of her business. That's exactly what she would have done in Rowlette, and that's what she was about to do here in Charleston.

"Major, if you don't mind my opinion, and a small suggestion, I would like to speak to you about Joey Lancaster. His ability to discern the correct line of questioning, his maturity to know when to talk and when to listen, and his dogged approach to completing the mission he has been assigned are refreshing, and he reminds me of a rookie that I had in Rowlette this past year. She and Joey could be twins, as far as their ability to accomplish so much as rookies with the limited experience and exposure that they both demonstrated under fire in the field. We promoted the rookie in Rowlette, and I believe she is going to make a wonderful investigator. She can work without supervision, but she doesn't mind working as an assistant, or even a subordinate to someone with more experience. She just soaks up everything around her," and Maggie paused a minute to catch her breath and continue her thoughts.

"I think you have the same type of potential officer in Joey. He is pleasant to work with, appears to be honest, loyal, and considerate of the feelings of those around him—even the perps. If he were my rookie, I would give him a vote of confidence by promoting him to corporal and letting him supervise Juliet and the other rookies you acquire in the near future. If he gets stumped along the way, I can all but guarantee that he will come to you for counsel. He's not the kind of officer that 'wings it' when he has serious questions. To be honest with you, during our investigation I almost forgot at times he was a rookie. As I said earlier, it's none of my business, because I am going to get on an airplane and fly back to Illinois once this case is closed. However, I think you have a diamond in the rough with this kid." Having said what was on her mind, she took Jonathan's hand, and they began to walk toward the door and Meeting Street.

Major Pinckney stopped her briefly and said, "Maggie, I will take your recommendation under serious consideration. I agree with you about Joey. He slips up on you, because he is so easygoing and appears to be laid back about everything. However, he is management material! Thanks for your suggestion. Now you two go get something good to eat at Anson's and enjoy your evening."

Jonathan and Maggie walked hand in hand to the Gaslight Inn, arriving at 5:30 PM. It was too early to go to dinner, but there was always the queen-sized bed and the Jacuzzi to entertain them until a respectable dinner time. They decided to enjoy the Jacuzzi, a bottle of fine white wine, and the finale—a brief visit to the canopy bed. They called Anson's for a reservation.

* * *

Seeing the sun setting in the distance behind the market from the front window booth at Anson's was almost enough to let them escape all their thoughts of the murders. Almost. The food and wine were the best food that they had experienced in Charleston, and they walked back by the Chocolate Factory on Market Street and bought "sinful," pure chocolate candies to take back to their room. And although they were aware of the shooting the last time, they walked along this street after dinner. It was peaceful tonight.

"You know, Jonathan, I could live in Historic Charleston except for one thing," she looked up at him with a contented expression.

"What?"

"I can't afford a completely new wardrobe! If we don't solve these murders and get the perp under arrest soon, I will never fit in my clothes again!"

"Just more woman for me to hug," he said lovingly.

"Rat's ass!" she said so emphatically that he almost jumped back from her side. "I am not going to be a happy little fat girlfriend or wife, waiting for my man to come home to see how much weight I have gained that day. I'll be eating yogurt, cereal, and fruit for weeks after this trip!"

"Like I say, that's not important to me, Maggie. But I am glad you're contemplating marrying me," and he leaned down and kissed her.

"What are you saying, crazy man? How did you get a marriage proposal from that comment?"

"You said 'wife,' and I just assumed you were ready for me to propose. I'm game when you are, Maggie."

"Let me get back with you on that point, OK? I think we need to stay focused on solving these murders—we can talk about romance and the future when we get back to Rowlette, assuming you still want to do so at that time."

"Oh, I will," he said, and he planted a huge kiss on her mouth. She didn't resist, but he knew he was pushing his luck.

Chapter 30

Polygraph and Hypnotism

"Just close your eyes, count backwards from one hundred, and think of sitting on a bench on a nice, warm day by the Battery," the voice of Dr. Harold Hemingway droned on slowly as he began to put Juliet under the influence of his hypnotic trance. Hemingway had been recommended by Dr. Hensley, who had researched some background on him before mentioning him to Major Pinckney as the clinician she felt had the best credentials for the task at hand.

Dr. Harold P. Hemingway definitely had great credentials. He received his B.S. in Psychology from Stanford University, a M.S. and Ph.D. from Yale University, and ten years of clinical practice at the University of Michigan-Ann Arbor prior to coming to Charleston to practice at the University of South Carolina Hospital. He was a very serious man, both in his professional life and his personal dealings with his peers. It had never been said of Dr. Hemingway that he was lighthearted or fun to be around. When you talked to him, it was as though he were looking through your eyes into the windows of your soul.

"One hundred, ninety-nine, ninety-eight, ninety..." Juliet's voice trailed off as her mind surrendered control to the good doctor.

"Juliet, you are going to go into a deep, deep sleep. Relax now, and go deeper, deeper..." he said, and his voice was as smooth as water in the Bay of Charleston on a calm summer's day. "You will only be able to respond to the sound of my voice. When I tell you to open your eyes, you will be fully asleep, but you will be able to recall things that have happened in the past. OK, now open your eyes," he commanded softly, and Juliet appeared to be awake.

"What is your name?"
"Juliet Robinson."
"Where do you live?"
"The Charleston Police Station Jail."

"Where did you live before that?"

"232 Radcliff Street, Apartment 13."

"Where do you work?"

"The City of Charleston Police Department."

"Do you know who Samuel Hogdon is, and what is your relationship to him?"

"Yes. He and I were good friends, and then we became lovers."

"When is the last time you saw him?"

"In the Rex Theatre a few days ago when he tried to kill me."

"Prior to that time, when did you see him last?"

"A few days before that date, when he told me that he was going to take care of the nosy detectives from Illinois. He bragged about wanting to shoot them and add them to his kill list."

"What did you do when he told you that?"

"I moved out of my apartment and went into hiding."

"Why did you do that, Juliet?"

"I was afraid that Samuel would try to hurt or kill me."

"Did Samuel tell you where he lived, or where he was hiding out?"

"No."

"Did he tell you the name of his grandmother?"

"Yes. Her name is Naomi Coppell, and she lives somewhere in Mt. Pleasant, just across the Cooper River Bridge. He mentioned Royall Avenue and Reid Street. He said she had a home there where he could hide if he needed to leave Charleston for any reason."

"Did you participate in any of the crimes that Samuel Hogdon committed that are related to the current murder spree associated with the Piccolo/Spoleto Festival?"

"No."

"Did Samuel Hogdon tell you anything about his plans going forward relating to the recent murders?"

"Only that he was going to get that bitch that had set him up with the cops."

"Do you know who he meant by 'that bitch'?"

"I'm not sure."

"Try to remember, Juliet. Did he mention anyone in particular that he wanted to get even with? Did he suggest where that person might work?"

"I can't remember."

"OK, Juliet. I am going to bring you out of this trance, and you will wake up and remember nothing of what we discussed. I am going to count to three and snap my fingers. At that moment, you will be wide awake. One, two, three..." and he snapped his fingers.

Juliet bolted awake and asked, "When are you going to put me under?"

"It's already done," Dr. Hemingway said soothingly.

"Was I helpful? Did I remember anything that can help in the investigation?"

"You will have to ask Major Pinckney or Lieutenant Watson, but I think they will be very pleased with the outcome of our session. You did just fine!"

* * *

Maggie, Jonathan, Joey, and Major Pinckney were observing the session from the other side of the interrogation room. As soon as Juliet revealed the name of Samuel's grandmother's home location, Jonathan slipped out of the room, went to the desktop computer and began pulling up all of the information surrounding that intersection. He slipped back into the room just as Dr. Hemingway was finishing the session with Juliet.

"Jonathan, we have two immediate issues," Maggie said. "First of all, we need to send someone over to observe Ms. Coppell's house to see if Samuel will show up. Second, we need to determine who the woman is that Hogdon felt set him up. I guess it could be me, or it could be Louise—I'm just not sure. The pressing situation is to see if Hogdon is hiding out in Mt. Pleasant. I'm going to take Joey with me and check out Mr. Pleasant. Why don't you hang around here and keep your eyes and ears open to see what develops?"

"That sounds like an excellent idea, Maggie. Do you think that Louise is in some kind of danger?"

"I'm not sure, but when you left to run down the address of Samuel's grandmother's house, Juliet said that Samuel had planned to get even with the person who had tried to harm him. The only person I can imagine that he could be talking about, other than me, is Dr. Hensley. I think she is probably safe, knowing that there is another layer of security available with the keyed elevator access to get to the morgue, but I would feel better if we followed up on the potential threat when Joey and I return from Mt. Pleasant. I doubt that it is an emergency situation, and I don't want to rattle Louise trying to explain all of this over the telephone. We'll go down to the hospital together when I return from Mt. Pleasant."

Maggie looked at Joey and said, "You and I are going to check out Naomi Coppell's house in Mt. Pleasant. We need to determine if Samuel Hogdon is sleeping there, has recently visited there, or is running his murderous campaign from that house. Jonathan, I will give you a call once we are finished interviewing Naomi, and you should call me if you find out something that I should know before I return to the precinct house." She and Joey waved goodbye to Jonathan, Major Pinckney, and Jill and headed for Pinckney's Crown Vic parked at the curb on Meeting Street.

Joey was excited at the suggestion that they were going to try to smoke out Hogdon in Mt. Pleasant. This is the kind of action that he had imagined when he joined the Police Academy originally.

"Joey, what I want you to do is to let me out in front of the house, and then I want you to park the car down the street, out of sight, and we will see if we can surprise Hogdon at his grandmother's house."

"Sure, Lieutenant, I can handle that. Should we call the Charleston County Police for assistance, since they are part of the county, but not covered by the City of Charleston police authority?"

"Absolutely, Joey. Good thinking. Do you think you can handle the request, or do you want me to set things up with the county sheriff's department? We need to make sure we have some backup if this guy goes berserk and does something really stupid."

"Let's see what I can do first. If I run into a buzz-saw or

something that keeps me from getting assistance quickly, you can be sure that I will contact you."

"Good man," Maggie said and clapped him on the back. "Now get your butt in gear and secure the rear of this house. By the way, let's be low-key and not go into this situation with guns blazing. Only use force if you have to. I don't want to give a little old lady a heart attack for no reason!"

"Yes, ma'am. I've got it. I'll radio you as soon as I have secured the rear of the house and the county backup officers are in place." He stopped to let her out of the car, and he was immediately on his way behind the house.

Maggie was thinking that Joey had really grown up a lot since all this began. She wished she could take him back to Rowlette to work in her detective pool, but she knew he wouldn't fit into the setting any more than she would fit in down here on a long-range basis.

* * *

Maggie had received a radio message from Joey that the county sheriff had a car in the area of Mt. Pleasant, and the two county patrolmen pulled up at the rear of Ms. Coppell's house within minutes of Joey's request. She was ready to knock and announce herself when the front door opened unexpectedly.

"May I help you?" a small, gray-haired lady opened the door and greeted her pleasantly.

"Yes, ma'am. My name is Lieutenant Maggie Watson, representing the City of Charleston Police department. May I come in for a minute and speak to you?"

Looking suspiciously, she asked, "What is this about, Officer?"

"We are trying to locate your grandson, Samuel Hogdon. Have you seen him recently?"

"Well, of course I have," she answered cheerfully. "He lives with me these days. What has he done that the police are looking for him? Come inside," Naomi said to Maggie, indicating that she should take a seat on the antique love seat in the living room. "Now, what did you say you needed with my grandson?"

"We just need to speak to him for a moment," she said, and her radio chirped, indicating an incoming transmission.

"Excuse me, Ms. Coppell. I need to see what my partner needs."

"This is Mama Bear," she answered, using the code name that she had established for her radio identity.

"This is Baby Bear," the voice came back. "There is no sign of an automobile or disturbance in the alley behind the residence. Is everything OK in there?"

"10-4. I will call you back momentarily."

Maggie directed her attention back to Naomi Coppell. "Can you tell me where I can find your grandson right now?"

"No, he didn't tell me where he was going. All he said was that he was going out and that he would be back this evening."

"How long has he been staying with you in Mt. Pleasant?"

"Only for about three weeks or so. He said that he needed to stay over here while the annual Piccolo/Spoleto Festival was in town. So, I gave him back his old room, and he comes and goes as he pleases."

"Do you mind if we look in his room, assuming we don't mess up your house or damage anything?"

"Oh, I don't mind, Officer. I don't have anything to hide here."

"Thanks," Maggie said and radioed back to Joey and the two county deputies. "Please come to the front door of the house so we can check out Samuel's room," and she ended the transmission.

"10-4," Joey replied, and in less than five minutes the three men were standing on Ms. Coppell's front porch, knocking on the door.

Maggie rose, opened the door for the detectives, and invited them inside. She wanted to get this done, and she needed to get back to the precinct to visit the coroner with Jonathan. The more she thought about it, the more she was convinced that Louise was the natural target of this maniac's anger.

Naomi ushered them back down a small, dimly lit hallway where she said Samuel's room was located. She tried the doorknob, but it was locked. Naomi looked up at Maggie and said,

"Something is not right here, Officer. We never lock our rooms in this house. It is a tradition. Do you think your men can open the door without breaking it down? I am concerned that Samuel may be hurt, or worse."

"That's not a problem, Ms. Coppell," Joey replied. He reached into his wallet and drew out a credit card. In a matter of seconds, Joey had sprung the lock, and the door flew open, revealing a bizarre sight. On one wall was a corkboard with newspaper clippings of the three murders, with follow-up stories about how each person died, the fire at the Rex Theatre, and several pictures of Dr. Louise Henshaw, the coroner. He had underlined several statements in the articles with a black highlighter, and he had circled Louise's pictures with a red marker and drawn a cross over the circles."

"Oh, my," was all Naomi Coppell could say as she looked at the many clippings posted on the wall, and the other notes and scribblings on the desk.

If Maggie had had any doubts of who the killer might be, those doubts were shattered when she observed this shrine that Hogdon had made to his murderous plan. She would get Jonathan on the phone and have him meet her at the hospital as soon as she could drive there from Mt. Pleasant.

Chapter 31

Terror at the Hospital

Jonathan was still talking to Juliet at the police station about what Samuel had said about the woman who had caused all of his problems. It was pretty obvious to her that Hogdon was referring to Louise, but she wanted to be sure of her facts before she alarmed the coroner.

"Do you remember anything else that Samuel might have said in regards to the 'bitch' that he was going to get even with?" Jonathan asked Juliet as they sat in the conference room, waiting to hear from Maggie about the raid on Samuel's grandmother's house. "You had mentioned those specific words in your hypnotic state earlier. We have reason to believe that Samuel is going to try and get even with whomever he has in his sights sometime this week, and possibly today," Jonathan told Juliet when they brought her up to date on the hunt for Samuel Hogdon.

Juliet thought for a moment and said, "I can't remember too much about it, but I know he was really mad at that woman for exposing him and his first and third murders. I didn't stay around much after he had disclosed that he had committed the murders, so I didn't hear any specifics about what the woman did or where she worked. I think it had something to do with the hospital. His uncle is a security guard there, and he said that he could get keys to access areas that most people couldn't get to without a password or key card. So, I guess it would be someplace in the hospital or clinic that has restricted access. Does that help?"

Just then, the dispatcher buzzed the conference room and told Jonathan that he had an emergency call on the radio band. She indicated that she would transfer it to the telephone desk set so he could put it on the speaker phone for everyone to hear.

"Jonathan, don't ask me anything—just listen," Maggie said. "We found Samuel's room at his grandmother's house, and his current plan is all about Louise. You need to get over there as soon as possible. I think he may be going to target her for tying the suspects together with DNA and leading us to him as the killer."

"Do you want me to wait on your return, or should I go to the hospital and meet you there?"

"Take Juliet with you to the hospital. He may talk to her, or we may be able to slow him down by distracting him. There is an outside chance that he has not arrived there yet, but I don't want to take any unnecessary chances that he is already in the building, stalking Louise or doing her any harm. Don't wait on me—leave now!" she said. "We just wrapped up a questioning session with Samuel Hogdon's grandmother in Mt. Pleasant. He has newspaper clippings with red circles around Louise's picture. He has crossed out her face in the photographs. It indicates to me that she is his next target and that she may be in a life threatening situation."

"OK, Maggie. We are on our way." He heard Maggie hang up the radio, and he turned his attention to the police chief.

"Major Pinckney, we need to get over to the hospital to make sure that Louise is aware of the potential danger she could be in with Samuel Hogdon," Jonathan told him.

"Do you need for me to go with you as a backup?" Pinckney asked.

"No, but I do need your help. This might be an unusual request under the current circumstances, but Maggie and I want to take Juliet with us to possibly help, assuming we get into a negotiating position with Hogdon."

"I haven't questioned your decisions so far, so I'm not going to question them now. However, if Juliet goes with you, she must go as an official officer, fully armed and protected with the same safety vest and equipment that you will be wearing. Do you have any problem with that?"

"Not at all. She's learned her lesson, and she can possibly redeem herself with these actions."

"Juliet, do you feel comfortable with these conditions?"

"Yes, sir," she responded and began to suit up for the encounter with her old boyfriend.

Jonathan grabbed his sidearm, protective vest, and handheld radio. Why would Hogdon want to go after the coroner? That made absolutely no sense to Jonathan. However, his job at this moment was not to figure out why Hogdon was targeting Louise, but just to intercept and stop him any way he could. He had just found her this past week, and he didn't want to lose her again.

* * *

Maggie left Mt. Pleasant with Joey, letting the county sheriff's deputies close out the visit with Naomi Coppell. She was a nice lady. It was very unfortunate that Samuel Hogdon was related to her. Of course, that was not Maggie's concern now. She had to get to the hospital and save her friend, Louise, if it was the last thing on Earth she would accomplish.

They were fully armed, protected with body armor, and speeding to the hospital in Major Pinckney's Crown Vic. It had been rumored that no one could drive safely in excess of forty-five miles an hour over the Cooper River Bridge and survive—she had the patrol cruiser on seventy-five, and she caught a glimpse of Joey's face out of the corner of her eye. His face was as white as the pillowcase in her hotel room. He also had a death-grip on the panic bar installed above the front seat passenger door. She smiled to herself and sped up even more. They exited the bridge, ran the traffic signal, turned left on Meeting Street, and flew down the street as if it were empty of other vehicles. She used the siren and lights until she was within a couple of blocks of the hospital. Then she turned both off, because she did not want to make a grand entrance and alert Hogdon, assuming he had beat her to the morgue. When she arrived, she left Pinckney's cruiser at the emergency entrance, sped inside and saw Butch Blakely sitting at his desk.

"What can I do for you, Maggie?"

"Butch, I need to speak to you in private for a minute. Can you get someone to cover for you for a few minutes?" Maggie asked.

"Sure," he said and lifted his two-way radio to get another guard to come to the desk and cover for him. When the other guard showed up, Butch told him that he had been called away on urgent business and that he needed to watch the desk and make sure everyone entering and exiting the building signed the register.

"What's this all about?" A worried Butch looked at Maggie and Joey, trying to read the reason for the expediency of this visit.

"Butch," Maggie asked calmly, "do you have a nephew named Samuel Hogdon?"

"Sure," he said. "He comes by from time to time and visits with me here at the hospital. Why do you ask?"

"Have you seen him recently at the hospital?" Maggie asked.

"Well, it's funny that you're asking that question today, because he has been here this morning. I just saw him about a half hour ago. Why, is it important that you find him?"

"Yes, Butch. Does Samuel have access to those areas off limits to the average visitor to the hospital?

"No, not normally. However, today he said that he needed to go to the basement to get something from one of the storage lockers that we allow family members of employees to use from time to time. He has had a locker down there for several months. What's going on, anyway?" and he began to get very concerned about his nephew.

Jonathan and Juliet had arrived at the hospital and were approaching the information desk. The temporary guard told them that Butch and some pretty blonde had stepped into the breakroom for a moment, and he pointed down the hall to the door that led to that room. They ran down the hall, and when they saw Maggie and Butch through the plate glass window, they opened the door and joined them in the room.

Maggie addressed Jonathan and said, "Butch tells me that Samuel is in the building, or at least he was in the building thirty minutes ago."

"Does he have access to the morgue?"

"Unfortunately, yes."

They quickly pulled their service weapons, alerting Joey that he should do the same. As they prepared to leave the small room, Maggie looked at Butch and said, "I need you to give us access to the basement, and then I need you to evacuate everyone in the hospital that can be moved."

"What are you saying, Maggie? I don't understand what's going on here," Butch said. He appeared to be very troubled and confused.

"I don't have time to go into it right now, Butch, but we have a very serious situation developing right now. Your nephew has been implicated in several murders, and he may be attempting to murder again. Just evacuate the hospital and put those who can't be evacuated in areas that can be protected by your security forces."

"OK, but I still don't believe it, Maggie."

"We don't require that you believe anything Butch, but if anyone else is harmed because of your nephew, this will not go down well for you. Do you understand me?" she screamed at him. She left Juliet in the lobby area to stand watch in case Samuel doubled back on them.

"Juliet, if Samuel appears, do you think you can hold him here and radio us to return from the morgue?"

"Sure, Lieutenant. That would be a pretty easy thing to do."

"What if he tries to convince you to help him, or even worse, help him escape from the hospital?"

Juliet spoke calmly and softly, "I would shoot the bastard in the chest."

"OK, I think you have your priorities right," and she smiled at Juliet.

"Obviously, we would like to take him alive, but we don't want another officer wounded or dead," Maggie continued. "Just hold him here and call us on the radio. We will be five minutes or less away from your position."

"Don't worry about me, Lieutenant. My head is screwed on straight this time!"

Maggie turned back to Butch and told him that they needed access to the basement. He activated the elevator with his pass key, and when they entered the elevator to take them to the basement level, Butch initiated the hospital's emergency disaster plan. There would be no one in the hospital, with the exception of those in critical care situations, after a few minutes. The hospital had initiated a unique plan a few years ago that concentrated a keyless entry system in a very secure section of the hospital. The operating room, critical care recovery areas, and ICU could not be accessed without a special electronic code in emergency situations. So, all of those people would be safe from a potential shooter or anyone who didn't have authority to enter those areas.

As they were descending to the basement, Maggie said, "When the elevator door opens, I want us to spread out quickly in three different directions. I will go right; Jonathan, you go left; and Joey, you move straight ahead. Of course, if we see that Hogdon has Louise in his grasp, we will have to react to the situation. Are you all ready?" she asked as the door was opening.

When the elevator opened, it was obvious to anyone who had been to the morgue in previous situations that the lighting was different. There was no evidence of any movement in the hallway, and Samuel Hogdon and Louise were not visible. However, the morgue door was closed, the lights that normally beamed out of the observation window were dark, and there was an uneasy quiet apparent to all three of them.

"Jonathan," Maggie whispered, "see if you can enter the morgue by that door down the hall, which is used to bring the bodies to the morgue from upstairs. It's by the service elevator."

"Joey, I want you to stand guard at the main entrance door of the morgue. If you see Hogdon with Louise, and if you are sure you have a clear shot, take him out!" Maggie commanded him.

"What are you going to do?" Jonathan asked.

"I'm going into the morgue to see if Hogdon is holding her captive. If he is, and if I can negotiate with him, I will give him a chance to live. However, if you get a clear opportunity to kill that S.O.B., take him out. I have a few concerns about Joey's ability to shoot straight and true, but I have no concerns about your ability. When you took that murderer out in Rowlette from two hundred feet, you made a believer of me!"

"You take care, and don't take any unnecessary chances with this guy. We will be backing you up all the way," and he squeezed her shoulder as she slipped into the morgue. Jonathan used the rear entrance a few minutes later, his eyes adjusting to the shadows in the room created by the blinking lights on the equipment monitors that Louise used in her autopsies. He had learned to shut his eyes for a few seconds when he needed to see things in a dark room after being exposed to bright lights outside. That would let his pupils in his eyes dilate to allow in more light. In a dark room, a little light can go a long way toward identifying items in shadows.

Maggie quickly spotted Louise, strapped to a straight back char, her feet and hands constrained with big plastic twist ties. The odd thing to Maggie was that she couldn't see Samuel Hogdon anywhere.

"Louise?" Maggie called out softly to her new friend.

"Is that you, Maggie? Don't come any closer—Samuel has placed a bomb in my lap, and if anyone tries to move it, it will detonate and blow us all up. What do I do?" she wailed to Maggie.

"Where is Hogdon?" Maggie asked Louise softly.

"I don't know. He was here until about twenty minutes ago, and then I think that I heard him climb the metal staircase to the main floor. Do you have someone up there that can help us?"

"Yes, we left a guard at the elevator. Where do the stairs exit the building?"

"He can either exit on the first floor, second floor, or third floor. If he exits on the first floor, the fire door opens just to the left of the guard's station. I think that's what he plans to do. It's what I would do if I were Samuel."

"The first thing we are going to do is to get you to safety. Jonathan, call the bomb squad and get them here as soon as possible. I think he used the bomb idea to throw us off his track so he could sneak out of the hospital and get away. What he doesn't know is that Juliet Robinson, spurned girlfriend and rookie police officer, is waiting for him to appear somewhere on the first floor."

"Is that good?"

"Yes and no, Louise. It's good for us, but it's bad for him. The officer I left in charge of security on the main floor is an excellent shot with a rifle or a handgun. If she gets a chance, she will put a bullet in him so fast, he won't know what hit him."

"Louise," Jonathan spoke softly, "all you need to worry about is staying calm." He looked at the crude explosive device in her lap and told her that there was not a fuse or timer to detonate the bomb. "This appears to be a motion-activated device. He cannot detonate it with any kind of switch or electronic signal. The bomb squad is on the way. Just hang in there!" he encouraged her.

Joey had gone to the main floor lobby, accessing the area by way of the staircase. As soon as he saw the bomb squad truck arrive, he slipped out of the lobby and told the bomb technician how to get to the basement. He led him back to Louise, and the bomb tech told them all to leave the floor and go outside the building until he had defused the device.

"I can't leave her," Maggie told the technician. "Let me stay to bolster her confidence. I will do whatever you want me to do."

"It isn't safe or wise for you to stay while I am working on this device," he chided her.

"Look, I'm not leaving here without my friend," and she glanced over to Louise and gave her a big smile. "I have confidence that you will get this done safely."

"You don't know anything about me or my skills. What if I screw up and we all go 'poof' before I get this thing disarmed?"

"I'm a risk-taker, and I'm not leaving my friend.

"OK, but I don't think it's wise for you to take such a chance."

"Yeah, yeah," and she winked at Louise. "Now get your butt in gear so we ladies can go to the bathroom and repair our makeup and hair!"

* * *

Upstairs, Joey and Jonathan had helped the few remaining people out of the building so the only people visible were Jonathan, Joey, Juliet and Butch Blakely, the security guard.

"Butch, you need to go outside with everyone else," Jonathan ordered when he saw him standing by an exit door just to the left of the guard desk.

"He can't! I won't let him," was the reply from a figure standing behind Butch, shielded by a tall, interior support column. "He's going with me, or he's going to die!"

"Samuel, wait a minute," Juliet spoke to him. "He is your uncle, and he has tried to help you in the past. Don't hurt him. Take me instead as a hostage," and she stepped forward a few paces to begin the proposed exchange.

"Not on your life," he snarled. "You are a little whore, and I don't want you as my hostage. You no longer have any value to me, or even to the police department, if the truth be known. Why would I swap this innocent old man for a useless bitch like you?"

It was obvious to everyone in the room that Samuel's anger was escalating. They had to distract him until someone could get off a clean shot and take him down.

"Why are you doing all this, Samuel?" Jonathan asked. "What have these people done to you in the past to make you want to hurt or destroy them?"

"You wouldn't understand—no one would understand," and he tightened his grip on his uncle.

"Try me, Samuel. Tell me why. I really want to know."

Everyone in the lobby had gone silent, with the exception of the exchange between Jonathan and Samuel. They seemed to sense that saying the wrong thing and angering Samuel more would not be a good thing to do, so they let Jonathan take the lead.

"I went to the College of Charleston with Lester Timmons and Terrell Swanson. I had an opportunity to become an actor or a dancer, leave this lousy town with a dance company, and become somebody important. But no, Lawrence Baker would have nothing of that. He insisted that I had two left feet, couldn't carry a tune in a bucket, and that there was no place in the artistic world for me, with the exception of cleaning up the venues before and after the performances. I pleaded with him to give me another chance, but he just laughed at me. It took a while, but when the traveling dance group came back to Charleston this year for the Piccolo/Spoleto Festival, I got my chance to pay them back for all of the bad things they did to me," and he paused to collect his thoughts before continuing.

"But why kill Swanson and Timmons? What did they do to you? How did they harm you?"

"If Lawrence Baker had not favored them with his attention, I could have been the star. Then I found out that Lawrence Baker and Lester Timmons were father and son. I checked into it when that coroner bitch linked them up with their DNA. I was right all along—Baker was showing special favoritism with Timmons. Well, I showed them both, didn't I?" Samuel's face was turning very red, and his eyes appeared to be growing larger and violent.

"Why did you kill Terrell Swanson? What did he do to deserve such harsh treatment from you?'

"He was a brown-noser. Baker gave him top grades and put him in every play and show when he was in drama class. Swanson kept his nose up Baker's butt until I couldn't stand it anymore. Then he graduated and moved away. But this year, he came back to town for the big festival. So, I got even with him. He'll not brown nose anyone else, ever again!" and he laughed maniacally.

"So, you did all of this out of revenge?"

"No, no, not revenge. They owed me. They cheated me out of a life of excitement and success. They deserved to die—all of them!"

Butch had become very quiet and was not moving, even though Samuel still had his arm around his throat, choking off his air and restricting his movements. Suddenly, Butch began to slide down in front of Samuel. Butch had passed out from lack of oxygen, and since he was a little heavier than he should have been, there was no way that Samuel Hogdon could continue to hold him in front of him as a shield.

"Die, you bastard," Juliet said as she suddenly put a 9mm round through Samuel's right eye. Before he hit the floor, she put another one in his left eye.

Jonathan rushed outside and got a physician to come inside the lobby to help resuscitate Butch. In a matter of a minute or two, Butch was on an oxygen feed, and he was being rushed to the emergency room. Jonathan announced to the crowd that the hospital was still dangerous and was an active crime scene, and he suggested to some of the physicians to send everyone home, with the exception of critical employees. He told everyone that as soon as he received the "all clear" from the bomb squad, they could enter and resume their duties. When Jonathan reentered the lobby, a physician had covered Samuel's body with a white sheet, and Juliet and Joey were securing the area for the forensic team to perform their investigation.

"Nice shooting, Officer Robinson. Remind me not to get on your bad side. How did you make those shots with a 9mm handgun from thirty feet away? Those were almost impossible shots to pull off," and he smiled broadly.

"Almost," she said proudly, "but not impossible."

"Look, you two, I am going back downstairs to be with Maggie and Louise. I want you two out of this lobby until the bomb squad has done their thing. You can help with crowd control for now. I know it's not as exhilarating as what just happened, but it needs to be done."

"Yes, sir," they both said and pushed through the revolving doors leading them out into the courtyard.

Jonathan sprinted down the stairs to the basement but slowed down and began to walk very quietly as he approached the morgue. The lights had been switched on, Louise was sitting with Maggie in her office, and they were both having a shot of whiskey.

"Now that's not something you see often in a morgue," he laughed. He went to Maggie, took her in his arms, and kissed her passionately.

"Wow," Louise said. "You two need to get a room!" and she laughed for the first time since she had arrived at the morgue this morning.

"Tell us what happened, Louise. We need it for our report, but I want to know because I am also nosy!" Maggie sat back down in her chair, and Jonathan pulled the other chair up beside her.

"Wait," Louise said, "Jonathan must celebrate with us!" She took a glass chemical beaker that she usually used to test chemicals in the deceased's blood specimens, poured a shot of whiskey for Jonathan, and said, "Cheers!"

"This is a first for me, Louise."

"Drinking whiskey in a morgue?" she asked.

"Well, that, too. I can honestly say that I have never drunk from a chemical beaker. Quite a novel idea."

"So, now tell me how all of this got started today. It has to be an interesting story. I will save it for my memoirs," Maggie said.

Louise settled into her chair, uncharacteristically put her feet up on her desk, and began her story. She recalled her horrific day at the morgue, relieved that it was over.

"I came into work around 7:30 AM, as usual. I turned on the lights in the morgue, put a pot of coffee on to brew, and sat down in my chair to gather my thoughts for the day. About 8:00, I went to the ladies room, brushed my teeth, powdered my nose, and opened the lavatory door to return to my desk. There, in the hallway, was a young man holding a sharp knife in his hand. He was within a few feet of me, and he motioned that I should come over to where he was standing. As you can see, there are only four doors off the hallway--the main door into the morgue, the back door where the bodies are brought into the embalming room, the far exit door at the end of the hall, and the door to the bathroom. There was simply no place to run, and I doubt that I could have outrun a strong young man with a sharp knife. At that point, I decided that I needed to try a different approach to survival than fleeing the scene."

Louise took another drink of her whiskey and continued her story. "He made me sit in my chair, he opened a gym bag, and he placed the explosive device on my lap. He twisted something on the device, and he declared that it was armed. He said if I moved, it would detonate. Then he sat in the same chair you are occupying, and he told me all about how he had been persecuted since he was in school at the College of Charleston. The funny thing, though, is that I had this strange revelation that he really didn't want to hurt me at all. He said that he would never have known that Lawrence Baker and Lester Timmons were related if I had not discovered the sickle cell characteristics in both of their blood samples. I asked him how he knew about that fact, since it had not been released to the press, and he said that he had a friend in the Charleston Police Department." At this point, Louise looked at both of them, questioning if his statement was accurate.

"Go on, Louise," Maggie said.

"He told me that he was sorry that he had to hurt me and that the bomb was simply something he needed to do to get everyone's attention. He said everyone would remember his name forever after today. He thanked me, and he exited the basement by the staircase, which you probably already know. You know the rest of the story, Maggie, because you were here when the bomb squad came down to neutralize the explosive device."

"Jonathan," Maggie said, "the explosive device was not a real bomb. According to the bomb squad, an aerosol can under pressure is more of a threat than that device in her lap," and Maggie smiled at Louise.

"Do you think he chose suicide by cop?" Jonathan looked to her with wonder. "I haven't had a chance to tell you yet, but we killed him a few minutes ago to keep him from harming his uncle."

Maggie looked at Louise, and then to Jonathan. She suddenly felt pity for that young man. Oh, he needed to be pulled off the street, tried for murder, and put away for life in a mental institution. But looking back on everything that they had learned about him and knowing that he thought he had no future in this world saddened her.

"What exactly happened up there, Jonathan? Was there no way to keep from killing him?"

"Not really, Maggie. I had told Juliet and Joey that if they got a clear shot at Hogdon, they should take it. As far as we knew at the time, he had planted a bomb in the morgue, threatened Louise's life, and was threatening to kill his uncle with the knife at his throat. How could we have known that he wanted us to kill him?"

"Who took him down?" Maggie asked.

"Juliet. Butch passed out due to lack of oxygen, slid down in front of Samuel, who had him in a choke hold with a knife at his throat, and Juliet put a 9mm round in each eye before he hit the floor. He died instantly."

"OK, here's what I want us to do. No one knows about his disclosure to Louise but you and me. I want to keep it that way. Agreed?" and she looked at both of them, only to see them staring at her in disbelief.

"Why?" Louise asked.

"Because he either did this for sensationalism and to be written up in newspapers and on television shows around the country, or he did it because of self-loathing. If it was because of the first reason, there's no way in hell he gets that coverage—even though he's dead. And if it's because of self-loathing, why bring that up? The only person he will hurt is Naomi Coppell, and it's just not necessary to tell the tale. Let's let her bury him in peace—for her sake."

Jonathan and Louise both nodded, and the matter was put to rest. Within a couple of hours, the hospital was back in normal operation. The emergency room was full of people complaining of runny noses, headaches, backaches, and every other kind of ache and disease conceivable. Louise had given Maggie and Jonathan her statement in the basement, so they let her slip out undetected through the stairwell to the lobby exit. Joey and Jill were writing up their reports of the takedown of Samuel Hogdon, and Major Pinckney was just relieved that he could assure the mayor that everything was back in order in Historic Charleston. And, according to the mayor's office, there were still ten days of festival left to celebrate and forget the city's recent troubles.

* * *

Jonathan and Maggie had put the closing touches on the investigation of the murders of the three Piccolo/Spoleto Festival performers, and they had booked a flight back to Chicago for tomorrow morning. They were tempted to extend their stay in Charleston to enjoy some of the jazz music and other delights of the festival, but their hearts were just not in it. Their ideal get vacation had blown up in their faces, and now all they wanted to do was to go home and recuperate from a hard week of "relaxation."

"I think we should stop by the morgue and visit with Louise for a few minutes before we leave the city, Jonathan," Maggie told him. "One thing that you found out on this trip is that you have a sister. You should try to get to know her better. She seems like a really nice person."

"It will take some time for all of the uneasiness between us to fade, due to my father and her mother's past relationship. I'm willing to work on it if she agrees."

They walked down Ashley Street to the hospital, a stroll that they had taken so often since they had been in Charleston, and they entered the lobby. The guard on the desk was not Butch Blakely, and Maggie asked the uniformed rent-a-cop where Blakely was.

"He's on leave," the man stated. "He's taking a few days off to get some things worked out in his head, and then he will be back. He's a good man, and we are going to miss him until he returns. He told me to tell you that he was sorry for everything that happened to you two, and he hopes to meet you again under different circumstances. He told me that you might be asking for access to the basement from the elevator. Come on, and I'll get the elevator ready to take you downstairs."

He used his passkey to access the basement switch. The security at the hospital had been increased since the incident with the bomb scare, and metal detectors had been installed at the main entrance of the facility to discourage blatant attempts to cause damage to the building or its occupants in the future. Of course, a criminal would never approach such a machine. Those machines were designed to keep honest people honest, and nothing more.

"Louise, Jonathan and I wanted to come by and tell you that we are returning to Rowlette tomorrow morning. We didn't want to leave without saying goodbye and good luck!" Maggie said, and she walked over to her and gave her a big, sisterly hug.

"Yeah," Jonathan agreed. "If you're ever back up in our neck of the woods, please give us a call so we can give you a proper welcome to Yankee-land," and he flashed her that impressive smile of his. "We simply must get together again before the next thirty years pass, now that we know we are kin."

"Well, you two could come to my cousin's wedding this fall in Birmingham. She's one of the few family members that I am aware that I have, and I'm sure she would like to meet both of you. What do you say?"

"When is the wedding, Louise?" Jonathan asked, and he looked at Maggie to see if she might agree to accompany him. Maggie nodded affirmatively, so Jonathan continued the questioning of his half-sister. "Maggie and I would love to come, assuming that it doesn't conflict with official police work in Rowlette."

"The wedding is scheduled for the Labor Day Weekend in September of this year. Let me know if you can come, and I will get you a room at the Parliament House Hotel. Doris Day was one of its original investors, and both Bob Hope and President Richard Nixon have stayed in the Presidential Suite from time to time. The wedding reception will be held in the Barron of Beef Conference Center following the ceremony. It would be great to have you two there to support me. Jonathan, you're as close a family member as I have these days."

"Count us in," Maggie told her, gave her another hug, and she and Jonathan left the morgue for the lobby. As they walked back to the Gaslight Inn on Meeting Street, they both felt a little guilty for leaving Louise down here on her own, but they had jobs and things to do that required them to fly back to Rowlette.

* * *

The flight back to Chicago O'Hare was uneventful, and they were pretty exhausted when they reached the valet parking lot, where they had left "Lucy," Jonathan's red, classic 911 Porsche. "Lucy" looked like an old friend to them as they got into the car to drive to Rowlette. This was a trip they would both never forget.

Epilogue

Lieutenant Maggie Watson and Jonathan Pembroke returned to Rowlette, Illinois, with a renewed spirit and an eagerness to get back to work. Jonathan had become Maggie's unofficial partner, although he was only an appointed deputy. That's the way they both wanted things to appear in public, although he became her sounding board and confidant on criminal intent by local offenders. The chief of police and mayor were happy with the arrangement, because he worked with no compensation and asked for no benefits from the department. It was a win-win for everyone.

The summer of 1996 was a quiet one in Rowlette. No additional murders were recorded after the cathedral cases were solved, no rapes or extortion, and only low-profile B&Es, a couple of manslaughter cases, and the routine altercations that generally happen when 150,000 people try to live and work in a restricted geographical area. Jonathan and Maggie looked forward to the wedding festivities in Birmingham over Labor Day, when they would see Louise again and meet her relatives. They booked their tickets, hotel reservations, and they were ready to escape to another potential rest and recuperation destination. Hopefully, this trip to Birmingham would be more restful for Lieutenant Maggie Watson and her deputy than the one to Charleston—or would it?